D0399796

Mercy 6

UNBRIDLED BOOKS

Mercy 6

DAVID BAJO

UNBRIDLED BOOKS

Copyright © 2014 by David Bajo

Library of Congress Cataloging-in-Publication Data

Bajo, David, author.
Mercy 6 / David Bajo.
pages cm
ISBN 978-1-60953-109-6 (paperback)
1. Quarantine--Fiction. 2. Los Angeles (Calif.)--Fiction. 3.
Suspense fiction. 4. Medical novels. I. Title.
PS3602.A578M47 2014
813'.6--dc23
2014003272

1 3 5 7 9 10 8 6 4 2

Book Design by SH · CV

First Printing

For Esme and her math

one

1.

Something brushed her cheek. She smelled cloves, something close. Both sensations passed in the night air. Mendenhall might have thought nothing of them, dismissed them as nerves, except that nonvisual hallucinations had come to interest her again, since a man had been brought into the ER last week exhibiting taste, touch, and olfactory alterations brought on by the DTs. He had died before she could finish questioning him. He wore a nice suit, was clean-shaven, the bristles along his nape tapered, pleasant against her fingers. He spoke—to someone who was not there—of butterscotch, a hummingbird's throat against his thumb, and the coarse scent of a horse's mane.

People—normal, healthy people—perhaps have more of these than they fully realize. They resist, filter out, reject, reconstruct, disown visual and auditory hallucinations because these indicate abnormality, threaten their sense of self, their standing. She had asked the clean-shaven man if he was describing memories or sensations. He told her they were sensations, clear and new. She was testing his lucidity as the EMTs hurried the cart to the bed. She knew that this high level of lucidity amid the DTs indicated imminent demise. He died before the cart arrived. Mendenhall directed everything; she held the man's nape. But it was all procedure. She felt him go flat, that unfailing surrender.

They injected, massaged, shocked, and recorded a lifeless body. The nurse and the EMTs appeared befuddled. They had enough equipment and meds and knowledge to revive a mummy, at least into a coma. But Mendenhall knew before the cart arrived. She believed in life.

She caressed her cheek, where she had felt the brush in the night, breathed, trying to reclaim the clove scent. But the air was back to mineral. She twisted her heel against the roof surface, still expecting the crunch of gravel. The surface had changed a year ago, refloored with a light industrial tile, good for walking, impervious to the elements. Her heel made no sound, nothing above the traffic hum seven floors below.

She was being watched. The figure she thought of as the Dutchman was on the roof with her, taking a break, standing as usual beside the remains of a telescope fastened to the low wall. The city glow cast him as a bit more than a silhouette. She could see his demeanor, his feigned interest in the horizon, his vague interest in her. She liked vague. That was where science often lurked.

It felt hallucinatory, walking toward him. He was no longer seeking solitude—that was clear. But was she no longer seeking it? Mendenhall walked into this question, its wonder palpable against the measure of her stride. She drew up next to him, shared his feigned interest in the horizon. He was tall; her eyes were level with his chin.

"You don't like the new roof?" he asked.

"It's okay." She looked at her shoe, twisted the heel against the tile. "I just keep remembering the old surface. Keep feeling and expecting it."

"Building memory," he replied. "My worst enemy." The last word revealed an accent, the *e* sounds too much alike. Maybe the Netherlands, maybe eastern Europe.

"I hate metaphor," she said. "Metaphors kill. Life is actual. Death is metaphor."

"I'm not speaking metaphorically. Buildings are memory. They are composed of and by memory. Buildings are the shape of memory. If you removed memory from this building, it would collapse beneath us." He remained in profile, watching the nightscape. "That memory is the main conflict in my work. Literally my enemy, that which I must attack and overcome. Or accommodate."

"Or surrender to."

He finally looked at her, though he did not turn his shoulders. "I never surrender, Dr. Mendenhall."

"You know me?"

"We met last year, though you won't recall. It was in the ER. You were busy. There was blood." He turned fully to her. "You are my enemy."

She angled her look.

"It is my job to redesign this hospital. Without interrupting. I started with this roof. Last year." His last two words smeared into one, sounding foreign, too short on the *a*, too deep on the *e*.

She motioned toward the telescope relic beside him. "Why'd you leave that?"

"I had to. By law. It was part of the original building. The doctor who founded the hospital was an amateur astronomer. In the 1930s you could see countless stars from this roof. Probably the Milky Way. Now you can count them."

They both looked at the sky. There was a lot of black space between few stars.

"Why am I your enemy?" she asked, still looking at the sky.

"Because the ER is my biggest challenge. And you, Dr. Mendenhall, are the ER. I told you this when we first met. I asked you for ideas. But you have no memory of that."

"Sorry."

"It's okay. I got ideas from you."

"How?"

"I follow you."

She stopped looking at the sky, stopped measuring the distances between the few stars. She looked at him. He stared at the city.

"Only here at the hospital." He smiled. "Though you always seem to be here."

She waited for him to turn to her. She could tell he was about to turn, a waver in his shoulders. When he did, she asked, "What ideas? What ideas did you get?"

"None that I could use. None yet." Again his last two words smeared into a single foreign sound.

"Why not?"

"Because every time I see something, something I can maybe use, you do something that trumps it."

"Trumps?"

"Sorry. I play cards." He curled his hands around an imaginary shuffle. His fingers were long. "But for instance, my main idea. I see that the ER is marred by its very function and space, by the fact that it is a harbor—collecting, assigning, treating, sending all at once. Chaos forms, a sense of chaos. So I think if we somehow divide it into smaller areas, areas that are still connected, we eliminate that sense of chaos. Incoming patients feel more like individuals, people waiting don't see the turmoil and trauma. Doctors and staff can focus. We reduce the sense of size, of overwhelm."

She braced her shoulders, not knowing why. It was almost a shiver.

He held up his hand. "Don't worry. I rejected this."

"Why?" she asked. "What was trump?"

"I saw you move from one stretcher to a bed across the bay. I see you do this once or twice a shift. You start to attend to an incoming emergency, something frantic. Things begin to steady, gather around the stretcher as you make decisions." He held his hand palm upward and curled his fingers. "Then you suddenly stand straight, freeze momentarily, and hurry to a bed across the bay, to an earlier patient. I see that you catch something, something in your periphery. Your peripheral vision. You figure something out about one case while taking on a new emergence."

"I had a mentor," she said. "He trained us to do that."

He spun the tube of the telescope relic. "The doctor who put this here—he knew. In astronomy it's called averted vision. In our field of vision, we see farther and stronger on the periphery—more clearly but without center. We can see the Andromeda Galaxy only with averted vision, while gazing directly at Pegasus. Averted vision is a great asset, responsible for many discoveries. It would be very bad to take that asset away from you."

She felt known. She felt cut. She needed to change the direction if not the subject.

"So it's back to the drawing board?"

"Yes. Literally. To save you from metaphor. That killer." He made air circles with an imaginary pencil. "Literally I go back to my drawing board."

"Are you the one who got rid of the geriatric ward and moved all the nurses' stations off center?"

"Yes."

She flexed her brow, considered him.

"You don't approve?" he asked.

"Oh, I approve. I highly approve. Most times half the hospital is a geriatric ward. And anything that puts nurses in their proper place thrills me. That was cold. That was brilliant. I approve."

"Thank you." He held out his hand and began to introduce himself, a dip in his right shoulder.

"No, no," she said, waving him off. "I know who you are. I remember now. You're Mullich. Something Mullich."

He drew his hand to his chest and performed a tiny bow. "Close enough."

"Can you put the surgeons in the basement?" she asked.

2.

A message buzzed against her hip. She kept her eyes on Mullich as she drew the cell to her ear. Her mentor had trained her to respond this way, to stay in the moment, to not let the buzz hurtle her forward. The added benefit of this response was courtesy. Mullich's expression changed from friendly to objective. In that transition he was handsome. The city glow cast his face in planes and angles. A night breeze passed over the rooftop.

She held the emergency to her ear. Four traumas just in. The voice was Nurse Pao Pao, which meant *Come now, come ready.* Mendenhall moved toward the elevator. Mullich broke with her.

"May I run with you?"

"Suit yourself. But you're on your own. You fall behind, you won't get through."

The elevator stilled things. She slipped her express key into the slot.

Mullich pointed to the slot. He pointed with his entire hand. "That was my idea. I had those put in."

"You stole it," she said. "From luxury hotels."

"All good ideas are stolen," he replied. "Yours especially."

She felt the drop in the elevator taking her to where she wanted to be.

"What are we falling into?" he asked.

"Four traumas. All in at once. Which indicates an event."

"You like it," he said. "Most doctors are put out by it. But you like it."

"I love it more than anything else in this world," she told him as the doors swooshed open and she began to hurry. She felt the tails of her lab coat tugged by the vacuum of the doors, her contrail forming.

It was easy to spot the call in the bay. EMTs were beelining to it, nurses gathering, causing their usual clutter of concern. Pao Pao, her arms ending in fists, was guarding a space for Mendenhall. Mendenhall heard Mullich stepping quickly behind her. He was wearing soft shoes, something athletic. For this, she thought. She slipped into the crease.

The four traumas were still together. This was not right, not this deep into the bay, not this close to the elevators. No attending was near. Mendenhall held back for a moment, not looking at any of the traumas specifically, just taking them in as four, as an event.

"Where are the other attendings?"

"You're it," said Pao Pao.

Mendenhall went left to right. The first was a black man with gray in his beard. He wore the brown shirt of physical plant. His eyes were open and still. The second was a sixtyish woman in a patient gown. Her eyes were closed, mouth open and slack. The third, a young man, had a visitor's pass stuck to his t-shirt. His eyes were open and still. They were very pretty eyes. He's dreaming, she thought. He's dreaming he's dead. The fourth was a surgical nurse. Peterson. Her eyes were closed, but Mendenhall could tell that someone had closed them. One of the other nurses, someone from the clutter and concern. Pao Pao would never have done such a thing. No veteran nurse would. Peterson's lids were skewed, one pushed too far down, one sliding up and exposing a sliver of white.

She felt all eyes on her. EMTs held raised paddles. Pao Pao's jaw was clenched.

They're dead, thought Mendenhall. "Go!" she said anyway. "What are you waiting for? What are you looking for? *I* look, *you* go."

She moved to the first, knowing that was the real way to start this. In the old days, in her mentor's time, they had DOA. She wanted to look back to find Mullich, to ask him: Could we have that back?

She pressed her fingers to the patient's carotid, the brush of his beard softer than anticipated. She pushed deeply, trying for any kind of flutter. The throat of a hummingbird. Anything. Peterson, she thought. This guy. This guy, too. We know this guy, too.

She drew back, looked for blood, for angled limbs or necks, for grimace, for posturing. All carts ceased. EMTs and nurses returned to ready positions. She spoke to Pao Pao.

"They're all from here."

Pao Pao nodded, frown parallel to jaw.

"No sign of injury or trauma."

Mendenhall looked across the bay to the entrance, the huge sliding glass orange from the night beyond. She sensed the gathering bristle, some of them following her gaze.

She carefully chose the order of her commands to Pao Pao. "Close the doors. Get Infectious Diseases."

Three of the EMTs and two nurses ran for the door. Others along the bay floor gathered what was happening and tried to escape with them. Mendenhall stopped caring about them. Pao Pao would get the doors sealed. In an hour they would open and everyone could drive into the night, eat sandwiches, drink, watch TV, go online, go still.

Mendenhall spoke to the nearest nurse and nodded toward those who ran. "Write down their names."

She then fingered the carotid of each patient.

"They're dead." She looked at her watch, the cheap digital she used for running. "Seven thirty-six."

Two of the nurses ignored her and made an EMT keep attending to Peterson. Those origami hats, thought Mendenhall. They should still have to wear those. She offered some vague expression to the two nurses, a kind of wince. It could have been a frown. It could have been dismay. She could have called them fools. All of these gave permission. Anything but "No, stop" gave them permission to try to revive Peterson.

Activity in the bay swelled near the closed doors. Outside, an incoming ambulance slowed, then sped away to another hospital, its lights pulsing against the glass, sirenless. Mendenhall spoke to Pao Pao, who had finished making the calls.

"Who was here before me? Who ran off?"

"Dr. Tehmul," said the nurse.

"How close did he get? Are they his? Did he touch them?"

Pao Pao shook her head. "They're yours. They're all yours, Dr. Mendenhall."

3.

She retreated to her station, which was just a three-walled cubicle at the far end of the bay. It was connected to another cubicle that three other doctors shared. They shared because, unlike her, they weren't ER specialists, they weren't permanent, they had other floors, they had careers. Her desk faced a side wall. She remembered when it had been moved away from the back wall. She liked it better this way because it gave her screen privacy. But now she knew the reason it had been shifted: this way gave her peripheral vision into the bay. Mullich was still following her. He stood at the entrance to her cubicle.

"What is happening?" He laced his fingers at his waist and leaned against the wall, first testing its strength with his shoulder. "I mean, I've seen this before, this containment. But I always had to surmise and read dry protocol. What is really happening?"

"Tag."

"Pardon?"

"Tag," said Mendenhall. "We're playing tag. That's what doctors do in ER. And I'm speaking literally. You touch first, you're it, they're yours. Right now I'm it. For all four. Tehmul ran away the moment he saw. You have to give him credit for surmising things so quickly. If he was real lucky, he ran outside. Escaped containment."

"But they are dead." Mullich tugged his ear. "What does it matter? To you?"

"It means I have to do all four charts. Until someone else takes them. In this case, Pathology."

"Maybe not for the one," Mullich told her. He was looking toward the bay floor. "They're pushing the one away. The nurse one."

Mendenhall brought the schedule up on her screen and touched ID, Infectious Diseases. She hurried but tried to hide it by smoothly moving her hand, not bending her wrist, an old bedside trick. She felt Mullich watching.

"Now what are you doing?"

"I'm seeing who's on for ID right now. If it's one guy, we might get out of here. If it's the wrong guy . . ." She saw that Thorpe was on for ID. She bolted from her perch and started weaving through bay personnel and equipment.

"The wrong guy?" asked Mullich, staying with her.

"But we still have a chance," she replied. "Because they split away Peterson—the nurse one. Thorpe will go there first."

"Where are *we* going?"

"To Pathology. The morgue."

"Shouldn't you go to Peterson?"

"Peterson is going to Thorpe."

When they reached the steel elevators, Mendenhall jammed her express card into the slot. The doors opened immediately. Inside, she waved the card at Mullich. "Can you make one that turns back time? Or vaporizes things?"

"Things like what?"

"Like Thorpe."

He flinched, crossed his arms, pulling his shoulders in.

"Sorry." She apologized in order to get an explanation. She wasn't sorry.

"It's okay." His accent bent and held the last syllable. "But I have worked on buildings where requests like that were not jokes."

The elevator was silent, felt still. Mendenhall wondered if they were even moving.

"I love basements," Mullich said, his breath still quickened from her pace. "The morgue is the only space in this hospital that makes sense."

4.

Pathology felt quiet. They heard music coming from one end of the ward, something spare, a contemporary chamber piece. Which meant Claiborne was on duty, which meant hope for Mendenhall versus Thorpe. She quickened her steps toward the music, enjoying the emptiness, the distilled basement light, no nurses. They saw a lab tech in mask, gown, cap, and gloves cross the center foyer. The glass walls were dark except for one section. Mendenhall led Mullich to that door and reached for the handle.

"Shouldn't we prep?" he asked her.

"Prep?"

"Like them." He nodded to the tech and Claiborne, who stood in full surgical garb behind the glass, their hands held still and curled above the bodies.

Mendenhall opened the door. "Just wash your hands after. And try not to breathe."

Claiborne pulled down his mask when they entered. "Dr. Mendenhall." The blue mask bobbed under his chin. He ignored Mullich.

The three bodies were uncovered but still clothed. A violin, a cello, and a piano took turns playing the same phrase. The janitor's name was Dozier, E.; the patient's name was Fleming, L. and the visitor with the pretty eyes was Verdasco, R. Verdasco's face was pretty, too. His hands, which lay straight along his sides, were delicate. He could be playing this music, thought Mendenhall. Any one of the instruments. Then she noticed something about Dozier. His shoulders were in slightly concave position, a tiny beckon in his arms.

"You see posturing there?" She nodded toward Dozier.

Claiborne dipped his shoulders side to side, sizing up the body. "That's a stretch. They found him on his ladder. He was about to replace a fluorescent. I mean, the ladder could be the cause of the shape."

"No," she replied. "It's posturing. Let's get scans of his head and neck. Right away."

Claiborne wagged his head. The tech looked at him. She was about to draw blood. Mendenhall had placed Claiborne in a moment, in a decision that might determine whether they all went home tonight or whether they had to spend a night in Castle Thorpe while his ID team ran blood work. If she could find trauma in Dozier, they might be free. Claiborne eyed her. They sometimes saw each other running on the exercise course, a path woven around the hospital grounds. This was the expression he gave her whenever she attempted to pass him. He would check her, a flicker of exasperation across his features, then increase pace and pull ahead. He had the waist of a sprinter.

"I was supposed to be done at seven," he said. "Surgery sent me three biopsies, then these came down. I got shows to watch tonight. My wife made pad thai." He widened his hands above the bodies. "But these really do seem to be Thorpe's. All from here in the hospital, all generally from the same time. All fast."

"Just give me this one? So we have some leverage on him?"

"They still yours?"

Mendenhall nodded, hoping. "I have to do all their charts. Except her. " She motioned toward Fleming, the one with the patient gown and bracelet. "She's somebody else's patient."

"No, her, too," he told her. "Seems she was officially checked out. Was gabbing with her roommate in recovery, having a Jell-O together, then collapsed across her roomie's bed. You get to start a whole new chart."

Mendenhall sighed, started to raise her hand to her brow, then thought better of touching her face. "What was she in for?"

"Foot surgery." Claiborne nodded toward Fleming's right ankle. The toes were thin and pale, the nails freshly painted red, post-op no doubt.

Mullich finally spoke. "How come you know everything?"

Claiborne only glanced at him before going back to Mendenhall. "Because this is Hell. We end up knowing everything that happens." He motioned toward the ceiling but kept his eyes on Mendenhall. "Up there."

He kept looking at Mendenhall as he spoke to Mullich. "Following her will give you the wrong impression of this building. I wouldn't advise it. Dr. Mendenhall still does the footwork. No one does that anymore. Not even the nurses. Just like now. Just like she came here." With his gloved hand still curled, he motioned to the laptop on a side table. "On that screen there are probably five requests—orders—sent by Thorpe. Blood work. But right there," he punched his hand toward Mendenhall, "is her. In person. Here to see me. Pay us a visit. Help us." He extended the last two words. "I haven't even seen Thorpe for over a year. To him, I'm a name at the bottom of a result."

"It's because I like people so much." Mendenhall looked at Claiborne's tech.

"It's because you like bodies. The body." Claiborne blew a hard breath, then gave orders to the tech. "Start blood work on Verdasco and Fleming. Zap Dozier."

"Thank you, Dr. Claiborne."

"Just get us out of here before midnight."

She started to reply, but Claiborne raised his hand and closed his eyes. He held a gloved finger near his lips, shushing. He pointed up to the music, the weave of the violin, cello, and piano. "This is the best part."

They listened to the quiet music and watched as the tech rolled Dozier to a corner of the lab. Mendenhall couldn't really see the posturing anymore, any real lift in his shoulders that might indicate trauma. Infection was most likely, given the timing, place, and disparate persons. A janitor, nurse, patient, visitor. But the timing was almost too good. All must have been found within the same five minutes or so. All must have died fairly quickly, fairly together, either before or during their transport to the ER. A janitor slumped over a ladder. A patient slumped over another's bed. Where had Peterson and Verdasco been found? How long had each of them lain undiscovered, unattended? . . . How bad was this hospital? She looked at Mullich, who was scanning the room, using Claiborne as a pivot for his gaze. How sick was this building?

5.

She returned to her ER cubicle to do charts. Mullich was no longer following her, no doubt more intrigued by Claiborne's Hell. Doctors hated charts because charts were menial, below a physician's station. Mere data entry, what her mentor had called paperwork. But the most profound cause of that hatred was the fact that charts acknowledged an overseer, reminded a physician that all her decisions and acts were up for assessment, even though 99 percent of those decisions and acts were repetitions, determined by precedent. And that last fact was the most difficult part of the acknowledgment, that what they were all doing was mimicking, robotics, child's play.

But these four new charts tagged on to the end of Mendenhall's long day were different; she saw them as an act of organization and self-checking, probably what charts were originally meant to be, way back when Mercy General had been built, when the telescope on the roof had been whole and aimed toward the Milky Way.

Enry Dozier was a fifty-three-year-old janitor with a clean work record during seven years of employment at Mercy. His medical history was in the system and showed nothing unusual, nothing more than a slightly elevated BP, almost average for a black male. He never missed the hospital's required checkup. He had been found slumped over his ladder in the seventh floor hall, one fluorescent tube leaning against a rung, the other shattered along the floor, presumably dropped. He was at the far end of the hall, past the patient rooms, so it was unknown how long he had been like that before being discovered by a patient taking a prescribed hall walk. He had been unresponsive during transport to the ER.

Lana Fleming, a sixty-three-year-old retired middle school teacher, had been admitted for surgery to scrape bone chips from her talocrural joint. The procedure had been successful. Her medical history was in the system and showed nothing unusual, nothing more than being overweight, average for a white female over sixty. The bone chips indicated that she had been athletic until her fifties. On the fourth floor, she had slumped over her roommate's bed while sharing tea and dessert. She had been standing over the woman's bed, making plans to get together after recuperation. Fleming had been checked out but hadn't changed out of her gown. The roommate had buzzed for the nurses immediately. Fleming had been unresponsive during transport to the ER.

Marley Peterson, a forty-one-year-old surgical nurse had been at Mercy for ten years. Her work record was stellar; her medical history, which was in the system, was marred by a smoking habit that had yet to exhibit any health repercussions. She had never missed the hospital's required checkup. The only prescription after every six-month checkup was to stop smoking. She had been treated for staph infections twice during her Mercy career: one MRSA, one VRSA. She had been discovered in a second-floor ventilation room that was also used for water storage. A worker from the physical plant, retrieving a jug for a water cooler, had found her slumped on the floor and alerted nurses. She had shallow breathing and pulse during transport to the ER.

Richard Verdasco, in his early thirties, had been visiting his mother in ICU. His medical records were not in the system. The mother, Lupita Verdasco, was in post-op ICU, not conscious after surgery to remove a brain tumor. Richard Verdasco had been found slouched in an armchair in the visiting area, a magazine across his lap. Another visitor sitting in the same area at first had thought he was sleeping but had alerted nurses after noticing that his eyes were open and unblinking. Verdasco had been unresponsive during transport to the ER.

It was infection, Thorpe's domain. She should take advantage. The ER would go still without incoming. She could run on the treadmill in PT, have a yogurt, granola, and apple at the cafeteria, take a whirlpool in fourth floor recovery, nap in the surgeons' lounge on Two. Claiborne would be furious about having started things with the Dozier case, but she never needed Claiborne because by the time stuff got to him, the patient was no longer hers, was either dead or parsed out to a real specialty. Claiborne needed her. He needed her for any decent consultation on trauma.

She petted her screen, scrolling down the four charts. Did they make it feel like skin on purpose? All first-year med students are assigned virtual patients. Some create avatars, whether allowed or not. That was one of the biggest changes in medicine, her mentor claimed. They often argued over whether this was good or bad, changing sides depending on what they'd seen that day in the ER.

She looked at Dozier's chart. Then she gazed unfocused over the bay. This was what she did instead of closing her eyes. She pictured Dozier three ways, recalling him in the ER and Pathology, then imagining him slumped over his ladder. She hadn't really seen any posturing, any signs whatsoever indicating disconnection.

We see what we are, her mentor had told her. Take one patient complaining of headache and fatigue and send him to four different specialists. You will receive four different diagnoses, four different prescriptions. Throw in one meddling aunt and receive another diagnosis and another prescription. Pathologists are different—different but not exempt. They see pathology. But is there always a pathology? Believe in life, Dr. Mendenhall, he told her. That there is something beyond diagnosis and pathology.

Pathology buzzed her, one word from Claiborne: Come.

6.

athology seemed darker. Maybe it was the increased coolness and the change in music, an even more spare solo violin piece. Maybe it was the bodies, now naked, with a fourth steel bed empty and waiting. Maybe it was the way Claiborne, Mullich, and the tech were standing. Claiborne now had Mullich in gloves and mask. At first she thought the architect was a cutter. The three stood in waiting formation, turned toward her entrance.

The mix confused her. The coolness meant Thorpe was setting things up for a long haul. The garb for Mullich indicated this also. The presentation of the bodies appeared Thorpe-ready, propped with limb angles measured and even. The empty bed—"Don't call them tables," Claiborne had insisted the first time she had made the mistake—held intrigue. Thorpe would keep Peterson alive on paper for as long as possible to get the best cultures, even if she had a DNR. Peterson was too young for a DNR. But she was a nurse, no doubt a human petri dish, perfect collateral for Thorpe.

Mendenhall put on fresh gloves when she entered but ignored the crisply folded mask. She eyed the empty bed, then checked Claiborne.

"That one's for you," Claiborne told her.

She'd been awake for twenty hours straight. This was a dream.

Claiborne motioned his mask and gloves toward Mullich. "His idea. A fourth bed just to give you the best perspective."

Claiborne went to Dozier, who was first in line. That was strange, too, the way the beds were ordered: Dozier, Fleming, Verdasco, then the empty steel for Peterson, the four aligned in a neat slant rather than squared.

"Him again," said Claiborne, nodding toward Mullich. "They're arranged according to the floors they were found on."

The others followed him to Dozier.

"Look at him first," he told Mendenhall. "Head and neck. Then go to the scans."

"Scans? You took scans?"

"You'll see."

She crouched to get a level profile of Dozier. The skull was balanced on the occipital, cleanly presenting throat and nape. His beard had been combed into a point. His lips were in repose, not yet slipping into grimace. With two fingers, she palpitated what could have been slight swelling beneath his Adam's apple. "Maybe something there." She shrugged. "Not worth a scan. I thought you would just run an X-ray."

Claiborne led her to the side table, a stand-up metal desk, out of place because of the lamp and pens and books and paperweights, little gifts. He flicked on one display above the desk, showing the X-ray. He left the one with the CT dark.

"I did what you just did," Claiborne told her. "I looked at him, pressed his throat, then walked to the X-ray." He nodded to the X-ray. "So I wasn't expecting that."

The display showed diagonal occlusion from occipital to throat, the point of minor swelling. Mendenhall squinted. There was a path of displacement and internal bleeding through the neck.

"So we ran this."

The scan clearly showed that the spinal cord and vertebrae were clean. The trauma was all capillary bleeding, all in the tissue, the major vessels and bone clean and undamaged. The skin appeared intact, certainly no wounds.

"Does that mean no infection?" asked Mullich.

"Nuh-uh." Claiborne kept looking at the scan. "It just seems a little too clearly defined for infection."

"You'd expect it to wander more," Mendenhall explained. "Infection."

"But I have seen linear infection paths." Claiborne drew the diagonal across the scan.

"Yeah," said Mendenhall. "Following a stab line. A long puncture."

"I've seen fungals a little like this." He looked at the tech. "I showed you that one. Absolutely geometric. Crystalline."

Mendenhall grabbed a horn-rimmed magnifying glass from the desk and went back to Dozier's body. Only after she began the move did she sense transgression on her part, a passing of Claiborne. The tech and Mullich turned with her but did not step, just broke formation, torn and hesitant.

She bent close to Dozier's throat, lens held above the tiny swelling.

Claiborne led the others to Dozier, bringing a wireless otoscope. With precision, he took the magnifying glass from Mendenhall's fingers and gave her the scope. It was laser-aimed. The halogen light was intense enough to turn Dozier's dark skin translucent. Mendenhall's pan was transmitted to a large overhead screen. They saw what she saw. The view was near-microscopic: dead skin cells sloughing, pores gaping, curled whiskers rooted.

"I see a line." Mendenhall drew the laser along a straight path of sloughed skin cells. She lifted her eyes to Claiborne.

"From shaving," he said. "A week ago, I'd guess. You can find a dozen of them on his throat. You'll find some more on the nape, especially around the occipital. When we turn him over." He nodded to the tech. "Tilt him."

With a delicate lift of Dozier's shoulder, the tech presented the nape and the base of the skull for Mendenhall.

"I need to get me one of these," said Mendenhall. She raised the scope a little to clarify that she was speaking about it, not the tech, though she might have meant both. She sought refuge in the close view of Dozier's skin, the epidural landscape. She did see more of those lines, not cuts, not scarring, just cells scraped evenly by a razor, days ago, weeks ago. She saw the salt crystals of Dozier's dried sweat.

Claiborne cleared his throat. The tech shuffled her feet. Mullich remained quiet. She could sense him waiting, not just watching.

She found a cluster of blood cells clinging to the corner of a salt crystal. Moving diagonally just below the occipital, she found another. Following the same line, she slid her view up the periphery and found a third cluster, dried purple, trapped in a sheer on the base of a salt crystal.

"I see a blood line."

She knew Claiborne was wagging his head.

"She found three dried blood-cell clusters on a hospital janitor. On a guy who'd been doing repairs all day. And the day before. And the day before that. In fact, you're just finding a case for Thorpe. Blood contact."

"The three form a line," replied Mendenhall. She traced the laser along the line. It wasn't quite perfect, with one cluster just on the other side of the line. Then she straightened to address Mullich. "Any two points form a line. But a third point determines, no?"

Mullich shrugged.

Claiborne stepped closer to her.

"You've gone myopic, Dr. Mendenhall. You've lost the big picture. You want to argue—*to Thorpe*—that maybe a microscopic blade lanced a janitor while he was on a ladder? Or that an intense burst of air went off inside his neck? And what about the others?" He motioned to the other bodies. "A serial killer with a light saber is loose in the hospital?"

Mendenhall passed the scope to the tech. She sighed and pressed the back of her sleeve to her brow. She badly wanted to rub her eyes with her fingers.

"The, what did you call it? Posturing?" said Mullich, his mask thickening his accent. "She saw that." He pointed back to the lighted displays.

Mendenhall looked down at her gloved hands, empty. She didn't know what she was doing. She couldn't really say that she had seen posturing in Dozier. We see what we are. She saw what she was. She was a dream-deprived trauma specialist, one who had never escaped the ER, forever moonlighting to pay off loans that no longer existed. She didn't even want to go home. She wanted the hospital to open, to let in more, to let in the outside.

"Can infection cause posturing?" asked Mullich. He was looking at the tech. She answered only with lifted eyes. Her eyes held still, almost black above the dark blue mask.

"Maybe a sudden bloom against the brain stem," Claiborne answered. "Something like that, I could imagine."

"Imagine?" Mullich pulled his mask down.

"Better than I can imagine a Jedi in a hospital."

Mendenhall was still bowed. "I'll go rest," she told Claiborne. "I'll come back down if you want."

Claiborne let his mask fall away with a simple stroke behind his neck. His expression opened to her. "If I do a bunch of digital scans before Thorpe's work, he'll send people down. I like it down here like this. Quiet." He pointed back to the displays. "You led me to that. We have that to show Thorpe. To put him on his heels a bit." He waved toward the other bodies and the empty bed. "You gave me something to look for in them. Later. Soon, but later."

7.

M endenhall returned to her cubicle. She fussed with papers and journals, squared them, then struck them all, swiping outward with both hands. Atop the resulting mess lay the most recent issues of *Tennis Magazine* and *Golf Digest*. She recognized the tennis player but not the golfer. She wouldn't have guessed that he was an athlete. Despite the airbrushing, she noticed a basal cell on the edge of his left temple. He should come see her. The subscriptions were gifts from her mentor, who knew well enough to have them mailed to the ER, where they would have some chance of being noticed. She had played tennis in college. Maybe the golf was supposed to be her future—her present.

She put the magazines on a stack of previous issues on the floor, all unread save for the letters-to-the-editor sections. She hunched into her space. The cafeteria had been too crowded, people gathering and lingering there during containment. She swiveled her chair to assess the bay. Pao Pao stood in the center, directing the EMTs on where to push the remaining gurneys, where to set up any new patients coming from within Mercy. A young woman with straight black hair interrupted the nurse. She wore a lab coat. Even from this distance Mendenhall could see that she was extremely pretty, exotic. The EMTs peeked back at her. She must have said something important to Pao

Pao because the nurse gave her immediate attention, no back, no resistance, no hesitation in her sturdy shoulders. The woman was even shorter than Pao Pao. She tapped notes into a hand tablet. When she finished with Pao Pao she came directly to Mendenhall.

She wore a name tag on her lab coat. The tag was porcelain with engraved black letters: Silva. She was the tech from Pathology, the tag a gift. It felt good to look at her face, oval now without the mask and cap. To look at her hands without the gloves, fingers balancing the tablet. Her expression appeared haughty, which also soothed Mendenhall. The tech was bracing herself.

"Forget something?"

"Dr. Claiborne sent me to gather info on the patients. Their situations."

"When they fell?"

Silva nodded, chin remaining upturned. "And how they were found. And where exactly."

"Exactly?"

"That was Mullich. He asked for that." Silva cocked her head. "And Dr. Claiborne okayed."

"Doesn't he need your help down there?"

"This will make things faster, give him clues as he examines. I send him the info as I go along." She raised the tablet. "Body to body."

"You and Dr. Claiborne should work with live people, Silva. Whole people. Up here. All that efficiency is lost on the dead and waiting."

Silva ignored this, looking flatly at Mendenhall.

"I can't tell you anything more than Pao Pao could."

"I didn't know you said it that way," Silva replied.

"Yes. 'Pow pow.' Like a gun."

"A toy gun, you mean." Silva straightened her gaze. "I didn't come here to ask you about the subjects."

"What, then?"

"Never mind," said Silva. "I should continue." She turned.

"No," said Mendenhall. "Tell me."

Silva faced her, again angled her head. "I joined Pathology to get away from what I don't understand. About this hospital, other hospitals. I don't understand how it's about avoiding the sick and injured. Avoiding charts. Not touching someone wheeled in for help."

"You wanted to ask me about *that*?"

"I thought you were different. Dr. Claiborne always said you were different. But you're not."

"And you are? You and Claiborne?" Mendenhall sighed to try to stop herself but continued, "It's a little straighter down there. The charts and the patient cha-cha are gone. But it's still all about power. Who has the most. Right? You're up here helping Dr. Claiborne keep his floor clean of Thorpe's people."

"He respects you."

"He uses me because I function as a challenge to Thorpe."

"I don't accept that. He wants your knowledge. He uses that." Silva brushed the tablet, read something. "I should go."

"Wait." Mendenhall almost reached for her elbow, the perfect, sharp angle of it. "Mullich."

"Mullich?"

"You said he asked for where. Exactly where they were found."

"Yes." Silva raised her chin. "Makes sense."

"To you, yes. I get that. Anything to help explain why it was so fast. Why they just collapsed, went from fine to out." Mendenhall felt a tired gnawing, doubt, a vanishing thread. "But what's it to Mullich, exactly?"

"This place is sick," replied Silva. "This place may be dead."

Mendenhall appreciated the way she then just walked away. As the tech moved across the bay, the EMTs and nurses and visitors parted for her. The elevators opened as soon as her small reflection appeared on the steel doors.

8.

From her cubicle, she watched Pao Pao. The nurse did not once look at her as she finished ordering the floor, but she was doing everything for Mendenhall. Twenty-five curtained stalls lined two opposing walls of the bay. Pao Pao had the EMTs put nine of the new patients in the stalls on one wall and five on the other side. The nine were Mendenhall's, all easily observed from her cubicle, all an easy walk-along. This arrangement made it a little harder on the nurses, a little more zigzagged. Mendenhall wanted the hospital to give Pao Pao another title, something other than Nurse. When the floor was completely cleared according to containment standards, Pao Pao did not stop. She proceeded to visit each bed, starting with those on Mendenhall's line.

Pao Pao worked her way along three patients. She spent a minute with each one, her firm expression unchanging, her arms always in motion: adjusting sheets, gowns, IVs, rails, bed angles. The motion, the flex of muscle, reassured the patients, maybe just hypnotized them. The patients would begin with lots of words. Mendenhall could see their mouths, their furrowed brows. Pao Pao's words appeared spare, about one of hers for every fifty of theirs. Then the patients tapered into silence beneath Pao

Pao's tucks and pulls. All of the other nurses on the floor were gathered at the station.

Mendenhall checked her watch and decided she had given Silva a good lead. If she let her get started with the interviews and investigations, the tech might be more at ease, might be able to stick to her own approach. Mendenhall would have to guess which floor Silva had chosen first, which subject. She would stay away from Peterson because Thorpe's people would be on Two. Fleming, on Four, would be the most static, and the witness was still there in the room. ICU, Verdasco's floor, would be more controlled, so it would be a bit easier to track down witnesses.

In the elevator, Mendenhall shoved in her express key and pushed Seven, right back to Dozier. This was better than trying to rest or eat cafeteria yogurt. She felt somewhat revived, the beginning energy of a reluctant run, blood quickening. Marking Claiborne, eluding Thorpe, trusting Pao Pao.

ON SEVEN, MENDENHALL thought perhaps she had guessed incorrectly. The end of the hall, beyond the last patient room, was abandoned. Dozier's ladder was still in position beneath the broken light, the glass and powder of the shattered fluorescent still not swept. No doubt someone from physical plant was presiding over a debate regarding whose job description required subbing for Dozier. Mendenhall crouched over the glass and powder. The splash pattern formed a line at the base of the ladder, oddly neat. The replacement tube leaned against the riser; Dozier's tool belt was looped over the little folding platform. There was a footprint across the line of glass, where someone had stepped to attend Dozier.

"They were more concerned with their shoes." Silva had appeared above her. "Than with him, I mean."

Mendenhall, still crouched, looked over her shoulder at Silva. The tech had fetched a CPR dummy and was cradling it.

"Yes. You'd expect more shuffling over the glass." Mendenhall looked at the dummy.

"Still," replied Silva. "Good for us. All this inertia."

"Us?"

"Pathology." Silva sat the dummy against the wall, readied her tablet with a brush of a middle finger. "We can use you since you're here. Instead of him." She nodded to the dummy.

Mendenhall rose out of her crouch, looked once down the hall, which was empty to the nurses' station, then out the window at the near end. The night view of the city held her for a moment. She pointed to the ladder.

"You want me to be Dozier."

Silva nodded as she brushed and tapped her tablet, lips parted in concentration.

"I interviewed the patient who found him. Her room is under containment, so I had her sketch Dozier. Had her tell me everything as she did that. She was kind of freaked by my mask and gloves, but I think that helped us get to the point. Then I interviewed the nurses to determine time as best as possible."

"Already?" Mendenhall was eyeing the ladder.

"I'm on a schedule. I have an hour. Then back down to the lab."

Mendenhall started up the ladder.

"Wait," said Silva. "I can be Dozier. I just thought you were closer to his height."

"No. No. It's fine." Mendenhall ascended the ladder. "Let's do these right. You can be the shorties."

"He was slumped over the top. Calmly. The witness said calmly. Like a rag doll."

Mendenhall looked around from the perch, not bending over yet. "A rag doll? You mean the arms were straight?"

"Yes. And out a bit. We followed up on that. Like a rag doll without elbows."

"So there was a trace of posturing?"

"Yes."

Mendenhall looked down. She could see the surface of Silva's tablet, that she was sending and receiving. She saw the line of broken glass. "The glass and the powder."

Silva bent her head to see. Her black hair divided cleanly over her nape. "What about it?"

"It's too straight. Right below this light. It fell straight down." Then Mendenhall pointed to the two sockets. "Look. The prongs are still in. Dozier didn't drop it. It rained down from here."

"Yes. That would fit," replied Silva. She brushed and tapped her tablet. "The patient strolled to the end window. Saw Dozier climbing to the burned-out fluorescent. He nodded to her, seemed fine. After she passed, she heard the glass falling on the floor, turned and saw him slumped over."

"His hand must've pulled it down as he collapsed."

"Yeah." Silva tapped the ladder. "You need to slump over. Like Dozier."

Mendenhall did this, positioned her arms.

"Hold still." With a cloth measuring tape, Silva plumbed a line from Mendenhall's waist to the floor. She marked the linoleum with a grease pencil used for skin. She then used a small digital camera to take a profile of Mendenhall. "Okay, Doctor."

"I feel like Claiborne's puppet." Mendenhall descended the ladder, flexed her shoulders.

"More Mullich's," Silva replied as she measured the distance from the floor mark to the walls. "He's the one who wants these exact locations and positions. We're more focused on time and behavior."

Mendenhall looked at the window view again and this time stepped to it, about a pace and a half from the ladder. She recognized the view. She pointed up to the ceiling. "I was somewhere there above him. Right up there on the roof, looking out at this." She waved to the nightscape of the city.

Silva said nothing as she entered and sent information. When she started to retrieve the dummy, Mendenhall stopped her.

"Leave him for the nurses. Which one next?"

leming's room, too, was in containment, the sliding glass door locked. All the front walls on fourth floor recovery had been converted to glass. Last year the floor had been closed for one month during conversion. Mullich. This made several things easier and better, including containment and patient monitoring. Mendenhall wondered how far Mullich would go with the glass.

She and Silva viewed Fleming's roommate before entering. The woman stared back, leaning forward, eyes wide. The cone of light from her bedside lamp appeared somehow domestic, yellow and shaded.

"We'll break her heart if we put on masks and gloves."

Silva put on fresh gloves and a mask. She handed Mendenhall a new set. "I'll be Fleming."

The roommate rose further from her recline as Mendenhall snapped on her gloves. The sliding door produced a soft breath as it opened. The room felt cool. Silva immediately moved bedside.

"We just have some questions. And you'll have to help us re-create Fleming's collapse."

Mendenhall would have let this approach continue, would have happily joined in, but the roommate was locking up. "Ms. Silva is a lab technician. I'm Dr. Mendenhall." She recalled the chart she had

done for Fleming. "I treated Lana when they brought her to ER."
She pretended to examine the screen showing the patient's vitals.

Silva turned to Mendenhall, tablet raised. "I'm sorry, Doctor. Dr.
Claiborne ordered me to ask, order, and go." She turned back to the
patient. "Tell us what happened."

Mendenhall took the patient's pulse anyway, figuring the touch
would offer some comfort. Comfort produced clarity. In the ER,
two seconds of comfort sometimes brought all the clarity anyone
needed.

"I don't know." The patient stared at the empty space above her
knees. "We were having some tea. From my tray. Lana was standing
about where you are." She looked at Silva.

"Was the tray over you?"

"No. Lana had pushed it aside and was serving us. Was saying
how we'd get together and have a proper tea somewhere nice." Her
eyes widened. "Somewhere they didn't serve Jell-O. Then . . . she
kind of blew out a little breath. Just a tiny puff. Then she fell over,
right across me."

"How did she present?" asked Silva.

The woman stared.

"What did she do right before she fell over?" Mendenhall
offered her a bottle of water. "How did her eyes look? Her arms."

"It wasn't sudden. It was calm. Like she had grown tired. Tired
from something she was remembering. She just looked down and
breathed that one puff. Her arms? Her arms didn't do anything.
She even held on to the tea mug. It spilled across my bed. Like her.
Just. Spilled."

"Her elbows bent?"

"Yes. Like when you lie down to sleep. Everything like that.
Like lying down to sleep when you're very, very tired."

"I'm going to place myself over you," Silva told her. "You direct me. Try to place me as best you can just like Fleming was."

Silva laid herself over the patient. Her hair fell across her face, covering her mask. The patient reached to adjust the cool black strands, but Mendenhall caught her by the elbow. "Don't touch, just direct. Let her do the arranging."

"One arm was out and over. The other was back and down. She fell more over than that, more over me."

Silva positioned herself much like a mourner would onstage, a daughter flung across the body of a mother. Again the patient reached, her palm nearing Silva's shoulder, before catching herself and gazing up apologetically at Mendenhall.

BACK IN THE hallway, Mendenhall relayed the measurements she had taken while Silva recorded them on her tablet. She had taken two photographs with the lab tech's cell, one from each side, of Silva lying across the patient. She had plumbed the line from waist to floor; then Silva had triangulated that mark with the walls. As they strode to the elevators, Mendenhall stripped off her mask and gloves and tossed them into a trash receptacle.

Silva spoke as she recorded. "No posturing. One prominent exhale. Relaxed fall."

Her tone was punctuated, so Mendenhall did not expect the quizzical look from Silva. She almost appeared sad.

"Can we do this by phone?" Mendenhall asked.

Silva shook her head as they neared the elevators. "My texts scroll on an overhead screen as he takes digitals and examines the body. If he taps a line of text, it registers here," she lifted her tablet, "as pursue."

"Tell him to take a lateral digital of her upper chest. Center on the lower trachea, right above the bronchus."

"I can't tell him that."

"He'll figure it out."

Mendenhall showed her express key. "ICU?"

Silva nodded as she entered her text to Claiborne. She winced at an immediate reply.

"What?"

"I'm fired."

The bell chimed, and the elevator doors opened. Two nurses were inside, confused by which floor they had been pulled to. They frowned when they recognized Mendenhall.

"He'll know it's me," she told Silva as they stepped into the elevator and Mendenhall hijacked it to third floor ICU.

Seconds later they were free of the scowling nurses. "They'll all end up in the cafeteria," said Mendenhall as the doors closed. The ICU hall was empty in the long stretch between the waiting area and the nurses' station.

Silva winced at another text, bit her lower lip. Anyone would have thought she was playing a game on the handheld. Anyone would have wanted to join her.

"And?" asked Mendenhall.

"He said to ignore you." Silva started for the nurses' station.

"No." Mendenhall touched her sleeve. "Let's go to waiting. Where Verdasco was found. I'll get your nurse to come to us. Save you that trip. That round of chatter. You having to submit."

Silva went with Mendenhall.

"How do you know it's the trachea?"

"The way she described that breath. Fleming's little puff. Then forward collapse. That's trauma right above the bronchus. Extreme trauma. Maybe involving the heart, too. A really hard punch to the middle of the chest or back. Commotio cordis."

"That kills boxers?"

"And schoolkids."

"You think that woman punched Fleming?"

"No."

"Then what?"

"Not an infection."

MENDENHALL STOPPED SILVA with a simple elbow touch. They stood midhall, that given privacy in hospitals. Silva squared herself to Mendenhall and raised her chin in a straight manner, not a tilt of skepticism, irritation, or humor. She just waited, open.

"Look," said Mendenhall, "that stuff with Fleming's roomie. I wasn't trying to counter you or put you in your place. Or get you fired. It's just more efficient sometimes to be . . . personable. It's not bedside manner. It's a form of examination, a safe way of opening up the wound. And I mean that literally. The psychological and emotional wounds start to clot immediately, too soon, screwing up memory, screwing up facts."

Silva remained still, her breathing thoughtful, her look searching. "Most cases of commotio cordis are caused by projectiles. There was no projectile."

"*All* cases of infection are caused by organisms. There is no organism. No virus, prion, bacterium, viroid, fungus."

"So far."

"Right." Mendenhall nodded toward the waiting area. "So far."

10

Mendenhall and Silva stood above the lounge chair where Verdasco had been found. The waiting area was empty. Mendenhall had called Pao Pao and told her what they needed from the ICU nurses' station. She knew what Claiborne must have been thinking as he scanned Fleming's chest and back. Internal trauma with no external signs. That would just intensify Thorpe's mission, give him evidence for a new infection. They were pushing water. The metaphor depressed her.

She looked at Silva for some relief. The tech brushed her tablet, reviewing, exchanging. She and Verdasco would have made a beautiful couple.

"You be Verdasco."

"You're closer to his height," replied Silva.

"Lie back. Be him. Use what you know. Before the nurse gets here."

Silva reclined in the armchair, leaned her head back, stretched her legs. Mendenhall spotted the nurse heading toward them, hustling down the hall with the fear of Pao Pao in her. She found a car magazine, thought of Verdasco's delicate fingers and pretty eyes, and switched to a local magazine featuring the city's symphony. She laid this across Silva's lap.

"It was more on his chest," said the tech. She realigned the magazine, then repositioned her arms. She held herself still, throat extended, lips softly closed. Light brown skin, black hair, red lips, pretty death.

"Eyes open," said Mendenhall.

The nurse yelped when she arrived at the scene.

When they were finished with the positioning and the nurse interview, Mendenhall led Silva toward one of the newest rooms in ICU. Some visitors had returned to the waiting area, coffees in hand.

"Where are we going?" asked Silva. "I'm finished. I can't go to Peterson."

"We're not going to Peterson." They arrived at the open entrance to the little arboretum. Mendenhall looked at her watch. "You still have ten minutes left on your hour. Thanks to me. Come."

By the way Silva assessed the room, Mendenhall could tell this was her first visit. The tech registered things with small, exact movements of her head, eyes aimed forward, blinking in between adjustments. The room was a tall hexagon. The entire ceiling was a soft amber light filtered through a lattice. One wall was covered by a smooth waterfall, its receiving fountain bracketed by dwarf palms. Ficus trees stood in the four remaining corners, shading the benches that lined the walls. Two visitors, a couple, sat together. They leaned forward, elbows to knees, gazing at the ceramic floor design, a kind of algebraic spiral.

"Welcome to Mullich's head," she said to Silva. "One corner of it anyway. It used to be a chapel."

They sat together on one of the unoccupied benches. Ficus shadows fell across Silva's neck and shoulders as she brushed her tablet. They hadn't learned much from the nurse who had been summoned to Verdasco by a startled visitor. He had presented a faint, irregular pulse, though Mendenhall wondered about that, coming from a nurse with quivering fingers. But they were able to get the positioning exact, the floor measurements for Mullich. Timing was just an estimation, as the visitor had only noticed Verdasco's glazed eyes when she had glanced up from her magazine.

"We might be able to verify a closer time," said Mendenhall, "if we can ever get to that visitor."

"Thorpe put her in quarantine," Silva replied.

"His bank, you mean."

"Why do you always question Thorpe? It's the right procedure. Why is it you against him? What about this hospital? People in this hospital?" Silva brushed something distasteful into her tablet. "What about the truth?"

"Okay. The truth is Thorpe's a narcissist. The worst kind—a smart one, a do-good one."

"You're no different." Silva tapped her screen, not looking up.

Mendenhall clenched her jaw, closed her eyes, and inhaled the smell of the waterfall and potting soil. She really believed that the best thing to do was let everyone go home and take hot showers and watch for symptoms, that the worst thing to do was seal up and mix the hospital's innards, its illnesses and emotions. This metaphor caused her to shudder. Why, really, were they doing this?

Silva misread. "Sorry."

"No. You're right." Mendenhall looked up to the glow of the lattice. "But lucky for you that I am. Lucky for you all."

Silva returned to her comfort zone, their comfort zone, the facts on her handheld. "The oddest thing is the set of times we do have. Fleming and Dozier fell within the same five-minute span, somewhere between seven twenty-five and seven thirty. Verdasco and Peterson could fit into that span as well. We haven't ruled that out."

"Verdasco." Mendenhall massaged her forehead, keeping her fingers from her eyes. She so wanted to press her eyes.

"What about him?"

"He's beautiful, no?"

"So?"

"I bet that other visitor looked at him. A lot. Snuck glances. Like clockwork. You know? We could figure out the time if we could talk to her. Then it would be points on a line. Two suggests a line. Three determines."

"There's Peterson. They found her in that ventilation room a little after seven thirty. A few minutes before they took her to you."

Mendenhall bowed her head and rubbed her neck firmly, tried to create some pain. "Thorpe kept Peterson alive on paper to get her to his wing. He needs a patient. But Peterson was just as dead as the others."

Silva probably never looked confused. But her expression was skeptical, one eyebrow lifted, nose angled to her tablet. She looked like she really wanted to go.

"When you get back to Dr. Claiborne, have him zap Verdasco's brain stem." With her finger almost grazing Silva's neck, Mendenhall drew a line following the angle of the tech's intricate jaw. "Center there. Tell him that's what I say."

11.

Mendenhall remained in the arboretum. She wanted to go to fifth floor containment, the Infectious Diseases wing, to interview the captive visitor and to examine Peterson and her chart. She had every right to do these things, and Thorpe would not prevent her. But doing so might bring too much attention, prompt Thorpe to send people down to Claiborne. The tech may have already stirred interest. The interviews and follow-ups were fine; the reenactments and measuring might have crossed lines. She pictured again how Silva had cast herself over the patient on Four, how elegant and still she had appeared, how she had drawn the patient toward touching. Thorpe could conceivably have Silva contained—herself as well.

A polite, professional consultation with Thorpe might prompt similar actions. Thorpe would be gathering the same data, the same confounding results. His conclusion would run counter to hers—containment. Infection had been the first call—her call—and thus would be the standing assumption. She felt driven to this room.

The young couple remained on their bench but were stealing looks at her.

"What's happening, Doctor?" the man asked. He had the same

expansive eyes and mouth as the woman, their largeness unnerving on him, fetching on her. Brother and sister.

"It's just a precaution. I think you'll be able to leave the hospital soon."

"We don't want to leave. We want our dad to be let in. We're visiting our mother."

"Soon," said Mendenhall. "I'm sure he'll get to see her."

"She's dying."

Mendenhall bowed her head and tightened her mouth. Protocol discouraged any reaction: the mother was not her patient, not her matter. Legally, condolence was affirmation; reassurance was disagreement.

"Can you get him in for us?"

"Who's her doctor?"

"He left," said the sister, one corner of her lips crimping. "He got out."

It was easy to imagine the hexagon contracting, the waterfall gaining volume.

"I'm—we're all trying to get the hospital open again."

IN THE HALL, she hesitated: once toward the elevators, then the waiting area, then the arboretum. She had known it would be a mistake to go into the hall without destination, but she had to get away from the already grieving brother and sister. She couldn't have the nurses see her like this. She strode to the elevators and inserted her express key. The elevator took a long time arriving, confusing her. And in this bracket of unexpected wait, she felt exposed and weakened.

When the steel doors opened, there was Mullich. He stood alone, arms crossed, wearing a lab coat. At first she thought he was wearing a stethoscope, posing as a doctor. But it was something else, a scope of some sort, some kind of viewing lens.

"Doctor," he said. He stepped out of the elevator and offered its emptiness to her. Cool air rose from the motion of his arm.

"You were outside." She stayed with him, letting the doors close. She looked up. "You were on the roof."

"I'm going to Verdasco's mark." He headed toward the waiting area and she followed.

"You got on the roof." She hustled to stay astride. "You took my elevator from me and got on the roof. I want *your* key."

"It will be helpful to have you along," he said, slipstream still fresh.

12.

Mullich genuflected over the floor mark and aimed his scope toward the long end of the hall, beyond the arboretum and the nurse's station. Mendenhall stood beside him. Visitors in the ICU waiting area watched as Mullich repositioned himself to take four measurements with the scope, Mendenhall turning with him, pretending.

"He never moved, then?" Mullich peered through the scope. On the near wall it cast three red dots, the middle one more pronounced, the two side ones faint.

"He was already in collapsed position. He went from life to death without moving."

"No. He traveled to the ER. To you. From here down to there."

"Look," said Mendenhall, "I kind of see what you're doing. Tracking a pattern. A pattern of . . ." She felt the attention of the waiting-area visitors and caught herself. "A pattern of demise."

Mullich took one more reading and stood. The visitors left with worried expressions, back to their loved ones or to the cafeteria.

"That's a good way of putting it." Mullich faced her. "Good enough."

Mendenhall shook her head and jabbed a finger toward the scope dangling from his neck. "It's not. You can't track death that easily in this place. I pronounced Verdasco dead down in ER. Time of death down there, too." She raised a fist to show him the cheap running watch on her wrist. "Using this. So what pattern are you tracking? Blood or paper?"

"Blood."

"Then forget ER. Verdasco died here." She pointed to the floor mark she and Silva had calibrated. "Dozier died on his ladder. Fleming died on her roommate's bed. See, Thorpe's going to use the paper one. But I don't care about some nurse's hopeful fingers taking a pulse that isn't there, about shoving eyelids closed, about some tired ER doctor pronouncing time of death because some other doctor ran away."

Mullich, as Silva had done, recorded information in his pad as Mendenhall spoke, focused on accuracy. She let him finish his entries.

Mullich stared at his pad. "And Peterson?"

"My guess is she died in that ventilation room. Right where they found her. But we couldn't get to Peterson because she's not mine. Not without pissing off . . ." With the heel of her palm, she pushed Mullich's forehead, forcing his gaze to her. "You. You can get me to Peterson. With that key of yours."

"That depends, Dr. Mendenhall."

"On what?"

"On what fight you're fighting."

She narrowed her look.

"Blood or paper."

She gave him an honest answer. There probably was no other kind for him. "I'm still deciding. I'll decide when I return to Claiborne. So give me Peterson. And that witness Thorpe has up there. That's your next stop, right? Dozier on Seven, Fleming on Four, Verdasco on Three."

"Not quite. I visit the roof in between each."

She retracted.

"For perspective." He raised his scope.

"I gave *you* an honest answer."

"Fair enough," he said. "I do go up there in between—to maintain and record perspective. But I'm also watching the containment. The shape of the containment. Its growth. I'll take you. I'll show you. But you have to agree to my conditions."

"You sound like Thorpe."

"No. I'm not like Thorpe. I've designed buildings—redesigned them—for people like Thorpe. But not this place. Not this hospital. Not this time around. Not anymore."

Stepping onto the roof meant everything to her. She could still smell it on Mullich, imagine its air trapped in the creases of his lab coat. Visitors approached the waiting area, then veered away when they neared Mendenhall and Mullich.

"What are your conditions?"

Mullich held up his card key. "Every time this is used, it's recorded. Yours, too. Thorpe's as well, and any like it. Anyone can see. That's how it is. That's how it must be. Transparent action."

She shrugged.

"No," he said. "You don't understand. You have to enter your key, too. Even though it won't open the doors. It will be recorded. Anyone, including Thorpe, gets to see where you go, where you tried to go."

"Thorpe won't play that way."

"I don't care. And I'm not playing."

13.

The roof door rejected her key. A tiny red light above the slot blinked twice. Mullich inserted his key, the light went green, a beep sounded, and the door opened, bypassing containment.

"Who gets to push the button?" Mendenhall asked. "The one that suddenly changes all the doors? Thorpe? You?"

"There is a chain of agreement. Thorpe is one link. My office just does the resetting because we know how. There is no single button." Mullich led her up the short flight of stairs and out to the roof. They headed to the telescope relic.

She paused to eye the stars. "Are you comfortable with all that? That chain of agreement? With policy, with Men Who Know Best? Containing things to keep the public calm."

"It might be the best first course of action."

She shook her head, continued to skim the stars. "First course of action becomes the *only* course of action. With policy and its makers and enforcers. Our nerves are built for power. They feed on it."

One step short of the low wall, Mendenhall closed her eyes and drew a full breath of night air. Cool and damp, it opened her lungs. She took the final step blind. She opened her eyes in exhalation, her look aimed toward the dark running trails below.

"Still," she said, "it all comes down to someone pressing *enter*. No?"

"You watch too much television."

They stood side by side, she tracing the trail run she craved, he aiming his scope over the parking lot.

"What will Thorpe think?" she asked. "If he notices I tried to come out here with you?"

Mullich was aiming his scope at a white truck blocking the parking-lot gate. "That I'm out here explaining things to you. I've already brought him out here. I told him I would bring other doctors involved."

She followed his aim as he glided it to other targets. The red dot spotted three more white trucks that she hadn't noticed: one parked in the center of the lot, one at the ambulance-only turn, another far down the hill road. The last truck was just a pale smudge in the darkness. The dot of his aim made a tiny red star.

"What is that thing?"

"A range finder." He continued measuring targets.

"How accurate is it?"

"Inside, at those distances, within two millimeters. Out here, within centimeters."

She pointed to the moon, a gray crescent. "Can you hit that?"

He took the scope from his eyes, which was all she wanted him to do. "Theoretically. But you would have to account for the refraction in the atmosphere, the bend of gravity from both moon and Earth, the time, and the scatter."

"The scatter?"

"Of light. By the time this reaches the moon, assuming we calculate all those factors, the light would dissipate into a large field several hundred meters wide."

"Circle or square?" Her thoughts were dissipating, what she had hoped for on this roof.

"A kind of X, actually," he replied. "Not quite axes, not quite perpendicular." He was making entries on his tablet, its blue illuminating his face, paling the angles.

"What did you see out there?"

"On the moon?" he asked. "Or here?"

"Here. Where I want to be. Not the moon—where I should want to be."

"Containment is increasing," he said.

She quit looking at the moon, the lot, the dark trails, and turned to Mullich. She parted her lips to speak but remained silent.

"It's to be expected," he told her. "When they brought me here, design for containment was a priority. This made sense. They showed me their patterns, and I showed them the patterns of my research from other hospitals around the world. The evolution of infections outpaces the hospital. That's no secret. Even something as common as staph trumps the Mayo. MRSA becomes VRSA. The infection grows increasingly resistant to control, though it remains the same contagion."

"You've spent too much time with Thorpe," she said.

"You deny those facts?"

She shook her head. "But another fact is that Thorpe fantasizes a world where everyone is contagious. The whole world his ID ward."

"As opposed to one big ER?"

"Yes," she replied. "Which is what it really is."

She rubbed her nose with the back of her hand, looked to the trails below. "I'm not going to Peterson with you. I don't care about Peterson. She's dead. She was dead when she got to me. She's Thorpe's specimen. Claiborne and I can approximate her time of collapse using Thorpe's requests."

Mullich raised a brow.

"It's simple," she explained. "His questions for the others will show what he knows about Peterson."

"But there is something, then," he said. "Something you want me to get. For you. Without letting Thorpe know."

"Just ask one question for me. When you're in there with your key. Ask that witness how many times she looked at Verdasco. How many times she looked before his eyes turned to glass. Beautiful glass."

Mullich made no reply, just stared at her.

"You can tell Thorpe exactly what you tell me. Tell him how many times she looked at Verdasco before she noticed something wrong. Would that satisfy you? Is that transparent enough?"

"If you'll come to one more place with me."

HE TOOK HER to a file room on the first floor. It was the room she had gone to after her very first shift in the ER. She had gone there to cry. She had gone there to hide. Her mentor had found her right away, two stale coffees in hand. The room's window faced east. Beyond the delivery trucks one could see blurry mountains rising from the city haze.

Mullich did not switch on the light and stopped her from doing so. The room was filled with the orange glow of the delivery bay outside, some pale reflections off the shipping trucks, too. Styrofoam cups littered the tops of the steel file cabinets. The room smelled of ashes, burned filters, and rancid coffee.

At first she was frightened; of what, she wasn't sure. Mullich, yes, but of what he could predict or of what he intended? Then, from the way he surveyed the room, she could see that it was his first time here. He went to the window, and she followed.

"Why here?" she asked. It was an ER question, one that suggested understanding, opened to possibilities.

"I want to help you decide. Blood or paper. I want to make sure you see."

With a very small flashlight, a key-chain thing, he illuminated the window. The light was icy, almost blue. It turned the window opaque. On the glass near the edge he focused on a cluster of smudges, angling the light.

"Someone tried to slide it open," she said. "So?"

"Not someone. Two people together. Very recently." He angled the light to sweep the broad plane of the window. Four handprints were clearly visible in the middle of the pane. "They shoved at it. From where we stand now."

"How did you know?"

"You can see by the handprints that they stood together. One shorter than the other, the taller one more desperate, his prints more smeared."

"Not that," she said. "I can see that. How did you know to come here? You've never been in here."

"Not physically, no."

She gazed at a single handprint, the highest one. The fingers were fully splayed, the thumb smeared along in a series of adjustments, a stop-motion effect. Mullich enhanced the effect by angling the light.

"In about an hour," he said, "there will be a few more."

"Or it will just be open."

"That would be impossible. All lower-floor windows were replaced. We don't use glass anymore. These windows don't slide anymore. They don't break."

"Are the blueprints in your head, or do you have to check?" She motioned to the tablet in his lab-coat pocket. "With that."

"I don't have to check." He evened himself to her, dousing the flashlight. The room became amber. "It's not that difficult, Doctor. Much less than what you have memorized. In your fingertips. How quickly do you go to the throat of a patient? Or the right kidney, a certain spot beneath the ribs, beneath an arm, into the ear? Without thinking, your hands moving on their own, two fingers ready?"

He illuminated the handprint again, singling out the highest one.

"I'll go in and get that answer for you." He lifted his face closer to the print, seeing something new. "If you make the fight about blood."

"It's never that simple. Sometimes you have to use paper. When paper trumps blood. And I'm good at faking when I need to get something from a patient. But I'm not good at fooling myself."

In the dimness, she could still see his gaze. He was looking at her face, her eyes, her mouth, back to her eyes. She was being honest. He remained silent.

"When you go in there," she told him, "she'll be scared. You'll be another doctor. You can't approach her like this. Like this, with me. She'll swear she didn't even touch Verdasco. She won't listen to your question. She'll want answers first. She'll want to know why things are attached to her." Mendenhall wiggled her index finger at Mullich. "Why this?"

She pointed to the range finder hanging from his neck. "And take that off before you go in."

14.

Mullich left the file room, pausing to offer the window to her, the space, kept the light off, softly closed the door. She watched the door eclipse his long shadow on the linoleum. The outside light from the loading bay reminded her of hard candy. Now that she knew where to look, she could see the four handprints on the window, the cluster of smudges where they tried to slide the pane. She could see them only with averted vision, her focus the supply truck beyond.

She was testing the effect, letting the handprints vanish and reappear, when a message pinged. Anything from outside her hospital life chimed that particular way. It was her aunt.

Cortez
?
He misses you.
Not fair.
Take him back.
You see why I cant.
Then when this is over.
Then no.
Are you ok in there?
Yep.
Safe?

And sound.

She slung the cell in its holster and pressed her wrists to her temples, rolled her jaw. She leaned against the wall and was about to let herself slide into a sitting position, stare at the window, when Pao Pao buzzed her. The zap on her hip made her clench her thigh, trailed the sciatic path. She let Pao Pao record her message. The nurse worked best that way, uninterrupted, no questions, no false assurances.

Mendenhall picked up when she saw that Pao Pao had finished. They had four new arrivals, all high fevers and pain. Mendenhall counted three even breaths in the resinous light before she left the file room.

PAO PAO HAD the four gurneys arranged in order of arrival, the EMTs kept at bay. Only one other nurse was working with Pao Pao, like her dressed in gloves, mask, and glasses. Patients in the beds lining the ER walls watched Mendenhall's approach. An EMT offered her a fresh protection kit. She took the gloves and waved off the rest as she headed to the arrivals.

Arrival one was a nurse, her expression widening as Mendenhall neared. Mendenhall looked at the nurse's eyes, then her fingers, then her length on the gurney. She eyed Pao Pao. "Let me guess. Third Floor. Pain . . ." Mendenhall palpated the sternum. "*Here.*"

Arrival one gasped. Mendenhall checked herself, took a breath. The EMTs had formed a line. Within this line gathered some of the ER nurses. Mendenhall wondered how they gauged their distance. What possible piece of medical knowledge had they gleaned that told them that twelve feet was safer than ten? What was gathering now in their sympathetic little nerve bundles?

She turned to Pao Pao.

"Fever 102, sudden fatigue," said Pao Pao. "Chest pain."

Mendenhall surveyed the three other arrivals, resting her hand on the sternum of the nurse from ICU. All three were focused on her, lips parted, heads lifted. One was an EMT; two were nurses.

Mendenhall moved away, tried to disguise her anger in quickness, and conferred with Pao Pao.

She raised a finger to stop Pao Pao from speaking. "Listen to my guesses first. If I'm right—pretty much right—then we'll know."

Pao Pao nodded once, jaw firm.

"The EMT's from here; one other nurse is also from Three, the other maybe from Seven. The one from Seven—neck pain. I'd say the other nurse from Three has the highest fever: 102 five, by the look in her eyes. Chest pain. The EMT, no pain at first, then neck and chest."

Pao Pao said nothing, blinked once, then waited.

"One came in about five minutes before the other from ICU. The other two right after."

"Cabral—the EMT," said Pao Pao. "He—"

Mendenhall raised a hand. "He. He just kind of joined in. When he saw them coming."

Pao Pao waited. Blinked.

Mendenhall spoke as softly as possible. "Here's what we do. We're going to give Thorpe one of these." She checked arrival one. "I focus on her, tend to her. You remove your mask and goggles and touch the other three, push them away, get that other nurse to join you. Get her to chat them up."

CABRAL SAT UP and scooted to the edge of his gurney before the nurses reached him. He was still in his EMT scrubs. He peeked at Mendenhall and inhaled through parted lips. Mendenhall said nothing to her patient as she palpated beneath the arms. She was tracking Pao Pao and the other nurse. They made a good tandem: Pao Pao silent, her arms swift and deliberate, the other nurse stooped and cooing.

Mendenhall felt something along the brachial crease, a spasm, realized too late that she had let her fingers linger there. A second later the woman convulsed, hips thrusting, head pushing back. Perspiration dampened her brow and neck, visible to all in the tendrils sticking to her skin. The nurse with Pao Pao lifted her hands away from their patient, held them there, her eyes widening along with the sudden spread of her fingers.

THREE WENT TO ID. Cabral would maybe escape. Mendenhall sat in her cubicle, trying to fashion her entries. She was hoping to just leave Cabral out of the charts. There would be more of these hysterics; he might be forgotten.

Pao Pao was clearing a corner of the bay for fever arrivals, forming slots between empty beds for incoming gurneys. Mendenhall felt the dull nausea of defeat, nearing surrender. She could just play this out, let Thorpe get everything he wanted. How long could this last? Three, four days at the most? But she had trouble imagining an end, Thorpe never managing to isolate anything.

Because there is nothing to isolate. She entered this on her screen. She needed to read it, to close her eyes, then open them and see it again.

Pao Pao stood at the opening of the cubicle. Her expression was one of flat assessment, the Samoan lift in her eyes checking the grim line of her jaw.

"Are you right?" she asked.

Mendenhall tried to nod but only lifted her chin, looked.

"Because ID is going to fill up," said Pao Pao. "They will start to pick and choose from these fevers, sending some back here. I plan to work through it. Working makes work pass quickly."

"Does it matter, Pao?" Mendenhall sighed. "If I'm right?"

"To me, yes."

Mendenhall pivoted her screen for the nurse, pointed to the last entry.

"Say it," said Pao Pao. "Please can you say it, Doctor?"

"I'm right," said Mendenhall.

"That convulsion," said Pao Pao. "That convulsion surprised you. I saw."

"That was my fault. I contributed to the hysteric. I left my hand in one spot too long. She thought I found something."

"Did you find something?"

Mendenhall shook her head. "I'm right."

15.

She tried to be Thorpe, to see as Thorpe. On her screen she brought up the latest studies on toxic shock and viral hemorrhagic fevers. When she read the descriptions, the symptom variations and anomalies, she could see the possibilities. Both could mirror sudden trauma. Both could strike a final blow suddenly, earlier symptoms hidden in the general malaise of grief, work, recovery. But when she let her vision rest on the ER bay, her self-doubt waned.

Two figures wearing the black and purple of ID entered the bay. Overdressed with surgeon's cap and booties, the leader moved directly toward Mendenhall's line of patients, the beds nearest the main station and elevators, the ones Pao Pao had arranged for her. Even with his exaggerated getup, Mendenhall recognized Dmir. She had never bothered to figure out his title, his position. She just knew him as a sort of containment executive, Thorpe's link to the profane. Dmir liked to dress up as a doctor, did that whenever he had the slightest opportunity. The surgeon's cap was new.

His trailing nurse appeared embarrassed by it, slouched and hanging back a half step. Mendenhall swooped into the bay. It felt that way; she didn't sense her legs, any of herself—on wings.

As she moved to cut off Dmir, she tried to reengage with her body, her thoughts, distill and purge the metaphors. Dmir was metaphor. Mendenhall was real. She sensed Pao Pao sliding in to cover the flank, drew from this.

"Doctor," she said to Dmir, stepping between him and his trailing nurse. As a child she had watched a show hosted by a purple dinosaur. She thought of that to gain some strength, some touch of earnestness. "Oh," she said when Dmir turned to her, "it's you. Just you."

"Dr. Mendenhall," he said, "we need this line of beds. We need this wall cleared."

This did not surprise her. But something about him did. Dmir had a freshness about him. Maybe it was all the purple, the way he filled it. Pao Pao was tending one of her patients along the wall, just tucking the sheets, tapping the chart, saying something low. But she was right on Dmir's flank, drawing a glance from him and halting his trailing nurse. Mendenhall took one full breath.

"I have nine. Two ballistic traumas we're stabilizing, three poisons we're dissipating, two ODs—oxy and alcohol—and two nearing DTs."

Dmir creased his brow, confusion disguised as concern.

"To answer the first question you should've asked," said Mendenhall, just loudly enough for the patients and the nearby EMTs and nurses at the station, "I cleaned, sutured, and medicated the ballistics. They cannot be moved yet. Getting shot—even in the arm or leg—is highly traumatic. The wound is nothing compared to what happens to the whole nervous system—but you know that." She lowered her voice, offered Dmir an inclusive raise of her eyes. "Moving the others would also compromise the stability of the first two. By attrition."

Dmir straightened a bit, though still appearing stooped, in costume. Mendenhall remembered the music from the show with the purple dinosaur. The show had been good for her. She had been too serious as a girl, too concerned with real life.

"But it's your call."

"Attrition," said Dmir.

"Yes. Attrition. The same thing that produced those three new containments."

Pao Pao moved down one patient, creating some distance from Dmir but widening the flank in this battle.

"Look it up," said Mendenhall. "You'll like it. Hysteria is highly contagious. It flies." She sensed Pao Pao's warning glance. She backed off, drew a discreet breath. "I'll clear the wall for you. As soon as we outpatient the ballistics." She raised her voice. "You concur?"

Dmir looked at his watch.

"Two hours," Mendenhall said before he could speak. "Tops. You can make the arrangements with Nurse Pao Pao." They both turned toward Pao Pao, who was looking flatly at Dmir. "Or I can do that for you."

Then she realized what exactly was new about him, the freshness. He had come in—after containment. Dmir never stayed past five—not like real doctors. He had night air about him, cocktail hour. His watch glittered. She could almost feel his pulse, measure its increase.

She remembered what she had hated about the purple dinosaur, the hate that made her want the show, need it. She would solve math problems during the episodes, lists of them, filling pages, all corners and margins, both sides, her fingers smeared with pencil lead. During songs she would draw the periodic table, delineate the inert gases, all subgroups. Babysitters stood horrified, their expressions not unlike those on the faces of the EMTs and nurses now watching her step once toward the station before cutting away from all of them, stepping to her patients.

Her patients. The longest anyone could be her patient was about two hours; then they were either discharged or assigned to the proper specialist. She had repeats—drunks, addicts, prostitutes, some ballistics. But ER repeats eventually disappeared. Into their lives, her mentor had told her, the lives they choose. See it that way.

Dmir lingered. Pao Pao was starting to leave, then halted between them. Mendenhall squinted at Dmir.

"What? What more?"

"Who's Cortez?" he asked.

"Who wants to know?"

"We," he said, "we want—"

"That was from my aunt. That was personal."

Pao Pao spoke, her voice low, her look flat, but there was relish in the angle of her head, the motion of her fist toward the floor between Dmir's shoes. "Cortez is her dog."

Dmir looked to Mendenhall for verification.

"Cortez," Pao Pao repeated. "A terrier, about the size of your Clarks. A little Scottie. Cortez. Cortez the Killer."

"The Killer?" Dmir raised his brow, not sure which woman to address.

"From the song."

"What song?"

"You don't know anything, Dmir. You don't know anything about anything," Mendenhall said. "Tell Thorpe to stay off my personal messages."

"You relayed information. Outside containment."

"I told my aunt I was safe and sound. It was for her. You tell Thorpe it was a lie. I feel anything but safe and sound. With him up there. I lied to my aunt for the sake of his containment. Because if I had sent her the truth she would be coming for me."

"Cortez, too," said Pao Pao.

They left Dmir in unison.

MENDENHALL VISITED THE first ballistic, joining Pao Pao bedside the bed. Kae Ng. Twenty-three. His name and age read like something from the periodic table. She looked at his slender wrists and knew he was only fifteen.

He was looking at her in a flirty way. He was high on the stuff she had given him. His black hair fell over his eyes, and he smiled with one side of his mouth. He peeked once at his shoulder, at the dressing she had applied.

"Can I have the bullet?" He had a smooth, low voice.

"You do have it."

He raised an eyebrow.

"I left it in. We usually leave them in. They're sterile. We only take them out on TV."

He seemed disappointed.

"I know," she told him. "The only reason I joined ER was for the bullet. So I could be that doctor who pulled it out and plunked it into the pan. That sound, you know? That finality. That cure. But it doesn't go that way. It never goes that way. It just melts inside you."

"Someone could use a nap," said Pao Pao.

n Pathology, Claiborne had the ventilation on full. Mendenhall could tell because the air was especially quiet. The vents did that, hushed the lab. Claiborne had once showed her the effect using a tuning fork he kept on his desk. He struck the fork—A, he told her. There was no sound. Then he fired the vents and struck the note again. The pure note emerged amid the gather of the ambient vents. So now maybe he had the vents on full for the music, which was a quiet violin solo drawing long single notes. But the lab was chilled, and the bodies remained on the steel, death grins forming.

Claiborne stood over Verdasco, looking from the young, beautiful body to an overhead display, then back to the body. Mullich was absent, but Mendenhall could see that he had set up shop in one of the lab's corners. Charts hung over his table, four showing drawings of the bodies in their respective found positions, floating. Four others appeared as blueprints of the spaces; one displayed the entire hospital cut into floors. The building had three basements, two more below this one. The one just below she had been to once or twice. The third was new to her.

Silva stood at Mullich's desk, bending slightly to make entries on the architect's laptop. The drawings of the bodies had lines through them. The drawings of the rooms and hospital had faint spirals on them shot through with blue dashes. A large chart beside the laptop was scrolled out on the desk.

The cold, thin air. The silent motions of Silva and Claiborne. They could have been on the moon.

Claiborne straightened to face Mendenhall. His mask was down. She started to speak, but he checked her with a look. She snapped on fresh gloves, exaggerating the last pull of elastic.

"I was right," she said. "Wasn't I? Trauma through the bronchus in Fleming. In Verdasco," she nodded toward the body, "through the brain stem and thorax."

"More or less," said Claiborne.

She sensed Silva's approach.

"Trauma," said Mendenhall. "So, trauma."

Claiborne shook his head. "Viral. Everything points to viral. Maybe fungal. I never rule that out too soon. But viral is the way to go. Hemorrhagic and sudden. Thorpe's fear."

"Thorpe's hope, you mean."

Claiborne closed his eyes and took a breath. There was a draw on the violin. "I want you to be right, Dr. Mendenhall. Like I want to be eating Thai with my wife. But he is right. You know it, too."

She thought, searched past the fatigue. She looked at Silva's face, relieved to find the tech's mask down, furtive lips and nose, eyes lifted. "No. I don't know it."

"Look, Doctor." Claiborne opened his hands, his arms. "You are very good at what you do. You made the call right away. You saw it."

She looked at the clean bodies, their skin reflecting the aimed light. "There should've been more bleeding, less isolation. Even in something fast. Dengue fever, even. Any VHF."

"That's what I thought. After you sent your predictions. So I searched. . . . I found this." Claiborne changed Verdasco's overhead to show a scan of his brain. Mendenhall saw a faint cloud along the edge of Verdasco's frontal lobe.

"And this." Claiborne changed the scan to Verdasco's left kidney. Another cloud.

"Those are pretty vague."

Claiborne shook his head. "They just got started. Then he died."

Silva stepped closer, almost getting between them. Mullich would have found that interesting, would have drawn the triangle, noted its slightness.

"We found similar hemorrhaging in the others," Silva said. "In other major organs. Dozier's liver and brain, Fleming's kidneys and brain. Thorpe confirmed something similar in Peterson's brain and lungs."

"You mean *incipient* hemorrhaging." Mendenhall eyed Verdasco's display as she spoke, trying not to lessen her tone.

"Don't fight this," said Claiborne. His gaze was that same look again, the one he gave her on the trail before he increased his pace. "You are the one giving us—including Thorpe—some of the best anticipations. Use them right."

He motioned to Verdasco's brain scan, then continued, "We most likely have a virus that produces trauma. We know viruses that do that—induce trauma, shock. This is new, yes. But it's in the continuum. New means nothing more to me than indication. Indication to find and identify. It doesn't mean panic. It doesn't mean containment. It means work for me. For us."

Mendenhall could not help inverting his first premise. It was what she did. It was what she had been taught. It was why she had gone to that abandoned file room. She closed her eyes and went there in her thoughts, just for the moment it took her to think out the inversion. Trauma that produces virulent hemorrhaging.

"I know what you're thinking," said Claiborne, "and it makes no sense. Not with what we have. Not with time and placement. It all happened here. Inside."

Mendenhall looked across the lab at Mullich's displays. Claiborne followed her gaze.

"He's doing it right, too," said Claiborne. "Using you right. Finding patterns. Hopefully a center."

Mendenhall looked at Silva.

"No," said Claiborne. "She's doing it right, too. Don't go there."

"You'll get me fired." Silva returned their looks.

"I want you to keep coming down here, Doctor." Again Claiborne opened his hands to her. "Because it will help you up there." He motioned toward the ceiling. "And it's helping us down here. But not if you're going to fight every finding. For fight's sake."

Mendenhall rubbed her own shoulders, kneaded them, resisting the urge to press her eyes and face. "When does containment end, then? Assuming no more outbreak. Assuming Thorpe disregards those last hystericals."

"All early cultures and tests are negative. But he staggered the patients. We'll go home in the morning."

She nodded as she looked down, felt Silva watching her. Mendenhall liked how Claiborne called them patients. His patients were neither dead nor alive. Even the dead ones, for him, kept giving.

"Thorpe's good," said Claiborne. "Maybe even a good person. He's just intense. How he should be—for what he does."

Mendenhall disagreed, felt it as the beginning of a shudder but let it go. She stayed there and looked at their scans, all of the clouds and lines and patterns. She found solace in the quiet movements of Claiborne and Silva, in the violin and chill and distilled air. But she went into her own world.

Cause of trauma affects treatment. A stab, a bullet, a toxin, blunt force call for distinct treatments. But only in the in-between, the sometimes long-between. First you treat the trauma itself. You hold a hand, say something, apply pressure, anodyne. Last you make sure to treat the trauma again, try to end it. If you don't, the patient is damaged forever, dies.

And the inverse of Claiborne's premise—his sound premise, the one they were all working under—stayed with her. Trauma produces virulent reaction.

17

B ut circumstance canceled trauma as the first cause. Circumstance allowed for virus as first cause, trauma as result, trauma as cause of demise. Mendenhall needed to do some research, five minutes on her screen. She stood aside in Pathology, still watching Silva and Claiborne. Claiborne, she could see, was getting ready to send the bodies into drawers. He was measuring Verdasco with a laser pen, the numbers scrolling onto the overhead. The thought of returning to her floor depressed Mendenhall.

Silva was starting to close out Mullich's laptop.

"Wait," Mendenhall told her, then stepped close.

Silva raised her brow.

"Can I use that?" Mendenhall asked. "Mullich won't mind. In fact he'd prefer it. So he can see what I'm doing."

Silva deferred to Claiborne. Claiborne fired his laser pen at Mendenhall's heart. She touched the red dot.

"I'm not fighting. Look, this way you can see right away what I'm thinking. Please, Dr. Claiborne. It's nice down here."

Claiborne returned to his task.

Mendenhall sat before Mullich's laptop, and Silva went to assist Claiborne. They listened to the single violin. Mendenhall felt her movements slow along with the rest of the room. She breathed, tasted the air as it dried her lips and tongue. The paper scroll beside the laptop was a blueprint of the hospital, a vertical. The ER was the longest rectangle. The roof was two brackets, opened to the sky, the empty blue.

On screen she brought up a recent study of hydrostatic shock. The accompanying video showed a rectangular block of gel being penetrated by a bullet in super slow-motion. The visual study showed a series of shots, each successive one lowering the caliber of the projectile while increasing velocity. The experiment aimed to demonstrate the value of velocity over the size of the caliber. The final demonstration showed a missile the size of a shotgun pellet passing through the gel at extreme velocity. On initial impact, a large cone of air instantly expanded the gel block, distorting it into an oval, almost exploding the entire block. Swirls of distorted gel spiraled outward, barely contained by the membrane, forming translucent waves. The pellet exited through a pinpoint at the tip of the cone, and the gel block returned to its original shape, but with coils of air caught along the perimeter and in the corners. These were trauma lines, vague and distant parentheses around the primary line left by the ballistic path.

It was pretty. It seemed to dance to the long draw of the violin bow sounding above the lab. The gel block was backlit with amber light to accentuate the trauma lines.

"Come see," said Mendenhall, softly, in case they were listening.

Silva came; Claiborne remained with Verdasco. Mendenhall ran the last video again, the highest velocity.

"It's hydrostatic shock," Mendenhall told Silva. She felt the lab tech near her shoulder. "It shows how high-velocity projectiles, even when very small, cause peripheral damage. Extreme damage."

Mendenhall repeated the demo.

"The body returns to form." Silva's voice was plaintive.

"I know that study." Claiborne spoke without leaving his position, the direction of his voice downward. Mendenhall imagined him behind them, talking to Verdasco. "You're fighting, Dr. Mendenhall."

"I'm not." She ran the video again, pausing at impact, the birth of the spiral. "I'm doing what I should do at this point. My expertise. What I know that causes peripheral hemorrhaging. Why people die from what should be nonfatal invasion. Why bodies die from impacts to nonvital tissue. Why I have patients die from getting shot in the shoulder, the thigh, the foot. Why I had one die from a piece of glass through her bicep."

"Those are extreme velocities," said Claiborne.

"We live in a world of extreme velocities."

"We have no ballistic," replied Claiborne. His voice was even lower, crouching closer to Verdasco. "We have no entry or exit."

"Okay. Okay. I'm just showing peripheral trauma. Peripheral hemorrhaging as indicator for extreme trauma. Hemorrhaging distant from the point of initiation. Bleeding in the most liquid organs." Mendenhall pointed to the amber swirls in the corners of the gel block, drawing Silva closer. "Far perimeter clouds in the brain and liver."

Mendenhall winced at her own words. Metaphor indicated lack of precision, a skip in the equation.

"Far perimeter clouds?" Claiborne knew what she was thinking.

"Okay. Perimeter bruising." Mendenhall turned away from the screen and looked at Claiborne, waited for him to quit Verdasco. After a moment he straightened and looked at her.

"That's what you have," she told him. "Something—a viral impact, if you want—that causes perimeter hemorrhaging in uninvolved organs. That's a valid assumption until you find something in those peripheral tissues. Those far tissues. I think you should focus on those samples first. While Thorpe's people go after the primary hemorrhages."

"I am Thorpe's people." Claiborne looked at Silva. "We are Thorpe's people."

"You know what I mean."

Claiborne joined her and Silva by the laptop. They stood together beneath Mullich's charts.

"Run it again," he said, nodding toward the laptop screen. "It's pretty. My eyes need a break."

Silva was the one who tapped it into motion. They watched the pellet pass straight through the gel block, the spiral of amber distorting the whole into a sideways tornado.

"I'm helping," said Mendenhall. "Increasing efficiency."

"Providing entertainment." Claiborne took control of the video, his hand dark and slender, freshly peeled from its glove. He made the demonstration run backward and forward, repeating. He darkened the screen, deepening the amber backlight. The impact seemed to bring the gel block to life, morphed it into a cell, quickening, seeking another.

18.

When Mullich returned to the lab they had to explain themselves. Claiborne had already moved back to Verdasco's body, drawing Silva with a nod. He must have sensed the architect's approach, the breach in his underworld. Mendenhall sat alone by the laptop, the video still looping, caught.

Mullich let the door ease shut behind him. He sterilized his hands with lotion, pulled on fresh gloves, all while scanning the others in the room, the screen displays. Everything was there for him. Mendenhall started to explain, then caught herself. This was Mullich. She returned his gaze and drew back from the desk, letting him see. Claiborne and Silva continued their work, innocent.

Mullich stood above Mendenhall and watched the loop. Intermittently he glanced back to the bodies. Then he moved to Claiborne's desk, studied the scans showing the primary trauma patterns.

When Mendenhall joined him, she said nothing.

"In these two," Mullich pointed to the scans of Dozier and Verdasco, "the cone is reversed."

"It's not the cone we're—I'm—focused on." Mendenhall found a laser pen on Claiborne's desk. She drew the bead of light across both diagonals, slashing the brainstems. Then she aimed it at the scans of the frontal lobes, Verdasco's lung, Dozier's liver, the vague clouds in each.

"These show incipient hemorrhaging in peripheral organs. Major organs." She let Mullich see, just see.

"You think that," Mullich pointed toward the video, "happened to them?" He held his hand toward the bodies.

"Not exactly." Mendenhall led him to Verdasco. Claiborne stepped aside, one eyebrow raised as he looked at her. Silva pressed Verdasco's chin, extending the throat.

"The body reacts in known ways, according to preset nerve patterns. We develop these as we go through life. Kisses, caresses, slaps, pinpricks, falls, dives into water that violently strain our necks. Innocent, little things we never really register. Things that begin in utero.

"These bodies didn't roil like that gel block. The nerve patterns just reacted as if they did, as if they would. As if they were shot through. The most vital and liquid organs anticipated hydrostatic shock, began to hemorrhage along the far nerve endings. The end of a whip. But without the whip."

She lunged toward Mullich, her fingers flashing straight to his eyes. He drew back. Silva gasped.

"Like that," said Mendenhall, keeping her hand raised, her fingers spiked before his eyes. "Actually, exactly that."

She lowered her hand. "Your body registered that all over the place. You closed your eyes, obviously. But feel. Look." She motioned toward Mullich's hands which had balled into fists.

"And your heart," she said as Mullich looked at his fists, opened them. "Well, maybe not *your* heart." She motioned toward Silva. "But hers, yes. And your toes, I bet."

Mullich had gone slightly tiptoe. He lowered himself.

"That's her theory," said Claiborne. "We're testing the tissue samples. We have lances from all areas of hemorrhage."

"I'm right until they prove me wrong," said Mendenhall.

She sensed Claiborne's amusement.

"At least that's how it should be," she told Mullich. "But stupid me. I reversed everything, right from the start. I made that call. So they get to be right until they prove themselves wrong."

19

She hadn't realized the dead were leaving. She didn't know until she stood in the lower bay with Silva and Mullich, until after she had followed them past the turn to the morgue. After the turn her steps numbed, turned to dreams. Silva and Mullich were in full cover, including caps. Mendenhall suddenly felt naked. She pulled up her mask, tried to disguise her ignorance. Silva didn't seem to notice as she stood near the sealed slider, hands crossed. Mullich did, watched Mendenhall adjust her mask, tighten her gloves.

The bodies were being turned over to Disease Control. Claiborne had shooed her and Mullich away, away with Silva. He remained with the bodies in the lab.

Mendenhall took her place in line by the exit, pretending. Something clanged on the other side. Silva pressed the buzzer. They heard the turning of the outside crank-handle. The steel slider lifted with a gasp, and the DC techs entered immediately, dressed in full gear, spacemen in Mendenhall's dream. She couldn't see their faces. There were four, one pointing orders, three heading back toward the lab to fetch the bodies from Claiborne. The suits slowed their movements. The leader handed Mendenhall a cap, which she put on immediately. She could tell by the straightness of his arm that there was nothing to say, no room for anything but the literal. He could have been expecting her, forewarned.

The waiting truck, with its door rolled up and its ramp down, was white inside, a lab almost, with beds bunked along its side walls. Looming behind the truck, just beyond the entry light, a camouflaged jeep idled, its occupants hidden behind tinted windows. The DC people returned to the bay with the bodies on gurneys. The bodies were sealed in white bags. Mendenhall tried to identify them, found that she could. Dozier was the longest, Fleming the widest, Verdasco the thinnest. She recalled his cheekbones, how they reflected his hip points, paled the color of his skin.

Soon after they were up the ramp, the slider closed and she was alone again with Mullich, Silva, and three empty gurneys.

20

When they returned to the lab they shed their masks and gloves. Mullich and Silva removed their caps. Mendenhall kept hers in place, wondering how her hair looked. Mullich appeared fresh from the barber. Silva's black hair cascaded into form and then shone even more as she pulled it into a ponytail. Who were these people? She calculated the hours of her current shift. She was due a shower.

High on the far wall of the lab hung four large screens showing the four bodies in 3-D grids, blueprints. Claiborne stood working the desktop that controlled the screens. Like his main desk, that table was also a standing one. She wished she had his posture. His shift was just as long as hers.

For a moment, the only real movement was the roiling display left on Mullich's screen. When Mendenhall focused there, she saw that it had been changed. She moved to it, felt Mullich and Silva turn with her.

On screen, the gel-block ballistic experiment had been replaced by another loop. This one showed the very old and famous clip of the circus strongman taking a cannonball to his stomach. Over and over, in slow motion, the cannon fired point-blank into the man's belly, the huge iron ball trampolining harmlessly away while the strongman stood his ground. Claiborne had muted the sound, but Mendenhall heard it anyway, the prolonged and hollowed groan. Mullich and Silva were kind enough not to chuckle, but Mendenhall felt their smiles behind her.

"Okay, fine," she said. "But it shows the same thing, just from the polar opposite. And I bet the guy died from it. Eventually." She paused the video at the point of impact, the ball buried in the man's stomach, just missing his lower ribs. "It's the fat that saves him. And those big legs. But look, in this second he's a bag of jelly with eyes and a mouth." She pointed to the grotesque flap of his arms, the impossible angles of his elbows, the lifeless hands. "And there in the extremities you see the most damage being done."

She felt the sting of tears, a mix of frustration and fatigue. She set the loop into motion again and sympathized with the strongman. "Screw them," she said. "Right, big fella? Screw them."

SHE HEADED TO the surgeons' lounge to take a nap. She would wake up and this nightmare would be over. Thorpe's quarantines would expire into mere advisory and high caution, controlled exits.

All the beds and chairs and couches in the surgeons' lounge were taken. On one bed two nurses had doubled up, both snoring. She considered waking them, claiming the space. But her heart rate was up.

Before she could leave the lounge, she felt a message ping. Two surgeons looked up from their magazines, one a cigar, the other a men's health. At first Mendenhall thought to take it outside. But it was the magazines, their sheen. And the surgeons, with their legs crossed, their eyes going from the shallow pages to her, the disheveled ER fool who might mess with a personal communication to the outside. Her aunt started with the dog again.

My friend loves Cortez.

Give him.

That cold?

Mendenhall clenched against a sad shiver, a hurt that dropped along her left side. The surgeon with the cigar magazine appeared to notice, recrossed his legs, and pushed his pages flat and away.

Give.

Wait.

She had nothing, no reply. She looked to the surgeons, and they turned back to their magazines, the health one first, then, a second later, cigar.

How are you doing?

Surviving. Scratch behind his ears for me.

SHE TOOK THE elevator to recovery, found an empty physical therapy room, took off her cap, changed into scrubs, and stepped onto the treadmill. She set the incline and pace, began her run. She closed her eyes and pictured the trails outside, orange-lit in the night, shadow-crossed, air something between cool and humid—but moving, brushing her face and neck.

When she opened her eyes she was startled by how much time had passed. Next to the LCD recording minutes was her pulse, the rate higher than what she felt. Her legs still thrummed with energy, ready to begin, amplifying her sense of disconnection, the illusion that the body is not the self. That particular defense mechanism. Even the sheen of sweat was not hers; it was cool and cleansing.

She had once had an arrival who had dragged himself with his elbows for more than a mile. In an advanced stage of alcohol poisoning—years of poisoning combined with one more final lethal dose—he had lost function in his lower body. He had dragged himself to her because he did not want to die alone. He remembered her but could not remember anyone else in his life. "How?" she asked him. An athlete in his prime could not have done what this derelict had done. He looked at her as she pressed two fingers to his carotid pulse. She eased the pressure, let it be just a touch, the last thing he felt.

She heard the door to the Physical Therapy room open behind her. She remained on the treadmill, waited to hear some nurse's apology, the "Sorry, Doctor" that always grated on her nerves. Instead she heard Claiborne's voice.

"Those things never quite cut it for me."

She turned to him but stayed on the treadmill, surfing a little as it eased to a stop. "You need to find your inner hamster."

He had shed his lab clothes, stood straight in his shirt and tie, thin leather belt neat about his waist. "You have a much better imagination than I do."

"I dunno. Cannonball Man was pretty imaginative."

"I apologize for that."

"No," she said. "I deserved it. It's your lab."

He let the door close. "Okay. Here we are on neutral ground." He opened his hands to her.

"How did you find me?"

"I asked Mullich."

"That's scary. He's scary."

"He guessed the surgeons' lounge first. If that's any consolation."

The ground did not feel neutral. The slant of the treadmill matched the tilt in her senses. She asked anyway. "What do you think it is? If you had to stop now, if all information stopped now? What would you say?"

Claiborne crossed his arms, angled his waist to one side. "Virus. Hemorrhagic, fast like dengue HF, but obviously much faster. Not very contagious. Has to get into the stratum basale, start there, burst there. They got it in some weird way that isn't being repeated. Mullich's work is actually perfect for us here, centering on locale, degrees of separation among the four. DC taking the bodies is good. They can do much better work than I. They should reduce Thorpe's control. They'll get us out of here faster."

She fingered the rail of the treadmill. "I imagine them to be just like Thorpe. Thorpe squared. Men with protocol are worse than men with guns."

"Protocol will protect us. Protocol will release us in the morning."

"Protocol is ego." She gripped the rail. "Literally. It's ego put into writing."

"Ah, right. Dr. Metaphor."

"You want me to think in metaphor. I can do that. I can drink that poison. I think what's most viral is the protocol and consensus. I think we just released it when we opened the morgue door. Now Thorpe is outside as well as inside."

Her workout scrubs had become clammy. Claiborne looked freshly dressed, relaxed in fine clothes. I run more than he does, she thought. I should be faster. I should look like that.

"Okay," said Claiborne. "Then what do you think it is? If we had to stop here?"

"I would guess you're right. But that shock is involved more. Toxic or physical." To think pragmatically lifted her. She rolled her shoulders. She guessed this was an extension of Claiborne's apology and liked him for that.

"You know a virus that induces toxic shock?"

She shook her head. "I'm not thinking that way. I'm thinking in terms of traumatic reaction. That the bodies responded as though toxic or physical impact occurred. Because it's new. Even if no toxin or ballistic occurred, the nerves reacted as though they had or were about to. Isn't that what TSS is? A physiological overreaction to a minor but unanticipated toxin?"

He considered this, or pretended to, pulled at the back of his neck and looked askance. They were first and last. She knew this. There would always be too much information in between their specialties. He knew this, too, was calculating that gap, how far to lean her way.

"I'm glad I found you. Like this." Claiborne rested his hand on the door handle. "Disease Control will find whatever it is before I do. I never find the new stuff. We just lead them to it. They'll find no reason for containment. We'll be running the trail tomorrow. Take a shower and a nap."

He left the room, turning his shoulders in that way doctors do, showing their expert backs.

Instead of a shower, she filled one of the metal whirlpools in the room with cool water, not mixing any heat. She stripped, dropped the scrubs into the hamper, and lowered herself into the water. The chill didn't hit her until waist level, then increased around her breasts, forcing a shiver. She saved her head for last, pausing for breath before complete submergence. Underwater, eyes closed, she felt the jolt of the chill melt into relief. Sweat and salt and oil lifted in ribbons from her skin. To her surprise, she wanted to remain there, down there at the bottom of the big bucket. She imagined herself first as a specimen in a jar, then as an experiment growing in an old sci-fi flick.

21.

M endenhall dressed, her clothes the same but at least freshly aired. In front of the PT room's sink and mirror, she pulled her hair into a ponytail. She found an elastic finger splint as a clasp, enjoyed the tight sting along her nape. She applied tinted balm to her lips, then wiped the excess over her cheekbones, raising some color there. Her cell buzzed on the counter.

Pao Pao. Mendenhall let the message come in and finish. She stared at herself in the steel mirror, thought she looked okay, still a catch because she was a doctor. This was a desperate ploy for normalcy. A message from Pao Pao could not mean normal.

Mendenhall held the cell to her ear, close but not touching. The nurse's flat tone was there, but the Samoan accent was in there, too, downward pulls: three arrivals, one very different. Hurry.

The "hurry" meant be the first.

When Mendenhall moved away from the counter, she thought of a blur of herself remaining in front of the mirror—staying, looking okay, ceding all control.

MOVEMENT IN THE ER was occurring in concentric circles, reminding Mendenhall of old swimming movies. The innermost circle contained three gurneys and spun with the direction and momentum of arrival. The outer circle of floor EMTs and nurses counterspun with the tangent of escape, with rubbernecking. The murmur swelled until Mendenhall broke through the circles.

Two gurneys were more hystericals, pain and fever, a nurse and an aide wearing ICU colors. The third gurney was still rolling, pivoted on back wheels. Pao Pao was reaching to catch it. She was the only one attending it—and it was clearly the reason for the this-way-that-way sway of the crowd. Mendenhall immediately recognized this arrival: Lual Meeks.

Meeks was physical plant, an experienced janitor like Enry Dozier. He was a guy all the doctors and nurses liked to identify as a friend, even though they knew nothing about him, nothing outside his ability to chat up anyone. Mendenhall was the only person in the entire hospital who didn't like him. She believed he was, at heart, a misanthrope. She didn't like the way his look lingered an extra second or two after his final good wish. She noticed that he did this with everyone, looked one or two seconds longer, his eyelids lulling, thoughts private.

But Lual Meeks was dead. He lay sideways on the gurney, which was absurdly wrong. Whoever had attended him first had just tossed him onto the gurney, brought him, spun him into the bay, and run. Pao Pao, in gloves, mask, and chest apron, was the only one near him, stopping the gurney's careen. No one had even bothered to help her tie her apron.

Mendenhall cinched it for her and then took the gloves and mask. She looked at Meeks as she prepped, pulled the gloves tight to her fingertips, ready for touch. Meeks's eyes were open, softened into that look she did not trust, as though he had just told her how young she looked today, how she looked like a goddamn Olympic pole-vaulter.

On the edge of her vision she saw the elevator open to reveal three figures from ID dressed in full garb, including head covers and tinted face masks. Even while focusing on Meeks, she could tell that the big one in purple was Dmir—leading the way.

If it had been anyone but Dmir—if it had been Thorpe himself—she would have done things right. Her legs and arms felt disconnected, moving with gut reaction. She sidestepped away from Meeks to hover over the two hystericals, their gurneys surrounded by attending nurses and techs.

When Dmir and the two others from ID entered the circle, Mendenhall almost bowed as she spoke.

"These are yours. Intense fevers." She nodded toward Meeks. "That one looks like an injury, a fall."

Dmir went for it. All the action and attention was there with the two hystericals. Mendenhall's lie had some truth to it; Meeks did look like a fall victim, frozen on his side, legs bicycled.

She returned to Meeks, joining Pao Pao. The nurse was glaring at her. She ignored this and pressed two fingers to Meeks's carotid. No pulse, but the skin was warm and loose. Her heart flipped.

She reached beneath his shirt and felt his armpit. Warm.

"They found him in the subbasement," Pao Pao told her. "Near the old boilers. Like this. Just like this."

"Who? Who wheeled him in?"

"They ran off." Pao Pao adjusted the gurney brakes, avoided eye contact.

"Pao?"

The nurse held still for a second, continuing to look down, before turning to retrieve a packet holding two syringes and a thermometer.

Mendenhall scanned the bay. The crowd of nurses and aides and techs had swelled around the others, was shifting to Dmir.

Mendenhall took the thermometer offered by Pao Pao and

inserted it into Meeks's mouth, counted to ten. Then ten again. She blocked out Dmir, all other action.

The thermometer read 101. About what she feared.

"Did they even give CPR?" Mendenhall could tell by how Meeks lay what the answer was.

Pao Pao shook her head. "Someone here got the call. When they got to him, Meeks was alone."

"Did *Meeks* make the call?"

Pao Pao shrugged. "His cell."

"You?" asked Mendenhall. "You had to go?"

Pao Pao shook her head. "The other two had come in, and I was directing there. It was Cabral. Cabral went by himself. Looks like he would only touch his clothes, a belt-and-collar hoist. Lift him, plop him, push." She checked the time. "Four minutes ago. At least he was fast."

Dmir and his attendings hurried their patients toward the elevators, pulling the crowd with them. But to Mendenhall it felt as though she were the one spinning away, out of orbit with Pao Pao and Meeks.

She looked at her watch but did not call time of death, did not do it right. It was the first time she had checked her watch since the last call. It was ten twenty-nine.

Pao Pao was holding the paddles.

"We're taking him to Pathology."

"Time?" asked Pao Pao.

"I'm not calling it."

"Then we have to do something, Doctor. I'm not joining you on this. Unless we do something."

Mendenhall rolled Meeks onto his back. Pao Pao put the paddles away and moved to help. Mendenhall shook her off. "No. Just stay close. I'll do it."

Meeks was looking at her. She pressed his sternum with both hands, precisely, released. Counted. Pressed. Released. Meeks stared at her. She pressed, counted, released.

"Let's go," she told Pao Pao.

"Call it, Doctor."

Time? There was no time. Time was suspended. She had stopped it three hours ago with the first time-of-death call, the closing of the doors. Pao Pao was beautiful. She never thought like this, acted like this.

"He's dead. Now," said Mendenhall.

Pao Pao held the front of the gurney, braking it. Meeks lay between them, now on his back, his clothes askew from Mendenhall's tending. His eyes were aimed at her.

"Do you always know why you do something?" she asked Pao Pao.

"Yes."

"What about when you can't know the why?"

"Then I do what I've done before. Or what others have done. That's medicine. Good medicine. What I see you do."

Mendenhall saw the ID people coordinating the elevators. She felt her entire body wince.

"Dmir," she called, "this one. This is the one."

22

S he went to the old file room to chide herself. When she saw that the lights were off, that the room was filled with the orange light of the outside loading bay, she knew she wasn't alone. She started to back out, to give privacy.

"Dr. Mendenhall."

She didn't recognize the voice, male, Filipino accent. She didn't see anyone at first, then spotted the EMT sitting on the floor beneath the big window, the one with the handprints. Cabral, that's Cabral. The one who almost went hysterical with that first wave. Him. The one who went down to get Meeks. The only one.

He remained on the floor as she looked at him. His knees were pulled up, his elbows resting there, head bowed, hands collapsed. She could smell his sweat, both the dried and the fresh. It was an ER thing. The old was from the hysterics, the new from hauling Meeks all by himself. He had a bald spot but looked very young, as though the black hair was coming in rather than receding.

"How did you find me?"

"A lucky guess."

He raised his head but not enough to meet her eyes. He seemed encouraged by her recognition, her interest. But still frightened.

"I was getting ready to see you," he said. "To apologize. To explain."

"You don't need to do that," she replied. "Either of those things. You need to show me where you found Meeks. How he was. How he looked."

Cabral nodded. "Okay, Doctor."

"I'll meet you down there," she said.

When he left she walked to the window. Outside, more vehicles had gathered beyond the supply trucks. Carved in shadows at the light's edge, their camouflage patterns drew the eye, framed the night. She pressed her forehead to the pane and shut her eyes. She pushed her hands to the pane also. Something for Mullich.

Learn to scold yourself first, her mentor had told her. Check your own pride before others do it for you. The specialist will always be coming down here to do that to you, to swagger into the bay and show everybody what needs to be done. All we have is our hands and eyes, our splints and Band-Aids and old crude drugs.

When she stepped out of the room and back into the bay, she sensed a creak in the entire building. Her mentor had told her about this. It's not really in the building. It's your body anticipating the change, adjusting. It sounds like vents activating, walls expanding. But it's you.

WHEN SHE GOT to the subbasement, Mullich was there with Cabral. The architect was explaining to the tech what they had done to the old boilers. Instead of cutting them up and hauling them out, they had stripped them down to their copper tanks and cut doorways into them, welded in shelves with the leftover copper. The new forced-air units loomed huge on either side of the old tanks. They hummed.

Mendenhall had been down here twice before to tend to injured janitors. One of them might have been Dozier. She had wondered about the boilers, put her fingers to the beaded weld lines. She remembered how warm they were inside, still trapping heat.

The long, narrow room was fully lit, though one fluorescent panel above the last boiler was blank. She looked at that. Mullich followed her gaze.

"It's not unusual," he said. "Each janitor changes an average of one fluorescent per shift. The new rods will never expire. It's cost-efficient to replace the old rods one by one, as they expire."

"You think he came down here for that? Was there a report?"

Mullich checked his handheld, startling both her and Cabral.

"No. No report." Mullich stared into his tablet. Frowned. "But Meeks was old school. He probably saw it earlier, came back down."

"Then where's the replacement rod?" she asked. "Where's the ladder?"

"They keep those down here." Mullich was still fussing with his handheld. "This is their domain. Everyone should have their domain. Even the janitors. Especially the janitors."

She went to the boiler beneath the dim fluorescent panel. One of the rods behind the translucent panel was still working, its bar distinct beside a dark twin. She brushed her fingers along the weld cut of the doorway.

"What do they keep in these things?"

"Snacks, little tools, magazines, coffee." Mullich joined her at the doorway. "Themselves." He would have to stoop to enter.

Mendenhall looked at Cabral. "He was in here," she said to him. "You found Meeks in here."

The tech nodded.

She stepped inside the boiler, felt the contained heat. She crouched near its far wall, where it curled below the shelves. She moved her hand along the curve, recalling Meeks on the gurney, his bicycling form. "Right here."

"Yes."

Mendenhall placed her palm against the smooth copper. It was warm. She guessed 101.5.

"I have a thermometer," said Mullich.

"Of course you do." She remained in her crouch, gazing at the smooth cup of copper that had held Meeks. "You can tell Claiborne Meeks was in here, against the wall. The wall is 101.5. You can double-check me with your thermometer. With your lasers."

"You should tell Claiborne."

She stood but stayed inside the boiler, felt the sweat from her workout returning, reblooming along her forehead. She stepped out and addressed Cabral. "His eyes," she said. "You didn't touch his eyes."

"No, Doctor. You caught me doing that once. Told me never to do that. Close their eyes."

She nodded. She didn't remember. She looked at his name tag, saw the A. after his last name. She had no idea what it stood for. "You did good work, Cabral."

It sounded okay like that, somehow equal. Egalitarian, Mullich would have said.

"Will they put me in Q?" Cabral asked her.

She put a shushing finger to her lips. She nodded for him to leave. He had a resolute bearing about him, not forced but new. She hadn't noticed it before. She saw it in patients sometimes, quiet internal decisions to go forth after seeing an X-ray, learning the extent of an injury, hearing bad news from her.

After the tech left she spoke to Mullich. "I can't tell Claiborne. I doubt he would even speak with me."

Mullich raised one eyebrow.

"I almost did a very bad thing up there. Which is the same as *doing* the bad thing." She pointed upward to the ER. "Pao Pao saw it. Dmir saw it. Everyone saw it. Don't even mention my name when you tell Claiborne. Unless you want him to hate you, too."

"What will Thorpe do?"

"Thorpe will be okay with it," she said. "He'll like it. That I backed down. That I gave in."

"I have a theory, Dr. Mendenhall. That you and Thorpe are the same."

She lifted her chin. "Yeah? I have a theory that you *are* Thorpe."

MULLICH TOOK MORE of his laser calibrations. Mendenhall leaned against the cool wall across from the boilers, crossed her arms, and watched. Mullich took a vertical measurement from the outside edge of the old boiler to the ceiling. He moved easily into a crouch, pivoted with no excess movement. But in between measurements, he repeatedly glanced at her.

"What?" she asked.

"Cortez."

"Those are personal. I offer nothing about what's going on in here. You and Thorpe can go—"

Still in his crouch, Mullich put his hand up, then brought it to his chest. "He showed them to me. I—"

"You what? You just did your job."

"No. That's not my job." He stood. "I only wanted to ask you something. Something about your dog."

Her anger turned to fear. How much of her did he want to peel away? "At least you knew he was a dog."

Mullich remained on point. "Do you miss him, or do you regret not having that life? That life one can have with a dog?"

"The second thing," she said. "But no. Both."

"People," he replied. The word heightened his accent, the *e* a bit short. "People like Cabral and Silva. They are drawn to you. They want something from you."

"Cabral and Silva are nothing alike. Cabral's a med tech, a hoddy. You don't even need a college degree. Silva's a research tech. She has that and more. She's probably Brazilian. He's Filipino. But you're right. They both have brown skin."

He bristled, which was what she was trying for. He remained in his crouch, his laser pen aimed at her. "I am not like that. You know this. But I don't like the joke. I meant they are both people who want to learn what medicine is. What it really is."

"They're interested in me because I'm familiar. I go to patients—to bodies—and put my hands there. Listen. They want medicine to be that. But it isn't." Without unfolding her arms, she pointed at his tablet. "It's that."

He looked at his tablet.

"It's that," she said again. "Until you get to the surgeons. Or Claiborne. I'm nothing, Mullich. Stop trying to find me."

"Your cynicism is false." Mullich stood.

It was difficult for her to remain relaxed against the wall.

"Your action betrays you. You hurried down here to see, to prove something. To yourself. Then to Claiborne, whom you respect."

"To prove what?" She tightened her arms about herself.

"Something you know. You moved like someone who knows."

"I don't feel like that," she said. "Like someone who knows anything."

"Come back to the lab. Let's see."

"Claiborne's?"

"He won't be there." Mullich checked his tablet. "Yes. He's up with Thorpe."

She eyed the tablet. He brushed it.

"Silva's there. That's all."

"She'll have orders," said Mendenhall.

Mullich put away his laser pen and raised his card. "I have this."

"Then you go in first," she told him. "Set things up for me, let me in. That will be most efficient. I need to make an appearance on my floor. I don't want to look like a runaway."

23

The building continued to shift. Arriving from the subbasement, Mendenhall sensed a gathering and sliding of weight in the important floors above, the strides of those assuming charge and knowledge. Others, she imagined, lingered close to doors and windows, false exits. Her own floor was escaping her. Her nine patients appeared pushed aside, separated now by a blank slot along the wall. They didn't look at her as she passed them, did not offer that expression of salvation reserved for the doctor. At the nurses' station, two dressed in ID purple had sequestered counter space. Both were focused on their notebook screens.

Mendenhall slipped into her cubicle. Someone, probably Pao Pao, had left her an orange juice. She drank it, felt the physical need rush through her. It was proper medicine to treat the Meeks case as evidence for further containment. She knew this, but she did not feel it. She was beginning to fear she couldn't trust her instincts, wondered how much they were skewed by what she sensed from the floors above and what might be happening outside.

On her screen, she entered the trauma forum and started a discussion thread for the five cases. She usually enjoyed this part of her profession. Rarely did ER specialists get to partake of such deliberation and exchange. Even in a worldwide exchange, their cases almost never lasted long enough for true discussion, ending in demise or reassignment to the real specialists.

She kept her information blunt and scientific, using Claiborne's summations, reserving her doubts. She merely asked for similarities. She knew Thorpe—one of his techs anyway—would monitor this exchange. She liked to imagine that her mentor checked them. She used that for control.

Within the moment it took her to rest her eyes on the bay, the Thorpe tech added corrections and extensions. Good wishes and promises came from ERs in Calcutta and Dublin. Then one more from Montreal, who had heard.

What usually emerged from these forums were strange ways that people died or didn't die. Patients hauled from the bottom of frozen rivers who were revived after several hours, unharmed, relating dreamy visions of the underside of the ice. Or the Phineas Gages of the world, those who staggered from death, dazed, changed, alive.

24.

ullich let her into Pathology. Claiborne was not there. Silva stood facing the far wall, the screens showing the hollow body outlines above her. There was already one for Meeks, showing the same trauma pattern, his passing through the left torso, the upper lobe of the lung and shoulder muscles. All five body patterns were gridded, set in sublimate position, arms and legs slightly spread, hands turned and open. She thought of the Da Vinci sketches. Silva said nothing, did not acknowledge Mendenhall's arrival.

Mullich stood before the adjacent wall, his screens showing floor and building diagrams, points of discovery marked by red dots. Mullich, at least, was facing her.

"I blame you," she told him. "Mostly."

He offered a confused expression.

"You and your building," she said, "for taking me away from my medicine. Away from where I should've stayed. Inside the bodies. Inside what I know."

"You don't strike me as the blaming type."

"I'm trying to be different." She turned to Silva, who remained facing her work, manipulating the overhead screens. "And you, too. For calling me out."

Silva did not turn around but flexed her shoulders. The black line of her ponytail remained still and straight down the middle of her small back.

Mendenhall gazed at the digital bodies, the tornadic patterns passing through them, the peripheral smudges marring the grid lines.

Mullich started discussing floors and then the bodies. Fleming, Verdasco, and Peterson, he said, were particular to single floors: Four, Three, and Two. Dozier and Meeks, by occupation, roamed all floors and subbasements.

"According to precedent, that indicates something airborne, the progression being strictly vertical despite the free roamers. Like Legionnaires'."

But it was as though she heard the outside of his words, only the echo.

"The odds," said Mendenhall. "What are the odds? That Meeks and Dozier happened to be on different floors? From each other? From the others?"

"Three to one," replied Mullich. Again the echo.

She had moved on. She spoke to Silva's back. "Can you shift the bodies to their found positions?"

From a laptop below the screens, Silva curled each body into its found position. Verdasco was the only one who hadn't moved, who hadn't fallen or collapsed. She studied the tornadic pattern across his bronchus. She looked away to refresh, caught Mullich's blueprint, felt her heart rate increase but did not know why.

"Move all the bodies into their positions before collapse." Her own words registered as echoes.

"We don't have the new one yet."

"His name is Lual. Lual Meeks." Mendenhall stared intently at Mullich's blueprints. "The ones you have, then."

Silva looked over her shoulder with a worried expression, then worked the laptop. The hollow figures shifted in quick increments, clicked into positions: Dozier on his invisible ladder, Fleming with her invisible cup of tea, Verdasco remaining at rest, Peterson and her cigarette.

Mullich probably saw it before Mendenhall did. The bodies coiled into their various ready positions, all different postures. But the tornadic patterns. Those. They went parallel to one another, all five, perfectly parallel.

Mullich looked at the body screens. Mendenhall looked at the building screens. She focused on the one showing the cross-section of the hospital.

"Draw it," she said. "You see it. I smell it on you. Draw it."

But he didn't have to draw it. The diagonal formed by the red discovery points reflected the diagonals on the bodies. Paralleled them. Mullich then connected them with a green line from Seven to the subbasement, from Dozier to Meeks, passing through Fleming, Verdasco, and Peterson.

Silva was now seeing it, gazing from her wall to Mullich's, then back.

"That's not possible. That's absurd." Silva checked her laptop, redid the contortions. The line through the building remained parallel to the line through each of the bodies. She finally looked at Mendenhall. "There are no straight lines in medicine."

"We all noticed," said Mendenhall. "Without prompting. We all see it."

The green diagonal passing through the blueprint was duplicated four times by the tornadic patterns through the bodies on the adjacent wall. That was what showed.

Mullich appeared fascinated. He gazed back and forth from the bodies to the building.

"The explanation is simple," he said. "Amazing—but simple. The two of you marked the calibrations on each floor. But you carried with you impressions of the bodies you had examined. Your floor marks were influenced by your knowledge of the bodies."

She hated Mullich. She hated when doctors were like this, so quick with their expertise. Let the patients have their moments, her mentor had told her, their moments of recognition. Let them be right. Learn. Learn with them.

25.

Silva touched the tablet beside the laptop, a graceful tap with middle finger. Her look excluded Mullich. Her eyes were stark, black as her lashes and hair. "Dr. Claiborne's on his way down."

She configured the hollow bodies back into their sublimate positions, all parallels gone. The diagonal through Mullich's blueprint now seemed aimless, out of place in a medical lab. There were no straight lines in trauma, either, especially not in ballistics.

"Thank you," Mendenhall said to Silva. "I'll go. I'll take the stairs."

"He takes the stairs. When he can't get in his run."

"Okay. The elevator." Mendenhall addressed Mullich, pointed to the green line. "Take that away."

She felt Silva's gaze, a wanting of exchange with her. We see what we are. They were two very different people yet had seen the same thing, constructed the pattern together, even argued a bit while doing this. As Mendenhall closed her eyes—she knew Silva was watching—she saw the diagonal, the slash of demise, through the building and the bodies, green turned to its negative, red.

WITH HER CARD, she commandeered the elevator to the top floor, closed her eyes and imagined it shooting through the lid of Mercy

General, a passage from a childhood book. She imagined, too, the iron tamping rod shot through the brain of Phineas Gage, recalled the photos from her medical texts, the bust of his head, the portrait of him holding the rod, the rod he had carried with him as a cane for the rest of his life. She imagined it erasing his thoughts. She thought of Phineas Gage relearning himself.

At the door to the roof she punched in her card. The red light blinked. She counted to ten and punched again, was refused. She repeated this four times, her forehead pressed to the door, her eyes closed. Beneath, the momentum of the building continued to slide away from her.

Ten more hystericals had come in after the discovery of Meeks. Pao Pao messaged her not to come; the ID people were there. Pao Pao had termed them hysterical, was still on her side. That was good.

She punched the card key again. She wasn't sure why or whom she was conjuring. Mullich could come, let her onto the roof. Thorpe's people could arrive, take her to quarantine. Maybe she was testing her value.

NO ONE CAME. She returned to the ER.

The ten new arrivals were fully curtained. This was a mistake. They had to be obvious hystericals. Thorpe would have taken anyone of interest. Closing the curtains fully around the patients would only increase their anxiety, heighten symptoms. Symptoms—even false ones—could injure and kill.

Her mentor had made her study psych wards. Among the catatonic and the wild, the doctors and nurses moved with rehearsed precision, every gesture a revelation. They did what they could do. They probably had an abandoned file room, somewhere they went to laugh, cry, push their weight into the glass.

She parted the first curtain, just the section at the foot of the bed, giving the patient a view of the bay. The patient seemed very fit, midfifties, a visitor. Beneath the sheet, his torso formed a wedge to his narrow waist. His face was lean and drawn, temples and cheeks forming hollows, a guy who ate plain tuna and nonfat cottage cheese and used his gym membership. A guy who believed the world was out to destroy his body.

In her early years she had felt no sympathy for psychosomatic arrivals, had seen them as selfish time-wasters. But by now she had developed some sympathy. It was their way of engaging with life, of acknowledging it. Her mentor had given her a book. The book's premise was that life is the perfect crime. She liked it because it denied the metaphor, denied itself, found purpose in that denial.

She sanitized her hands, introduced herself, and took the patient's pulse. The curtained nook seemed quaint: no equipment, no technology, light filtered through gauze, a neat stack of cool towels, and a cup of water. She pressed his forehead: 101.5.

"Do you know what it is?" he asked.

"I know that what you have is completely different."

"You know that?"

"Yes. I was the first one. I've been working with Pathology. And everybody."

Across the opening in the curtain, Cabral passed. She recognized him from his posture, downward and thought-filled. She was not surprised to see him return to the stall.

"Dr. Mendenhall."

"Yes, Cabral. Open the other stalls. Like this one."

He nodded. There was something about him. She sensed a retraction in her vision. When she looked back to the patient, she recognized what was happening to her. The familiar dizziness, one-sided, a physical click, pleasant above her brain stem. She needed to sleep. Stop everything and sleep. Lie down. She already yearned for the waking moment, that fresh blare of thought.

She smiled at the patient and told him to drink his water. As she passed Cabral, she told him not to open the drape to her stall.

SHE CHOSE THE stall three removed from the last hysterical. She enclosed herself within the curtains. As she sat on the bed, she removed her lab coat and readied it as a blanket. She knew Meeks had fallen at the same time as the others. She knew the rattle and thrum of the bay would lead her to sleep. She knew she would lose consciousness within seconds of sublimation. She knew how soft the pillow would feel. She knew there was something wrong with Cabral.

What she didn't know was how long she would sleep.

two

26

The first waking was false, surfacing to dream glare. The stall hung white. She heard static. The sharpness of the real waking verified the first as dream. Eyes open, head lifted from pillow, she had trouble discerning between the two. Her heart rate, which had jolted her out of the dream, increased. Outside the gauzy enclosure of her stall, it was not quiet. Someone—a nurse—had screamed. Carts rolled, running shoes squeaked. Nurses tried to give orders. Finally one asked, "Where's Pao Pao?"

Mendenhall knew Cabral was dead. She knew from the waking dream. This realization was what that two-second dream was about.

But it was hard to get her body to work. She had no grip. She needed to focus just to turn her wrist, to see her watch. She had slept for three hours, a stunning amount for her in the ER.

Dread sharpened her logic. If she stepped out there to do her job, to take charge, chances were high that ID would quarantine her, connecting her with Cabral, Meeks. If she left the ER along the periphery of the bay, took the elevator somewhere quiet—like Physical Therapy—only Mullich would find her. She would have to go into hiding. The only way she could survive that emotionally would be to stay involved in these cases. That involvement would reveal her.

Thorpe was the unknown factor. How accurate was her

assessment of him? Was he power or science, more paper than blood? How strongly did she believe her claims about him, the ones she had voiced to Claiborne and Mullich, that he was paper? That he needed her science, their science, their blood work?

UNDECIDED, SHE SLID through the curtain opposite the commotion. She knew all of the bay's blind spots, every crease. Pao Pao spotted her immediately but said nothing. Mendenhall raised a staying hand. The nurse stood along the inner circle surrounding Cabral. Again, that series of Busby Berkeley dancers swayed this way and that, people afraid but wanting to see. There were more ID people than Mendenhall had expected, purple and done up as surgeons, none of them where they were supposed to be. Only Pao Pao was positioned correctly, ready for orders. Dmir stood in the second circle, hesitating.

Cabral had not even been transferred to a gurney. Someone had spun his bed into the bay. The brakes were still set on one of the wheels, and so his bed angled in throwaway position, his body uncovered. His hands were clasped beneath his chin as he curled on his side, a child saying bedtime prayers. His eyes were open. She could tell from across the bay. The curtains and rods of his stall lay collapsed, ruined by panic.

Mendenhall spied the nurse who must have found him. She was slouched in the third layer, peeking around Dmir. At least have the courage to run, thought Mendenhall; at least have the decency. Mendenhall shifted into another crease, maintaining the same distance. Pao Pao checked her.

Mendenhall sensed her about to move in. None of the purples from ID advanced. Once a man had been thrown into the bay, a drunk who had fallen asleep hitchhiking in the middle of a night highway, had gotten caught beneath a speeding semi and been filed down by the friction of the asphalt, the half of him that remained still somehow alive, the one arm pumping, the one eye looking in wonder. No one had moved to him. Mendenhall had to break from a patient to go to him, to get to his last breath, such as it was. Never bring your fury with you, her mentor had advised.

She measured the distance to Cabral. She took a breath, the filling kind right before a run, getting oxygen to the muscles, relaxing nerves into readiness. She donned gloves, the snap turning heads. She stepped out of hiding and cut through the circles. She took the opportunity to hard-shoulder someone from ID as she passed, digging her forearm into the purple garb.

Pao Pao waited until Mendenhall had driven through the final circle, then moved with her. The nurse pulled up her mask, offered a fresh one to Mendenhall. Mendenhall let her tie it as she bent toward Cabral.

She pressed her fingers to Cabral's carotid, knowing there'd be nothing. "Temp," she ordered.

Pao Pao slipped a disposable thermometer into Cabral's mouth. It rattled on his teeth, the nurse's jab kind and relentless. Mendenhall called time of death and pointed to three ID people. "You, you, and you, get him on a gurney and get him to Path. Warn them."

As they moved, Mendenhall crouched closer to Cabral, rested a hand on his shoulder. She looked at his face. His expression was in a dream, a knowing dream. From behind, she heard Dmir clearing his throat, popping forward.

"I—"

"You," she said turning to Dmir, catching him directly with the first shot of her glance. "Take it to Thorpe."

She had very little hope of keeping Cabral with Claiborne. But maybe for a few minutes she could get him there, in that right place for him, in that decent and distilled air. What he deserved.

If it was airborne, they were all as safe as was possible; Cabral had stopped breathing long ago. If it was fluids, there was no added risk. No one was touching him. But she knew that it was neither of these. She could put her tongue to Cabral's tongue. She could drink his blood. That was how strongly Mendenhall knew what she knew at this moment. She brushed the young man's thinning hair across his temple and around his ear, then stood back. She eyed his whole form and tried to gauge where the pattern of occlusion would be, where it had slanted through muscle and capillary, roiled through nerves.

She took two steps back and gave herself to ID, to whatever would take her. She bowed her head and shook her arms, elbows loose, run finished. Dream over.

27.

Nothing and no one took her. She made one more backstep, anticipated a hand on her shoulder. There was nothing, and she swayed. The ID people were following her orders, though Dmir now stood in charge. He was on his cell, not looking her way.

If Cabral was to make it down to Path, it would only be for a quick pass. She had very little time. And Thorpe could still send her to Q. She had messed up with Meeks and in an even bigger way, it seemed, with Cabral. Her position was extremely weak. Thorpe might have liked it that way; better having her loose rather than sealed.

She looked for the nurse who had found Cabral. She scanned the creases in the bay, the first blind spots nearest the station. She moved to cut off the nurse in the path toward the elevators. How smart could she be? How frightened?

Mendenhall would have liked nothing better than to have her sequestered and taken to Q, pushed behind glass and strapped to a bed. She could picture the nurse finding Cabral, her silent scream within the curtains, the panic that had made her shove the bed through the stall, one brake still locked, the bed spiraling away from her, twisting her wrists. Abandoning him to another's scream.

She closed her eyes and inhaled. The nurse stopped when

Mendenhall appeared, took one sidestep. Mendenhall eyed her name tag, raised her hands.

"Nurse Amihan. Get us some coffee. My desk. One minute."

AMIHAN GOT THERE faster. The cups shook in her hands. Mendenhall stood at the opening to her cubicle and motioned for her to set down the coffees.

"Have a seat." She offered the only chair in the cubicle.

"Thank you, Doctor." Her accent was heavy, even with this simple phrase.

"Everyone's shaking right now. Just sit. Just don't spill anything."

Amihan sat and looked at her lap, her hands twisting there. She was young. Her hair was black and straight, a shine to it.

"Were you in Manila? Before here?"

She nodded, still looking down.

"Did you know Cabral there?"

She shook her head.

"Try to speak."

"No, Doctor. He was here before me."

"But you knew him."

She nodded.

Mendenhall tapped her lips.

"Yes, Doctor. A little."

"Tell me about him."

"Tell you what?"

"Just something. Was he funny? Did he tell jokes? Did he smile? Was he quick?"

"Yes. He made little jokes. Little faces. He was quick. He made little—jokes—with his hands."

Mendenhall squinted. "Jokes with his hands?"

"Like this." Amihan fashioned her hand into a beak and made talking motions.

"Hand puppets."

"Yes. Those. But on the wall."

Mendenhall smiled. "Shadow puppets."

"Yes. He talked for them but without moving his lips."

"Good." She checked her watch. "Now, just one more thing. Then I'll leave you alone. How was his posture?"

"Posture?"

"His shoulders?" asked Mendenhall. "Did he keep them straight? When he moved quick?"

"Yes, Doctor. He made them straight. Always straight. Tried to look tall, maybe."

Mendenhall hurried from the cubicle, left the nurse without word or wave. It was the only torture she had time for, the only one she could imagine.

28.

ilva was waiting for her in the Pathology hall. The tech's mask hung loose about her throat. She stood before the closed door. There was an invitation to her stance, an angling toward the handle, exposing it. She lifted her chin—too high.

"How furious is he?"

"You are not to be let in."

Mendenhall neared Silva, was careful to relax her expression. "He must be curious."

Silva looked perplexed.

"Why not just lock the door? Why not just listen to me push the buzzer, bang on it?" Mendenhall raised her chin, level with Silva's brow. "Why have *you* out here?"

"To avoid unnecessary contact with Cabral."

"But right *here*," said Mendenhall. "He told you to stay right here, no?"

Silva nodded once, then twice.

"Then he's curious." Mendenhall wanted to be more graceful, to ease her way through the exchange. Silva—her intelligence, its devotion—soothed her. But she felt a press from above, ID buzzing about the ER, coming down to take Cabral.

"Ask him to let me in if I can guess the occlusion, its location and position."

"I have orders not to do that."

"Then go in and tell him. Just walk in and say, 'Renal membrane to gluteal. Through the pelvis. No major vessels."

Silva flinched, a pretty inhale, gathering.

"Come on, Silva. Just do that. He'll be disappointed if you don't. If there's no try."

Silva applied her mask, opened the door, which wasn't locked, and went in. Mendenhall could only hear the sound of Silva's voice, not the words. She could hear the effort, pulses of forced volume. Then silence, nothing from Claiborne.

Silva came back out, mask still covering her nose and mouth. There was hope in this; she was going right back inside. "Which side and which direction?"

Mendenhall recalled Cabral's position on the bed. He had rested on his right side. So left, he had been favoring his left, whether he knew it or not. The direction? Up or down? At about seven twenty, when the others had fallen, had he been standing or sitting or lying down or crouching to make shadow puppets on the bay wall?

"Left side. From renal membrane—but not the kidney, not even grazing the kidney—down through pelvis." Almost confident of the location, she was guessing the direction, going with her initial claim, which had not been thought out. She guessed that Claiborne was testing her doubt. Mendenhall was all doubt, every word weighted with it.

"Okay, come in." Silva drew mask and gloves from her lab coat and handed them to Mendenhall.

WHEN MENDENHALL ENTERED the lab, Claiborne was extracting marrow from Cabral's left pelvis. Cabral was naked and positioned symmetrically on the steel bed, arms open, legs open. She knew not to speak and took the seat arranged for her, a stool with wheels locked. She was careful with her posture, mimicking Silva's straightness as best she could, the level shoulders.

Claiborne continued the extraction as he spoke, mask pumping. "Six dead, four at once, maybe one later, one more definitely later. What does that indicate?"

Mendenhall did not hesitate. "Infection."

Claiborne nodded for Silva to approach the body. The tech began entering readings on her tablet. The readings appeared on an overhead screen beneath a figure of a digital scan revealing the tornadic occlusion through Cabral's left pelvis.

This was what Mendenhall needed most, to see Cabral in this light, caressed by this air, saved from the humiliation in the ER. She saw his first name on the overhead screen. Albert. Albert Cabral.

CLAIBORNE WAS SCOWLING as he worked, his dark brow furrowed into his mask, eyes aglare. But maybe that was from the extraction, the precision and force required to needle into the pelvis. From her stool Mendenhall examined the overhead screen. The occlusion appeared in the marrow but not the bone.

"What are you thinking, Doctor?"

Mendenhall started. She should have been ready with her phrasing. Maybe this was what she wanted also, what she needed in getting here with Cabral, Claiborne, and Silva. Focus, a hard external counter to her doubt.

"I'm thinking it . . . the infection . . . burst in all six at the same time—about the same time."

Silva stopped entering data, looked at Mendenhall. Claiborne kept working.

"Meeks collapsed against warm metal, affecting temp and rigor.

Maybe," Claiborne said. "But Cabral here? He survived. Why? No major organs?"

"No," replied Mendenhall. "He didn't survive."

Now Silva dropped her arms and looked at Claiborne, perhaps awaiting orders to escort Mendenhall out.

"Explain."

"Neurogenic shock. He was walking dead."

Claiborne wagged his head as he focused on the final draw of the extraction. He treated Cabral as living, feeling, removing the needle with a graceful push-pull, push-pull.

"You've never seen it," Mendenhall told him. "Only in charts, written. Neurogenic shock. *I've* seen it. Many times. I should have seen it in Cabral."

"You're stretching again." Claiborne sealed the extraction in the syringe, carefully snapped the needle into a disposal bag, and handed the sample to Silva. "You're fighting."

"I did see it in Cabral. I just didn't register it. I should've registered it. If I'd known him . . ."

"Stop." Claiborne gazed upward. "We're out of time. You need to leave here before ID shows up. They catch you here, you're done. I'm done."

She stood, hesitated. "Close-scan the sinoatrial node. Before they take him. We know there'll be incipient hemorrhaging in the brain, like all of them. We'll see that again. But the sinoatrial . . ."

She hurried from the lab. Before closing the door, she looked at Silva, offered a nod of thanks. What she could muster.

29

A lone in the wide hall outside Pathology, Mendenhall heard the elevator arriving. She turned the nearest corner, found herself atop the ramp to the exit, where they had delivered the bodies to the outside. She pressed herself to the wall, near the edge, turned her head to the sounds. The elevator opened. Three sets of footsteps pattered on linoleum—a leader and two techs. Whom would Thorpe send to confront Claiborne? Maybe himself. She was tempted to look.

"When we go in," said the leader's voice, "remain behind at ease. It's his lab. If *she's* in there, call for removal; don't make me say it." The voice was hollow. They were wearing full hoods and face visors. There was no point in looking.

She had seen Thorpe once, from a distance, from the rear of an auditorium, a doctor sitting in a line of experts onstage. She had stayed only to hear the first speaker, to show her face at a mandatory conference. She hadn't paid attention to the introductions, never figured out who was who.

But that was him out there, no doubt. Why? For Cabral, the clear signifier of outbreak? For Claiborne, to lay some claim in Pathology? No, he was there for her. She turned the other way in order to trail silently down the exit ramp.

A body was there. On a gurney angled toward the sliding door, it was sealed in a white bag. On tiptoe, in a slow-motion sprint, she moved to it. She crouched behind it in case they checked around the corner before going into the lab. She counted to ten, then straightened and examined the bag.

It was Peterson. Marley. Mendenhall knew this without looking at the tag. Beneath white vinyl the nurse's arms lay straight along her sides, her chin stiff, her stomach a soft rise, her feet at symmetrical angles. She and the other smokers used to wave as Mendenhall ran by them on the trails, laugh and raise cigarettes, try to get smoke in her face. "That will kill you, Doctor."

She adjusted Peterson's gurney, setting it perpendicular to the sliding door, less abandoned. Mendenhall was glad that she had found her, could wait with her. Mendenhall was screwing up everything. At least she could do this.

The slider buzzed and then rattled open. Mendenhall swung to the other side of the gurney and braced herself. The Disease Control truck was ramped open, its portable lab soft and white. Two space-suited figures hurried to the gurney, ignoring Mendenhall.

Another appeared from somewhere. He was tall, no face visible behind the tinted visor. He looked Mendenhall up and down. She saw her face reflected in the black plastic—wonder, fear, recognition.

"Mullich?" she said.

The figure only breathed. He stood guard as the others transferred Peterson to the truck. He slammed the button that dropped the slider, divided her from all of them. The drop softened at the very bottom, whispered shut.

SHE HEARD FOOTSTEPS from atop the ramp and looked up, expecting to be caught by Thorpe and his techs. But it was Silva, her form slight in oversized scrubs. The fluorescent lighting seemed to press her against the wall. She let her back slide down the edge, folded herself into a sitting position. She put her hands to her face. Her black hair fell forward. Mendenhall could tell Silva had been resisting her hands, putting them there. She could have been drinking from them, pulling cool water to her skin.

Mendenhall walked up the ramp and sat perpendicular to Silva, let her legs angle down the slope.

"If we had cafeteria trays we could slide."

Silva opened her fingers but kept them to her face. "We'd need ice."

Mendenhall nodded.

"Rough in there?"

"I've been ordered to rest." Silva smoothed her eyebrows, blinked, let her hands fall.

"That's a challenge," replied Mendenhall. "To find a place. These days."

"Not down here. No one comes down here to rest. You can find empty beds in the labs. They're not all steel."

"But you're *here*."

"I was hoping to find you."

"I'm never one to talk to."

"You have Dr. Claiborne confused." Silva looked toward Claiborne's lab. "Confused and muttering. He didn't try for slices of the sinoatrial."

Mendenhall shrugged. "It was just a stab. Before I had to run."

"He sliced the basal ganglia instead. The amygdala."

"Did they catch him?" Mendenhall straightened her feet, bounced them a little on the ramp.

"He didn't seem to care. He let them."

"Thorpe. What did he say?"

"He just asked why he was doing that to a dead brain. If he had previous scans from when the patient was alive. Then they bagged Cabral and took him."

"You found that strange?"

Silva flexed her jaw, muscles fingering between slender bones. "Why not just stay there? Complete the scans and samples there? Then take him."

"Don't expect any spontaneity from them," said Mendenhall. "Don't expect good medicine. From them. Outside their own labs anyway."

Silva looked at her, waited for her to turn more to her. Her eyes were almost black, but that was because of the darkness of the lashes, the even brows. Her lips hung in a pretty frown.

"But me," said Mendenhall. "You want to know if my medicine is good."

"I need to know it."

"It is." Mendenhall took hold of Silva's foot, squeezed the small running shoe and wiggled it. "I observed Cabral the way I should've. I reported it. To the pathologist. He exhibited signs of neurogenic shock. Delayed."

Silva offered the other foot, and Mendenhall held it, with her thumb palpated the metatarsal slope. Silva lulled her eyes. "What good are scan slices from a dead heart, a dead brain? With no live comparisons?"

Mendenhall shrugged. "Probably none. But your boss is very good. He sees things in dead tissue the rest of us don't. I presume. Just like I see things in trauma behavior. I'm not as nuts as you think."

"Will he let you back in there?"

"I can only try." Mendenhall nodded back toward the hall. "Go find one of those dead beds. Sleep for a good hour. Like he ordered. You'll make better decisions, better observations."

"How did you know he said an hour?"

"He's a man who knows the value of time. Better than anybody. He runs miles paced to the second. Bodies are clocks. Dead or alive, they are clocks, more intricate than any mechanical ones."

30

Claiborne was working the laptop beneath the far wall of the Path lab. Above him were the gridded forms of the six patients, sublimate, occlusions marked as long red triangles. Two screens held three bodies each. A third screen illuminated two stochastic equations: one for continual progression, one for burst. The one for continual had four lines, the one for burst only three. The four steel beds were empty.

Mullich sat in his corner, below his screens showing the building grids. Had he been there all along? He sat as though he had, a mask hanging loose from his neck.

"Are they after me?" asked Mendenhall.

Claiborne turned to her, an elbow to the desk. "I told Thorpe what you said. Suggesting viral burst. He's on the same page. We're on the same page."

"You tell him about the neurogenic shock? About Cabral and the others being struck close to the same time?"

"I'm not stupid. I'm not crazy."

"It'll show," she replied. "Eventually."

"Then let it. Let him find it."

"He's a virologist. Everything will show viral to him. He'll always go forward, seeing everything as progression. Outbreak."

"Everything *does* show viral."

"Except there's no virus."

"That happens."

"So does delayed demise due to neurogenic shock."

Claiborne's gaze held steady. His unfurled mask hung neatly over his tie and the lapels of his lab coat. "I saved you."

Mullich turned to them. "She's lying."

"She's withholding." Claiborne kept looking at her, not even glancing toward Mullich. "She's withholding what she should. For me. For herself."

Mendenhall didn't feel that she was lying or withholding. She just felt open.

"Thorpe asked me—us," Claiborne nodded toward Mullich as he continued, "about Cabral coming to ER earlier. With that first wave of fevers. He heard something."

Mendenhall returned his gaze. Only Pao Pao knew for certain what had happened. Only she had confronted Mendenhall. Pao Pao would not have said anything to anyone else. But plenty of other nurses and techs had been there, maybe noticed Cabral on that gurney, getting up from that gurney and scuttling away.

"We told him what we knew," said Claiborne. "Nothing."

"I appreciate that."

"Okay. Now you tell me."

Mendenhall stepped closer to Claiborne. "Cabral was on a gurney. I noticed him slip away. I did not start a chart for him. He was healthy. Scared. But fine."

"You said yourself he was off."

"Later," explained Mendenhall. "I realized later. Suspected later. That's the truth."

"He was with us in the boiler room," said Mullich. "He was the one who fetched Meeks."

Claiborne's expression remained flat. "Anything else?"

"I spoke with him after. Alone in a side room. I sent him back down to the boilers. I met him down there."

Claiborne stood. He motioned to the first empty bed. "There," he told her.

Mendenhall removed her lab coat and sat on the steel. The brakes weren't set, so the bed scooted away from her weight and she had to restraighten it. She composed herself, adjusted her posture, rolled up her left sleeve, pumped forth a vein.

"Lie down." Claiborne tied his mask and snapped on fresh gloves.

Mendenhall positioned herself, the steel cool against her shoulder blades. She flinched, confused. "Careful," she said as Claiborne approached with the syringe. "I'm a live one."

"I'm doing scans as well," he said as he swabbed the insertion point. He drove the needle, his grip firm around her elbow. "Anywhere I should focus?"

She watched her blood fill the syringe, was startled, as always, by the darkness of it. Not the color of the wounds she saw every day. Not the bright red of movies. "No. I feel fine. You'll find nothing in me."

31.

Pao Pao called her to the ER. A surgical tech had been injured trying to break through one of Mullich's windows. One of the security officers who had restrained him was in, too. Mendenhall took solace in the call and the exit it provided. She paused outside the door to the Pathology lab. Claiborne and Mullich were in there with her scans. They would get to see them before she did, turn her, fold her, render her, float her above the room. Thorpe, too, would see them before she did, have them.

When Mendenhall got to the bay, to her remaining section along the wall, Pao Pao and an EMT were with the injured tech. The tech's complexion was waxy, and he was sweating as he lay back on the gurney. Pao Pao was pressing a wound above his left eye. The nurse eyed Mendenhall hard as she approached. Mendenhall donned fresh mask and gloves. One bed back was Ng 23, her gunshot patient. She felt his gaze, too.

As she neared, Mendenhall could see everything. The position of the wound, the paleness, the quiver in the patient's fingers. His head had struck a wall, maybe Mullich's window, shoved there. One bed over sat the security officer, slumped to one side, arm hanging long and low. A separated shoulder, lots of pain.

She bypassed the tech and swerved toward the guard. "Sterilize and numb the wound," she told Pao Pao. She looked at the EMT. "Ready sutures."

The security guard appeared startled even as he clenched against the pain in his shoulder. With a stiff arm, Mendenhall pressed him against the recline. He was big, his chest thick, his groan hollow inside it. She broke the seal on a foam bit and inserted it between his teeth. He seemed to know. His eyes widened. She palpated the inside of his biceps, checking against fracture. Without hesitation she pulled the arm, rotated, and shoved. The guard hummed loudly into the bit, eyes bulging. There was a wooden clunk as the shoulder set and the guard spit out his bit in a hard exhalation. The bit struck Mendenhall's mask as she closed her eyes against the spray.

She glared at the guy. "Every time. Ev-e-ry time."

His entire body relaxed, though his face appeared ready for pain, his eyes wide to the ceiling.

"It never gets old, does it?" she said.

He blinked, wiped tears with his good arm.

She offered him a Percocet and a cup of water, ordered the nearest nurse to dispose of the bit. She moved to the wounded tech.

Pao Pao dabbed the wound once more before clearing space for Mendenhall. The bleeding was still active, perhaps too heavy. The cut was maybe too close to the eye, ranging to the end of the brow. Mendenhall changed into new gloves without looking away from the tech's face. Pao Pao slapped the stapler into Mendenhall's palm.

The patient's eyes were glassy, his skin moist and white. His left eyelid drooped from the local. Mendenhall pinched the top end of the wound, where the blood was thinnest. The patient registered no sensation. She punched the first staple, beginning near the eye, where she had to be most intricate, where the bleeding was heaviest. Pao Pao dabbed between staples. Mendenhall folded the skin carefully, slightly inward but only just enough, hope against the scar. She made sure the eyebrow was not affected, not crimped in any way.

She laid out orders as she worked. "Send him up to Two right after. They can rework my suture if needed. But they'll have to measure his concussion first. He may have to go with my work. For a while."

The last four staples were easiest, curling upward across the temple. Pao Pao's dabs fell in sync with Mendenhall's staples. She could hear the soft breath puffs inside the nurse's mask, feel her shoulder pivoting firmly against her own but never pressing, steady. Mendenhall could brace her intricate movements there.

She imagined the scar she was creating.

SHE DOUBLED BACK to the guard. He reclined on his gurney, already mellowed from the pill. His eyes followed her, swam toward her edges. A nurse approached, and Mendenhall nodded for her to leave, all the while focused on the guard's eyes. She took his pulse: 60. He worked out, an athlete. His uniform had a kind of piping along the pockets and cuffs, yellow.

"You're not from here," she said.

He just looked—at her face, at her hand on his wrist, back to her face.

"When did you come in?" she asked. "When did they bring you in?"

Someone approached the gurney, a shadow over her left shoulder.

"He's DC." It was Mullich's voice. "They sent them in with some specialists. After Meeks was found."

She stared at the guard's shoulder, aimed. She resisted turning to Mullich.

"Them?"

"Six per floor."

"That's an army."

"From how you treated him," said Mullich, "that's what they'll need."

"Do you have secret tunnels or something?"

"I'm not the one with secrets."

She turned to Mullich, raised herself to his chin, pulled down her mask. She pulled off his, too.

"Doctors withhold," she told him. "It's proper medicine. We examine. We consider. We let one another do the same. We consult. When ready. I have nothing ready for Claiborne."

"Then for me." His breath was clean and sharp, with tea or something, but cool. "We can go to the roof."

"I have to tend to patients. Here. I need to get my floor back."

"I'll be up there," he said. "Alone."

She broke away first, leaving him with the high and wounded.

SHE MOVED TO Kae Ng's bed, the bullet wound who claimed to be twenty-three but was really fifteen. His latest readings indicated he was fine, could be released. Released into what? She pressed two fingers to his wrist. Her arrival had quickened his pulse. His hair was swept back, no longer hiding that one side of his expression. Confidence was gone from his eyes, though they were clear. He was trying to form his usual sneer, but one corner of his mouth creased further downward.

She exposed his shoulder and removed the dressing. The bullet wound was sealed with a single staple, her own neat work, the scarring forced to the inside where it would never show. His creamy skin was hairless, the contours of his clavicle and shoulder sharp.

The final scar would look no bigger than a punctuation mark, a semicolon, no doubt a disappointment for him.

"Roll your shoulder twice."

He hitched his shoulder. "I don't feel it."

"I'll send you home with the X-ray."

He nodded.

"Is it close to the heart?"

She found that strange, how he disconnected from himself. Usually patients only did that when they were actually looking at the X-ray. "No," she answered. "Not in medical terms. But, yes, it'll look that way."

"Instead I'm just gonna die from that." He nodded toward the beds that were not hers, the hystericals across the bay, sent from Thorpe. They were all in recline, nurses and techs and visitors.

She pressed his forehead. It was cool and dry.

"Don't even consider them," she replied. "I don't."

She would say the same thing to Mullich.

32.

The roof door was left ajar. She would not have to punch her key. Mullich was letting her bypass Thorpe's watch. She entered her key anyway, the red light blinking. She shut the door behind her. It was still night. The few stars had shifted, the sky deepened, the city quieted. A helicopter circled with a distant popping. The roof surface shone silvery, segmented into large rectangles. Mullich was not in his usual place by the telescope relic, his silhouette nowhere along the low wall.

"You've turned on me," she called out. She scanned a far corner.

A red dot of light quivered on the lapel of her lab coat. She cupped it in her palm, then found him in the darkness of the opposite corner, a gray shadow in the black.

"I fear you," he said.

She walked to the telescope, sensed the red dot on the back of her shoulder. The helicopter orbited, swung outward, its sound faint and hollow, trailing. She was startled to see the red line of Mullich's laser flash in the copter's exhaust cloud. She half expected an explosion.

"How far away are they?" she asked when he drew up beside her.

"Three kilometers."

"What does that mean?"

"They've found something on the outside."

"In the bodies?"

He shrugged and let the range finder hang against his chest. He brushed some entries into his tablet. Watery colors from the screen washed over his face, deepened the angles. He cut her one look.

"How can *you* fear *me*?" she asked.

"You present me with the unknown. The un-accounted-for."

"You seem to account for everything pretty quickly. Especially with me."

He held the tablet to her. On it was a cross-section blueprint of the hospital. The red diagonal showing the vertical path of demise slashing a straight line, following the pattern she and Silva had marked out for him.

"You already explained that. How we projected our knowledge of the bodies. How we took what we knew well and used it to describe what was new to us. I was impressed. I was decimated."

"What if I'm wrong?"

"You're not." She waved her hand over the screen. "That's impossible. The fact that it reflects the same angle of the occlusions—all the occlusions—proves our mistake."

"Why is it impossible?"

"Because there are no straight lines in ballistics, certainly not with these distances. And there is no evidence of a projectile—outside the bodies. Outside the skin."

"Why, then, do you keep resisting?"

"I just see what I see."

"Out here," he opened his arms to the nightscape, "away from the doctors, I hoped you could think. More. About what you see."

She hooked his wrist with two fingers and brought in his outstretched arm, brought the screen to her face. With a crook of his thumb, he toggled between the blueprint of Mercy and a scan of the occlusion. The occlusion was struck through with the same red diagonal. He did this three times.

"Whose are you using?" she asked.

He toggled three more times. Hospital, occlusion. Hospital, occlusion. He blinked slowly at her between each crook of his thumb. Hospital, occlusion.

She felt used. He had her vision in control. She tore it away, looked to the stars. She answered her own question, an unexpected tremble in her words.

"All six. You're using all six." Still looking at the sky, she felt sad for them. "Dozier," she said. She found the Dipper, faint but there. Named them as those stars. "Dozier, Fleming, Verdasco, Peterson, Meeks, Cabral."

"Explain them," he said. "Not as viral. As ballistic trauma only. Not virus induced."

"They'll say that's a leap."

"Put *my* work in there. What you've learned from this building. Consider all cases you know, any possibility, but only linked to ballistic."

That made her look away from the constellation—to him. He was staring hard at her.

"You'd need momentum. A huge amount."

"Kinetic energy," he said. "One-half the mass times velocity squared."

"We would be talking very, very small mass," she replied. "Almost nothing. Lots of velocity. Almost all velocity. There is no such thing." She thought. "Except in some studies. Aftermath studies in Hiroshima and Nagasaki. The lines from point zero—lines through the ashes of bodies and buildings—are straight lines. It was one of the first things they showed us. In lecture, in ballistic trauma. I remember. On the overhead, how they looked, white lines through gray. Thousands of them shooting outward. Etchings. Pretty. Before we realized what they were. Before they panned out and we saw."

She looked at him and laughed. "You suggest some sort of particle. A god particle zooming its way right through everything."

"No." He pocketed his tablet and rested a hand on the telescope relic. "The God Particle is elegant, subatomic, constructive. This would not be that. This would be crude and molecular. Destructive."

"Like me." She laughed again. "Crude and molecular. ER."

"No. But yes—molecular. One element. Near–light speed."

"Iron," she said. "Nickel. Flip a coin."

"Something less transitional."

She was in the periodic table. She was scribbling it out, scratching herself with it.

"Silicon," she said. "Then, silicon."

"Yes. More like that. A metalloid. The tiniest shard of glass shot through."

"You've thought this out." She almost reached—to shove him. Hard, into the relic, over the wall.

"It was the fluorescents," he said, "that got me thinking this way. Those plus my fear of you. My eyes followed yours to those shattered lights."

She twisted her lips, skeptical. He continued.

"The odds are good. There are enough fluorescents along each ceiling to make it very probable that at least two would be struck along the same line. The one above Dozier, the one above Meeks."

"That doesn't fit," she said. "Your particle is becoming God again, shattering glass but nothing else. Not bone, not plaster, only what suits you."

"The particle doesn't shatter the glass. In fact, glass is a liquid. Technically. The particle would pass through it easily, without disruption. It's what's inside the fluorescents. You know how they work?"

"Yeah," she said. "You throw a switch and they go on. Sometimes not so much."

"The tiny shock of energy excites the mercury vapor and oxygen. They move around and release photons. Light. Too much energy and they move way too fast, and the tube bursts. See?"

"But the tube above Dozier was dead. He was replacing it."

"Dead tubes are just low on vapor. There would've still been plenty in there for this."

She raised a hand, but he spoke before she could.

"Now, you explain."

"Explain what?"

"What happens inside the bodies."

"The patients," she said. "They're more than bodies."

"Okay," he said.

"No." She raised a finger between them. "It's important. Because if they were just bodies, then nothing would happen. They would just be like all the other stuff. Like the walls and ceilings. The building."

"Yes," he said. "Then, yes. People."

"Persons," she said. "With memories. Memories. Memories in nerve patterns. That trigger heartbeats and brainwaves and capillary dilation."

"Cabral," he said.

"What about him?"

"He's the anomaly. For me. But not for you. Not for Claiborne, either, I think. You made him fit. Fit enough for Claiborne, even. That's what struck the most fear in me. Fear of you."

"It's common," she told him. "Neurogenic shock. Delayed. It's why so many people die in the morning. The early morning. They wake and they die; it all starts to finally happen. From what they should have died from earlier. What their body believed, what their body was ready to do. Sometimes they make it to ER, to me. No one wants the night shift."

"It works," he said. "You see it works. No more than one per floor. Demise is not just vertical—it's strictly vertical."

SHE LOOKED UP at the Dipper again. He toyed with the telescope, adjusted the hollow tube, aimed it. She could name the stars. There were eight, not six. Mizar and Alcor were the twins that formed the angle of the handle. Alcor was the one often missed because it was so faint, so close to its brighter twin. It used to be prescribed as an eye test. By doctors, back when physicians used things like stars.

"It doesn't work," she told him. "Your God Particle. Because of the velocity. There is no detonation. Nothing that creates that kind of velocity. Nothing outside Hiroshima. And we would've all felt that. The whole world."

"But there is." He nodded to the sky, to the stars she had named.

"The fastest possible speed for a meteor is seventy-three kilometers per second. That would require a solar orbit plus retrograde into Earth."

"You know this? You've thought this out?"

She shook her head. "Only from reading my medical texts. There is one documented case of a meteor striking a person. Alabama, 1954. It crashed through her roof and bruised and burned her thigh. NASA has other studies. One of their biggest fears for space exploration was high-velocity micrometeors, something that would pass right through any helmet, any skull. It's still a valid fear but distant enough. We just take the risk."

"There are other kinds," he said. "There are faster ones. Extrasolar ones, yes? With near-infinite velocity."

"Look, Mullich." She took the range finder, pulled it to her eyes. It was still looped about his neck, and he had to lean in to her, shoulder to shoulder. She only used it as binoculars, to look at Mizar and Alcor. "I like this. Talking about this. Out here. It's good for me. I get what you're doing. But if you go too far, you'll become a patient."

He shifted, relaxing the strap by moving his shoulder behind her shoulder. He could just about whisper in her ear. "Those detonations. The ones you need for velocity. There are billions of them out there. Happening billions at a time over billions of years. The odds are better than you might think."

She kept the scope pressed to her eyes, gazed at empty space. "That *I* need? Velocity that *I* need? Don't make this about me."

She returned the range finder to his chest, pushing him away with the motion.

"It's a virus," she said. "Hiding inside us. The way a virus must hide. If it is to survive and evolve. If it is to survive us." She motioned to the sky. "It's not out there." She jabbed a finger into his ribs three times. "It's. In. There."

She meant none of it. The third jab felt desperate. Mullich raised his arm to give her a clear shot, but his expression was matter-of-fact. She dropped her aim and looked to the sky.

33

Mendenhall went directly from the roof to Pathology. The lab door wasn't locked. She entered. Claiborne was slumped over a side desk, head resting on arms. His feet had dolled outward, nothing holding him up but the stool, which appeared ready to slide away and spill him to the floor. Cello music played, a soft, pulsing solo. Above him two screens displayed full-body scans. Each body was shown in both profile and sublimate position. She felt herself already gone into ER mode, three seconds of assessment before moving.

"When it's crazy bad," her mentor had explained, "count to three before moving. You'll save time. You'll spare yourself, the front end of your nerves."

But this shouldn't have been crazy. There was only one thing—Claiborne. The scans above, the two bodies multiplied, were throwing her, casting her perception into a high wind. She snapped on fresh gloves and rushed to Claiborne. His lips were parted, his fingers in a gnarl, no respiration. But she wasn't waiting that long, long enough to watch for breathing. In front, her gloved hand felt disconnected, leading.

He bolted upright before she touched him, and she froze, hand raised, two fingers ready. He blinked and then focused on her hand.

"You put on gloves. You were going to check for pulse."

She nodded upward to the screens. "It was them, the other bodies. Sorry."

Claiborne pulled at the back of his neck, flexed his shoulders. "Don't be. It shows there's hope for you. It shows you kind of really might think it's viral."

"I've been thinking that," she said. "Mullich got me thinking. I told him it was in there. In him. In them. Us."

"Well." He motioned to the screens. "It's not in you or him."

She realized the one screen was her. She flinched and turned to the one for Mullich.

"What?" asked Claiborne. He nodded to the scan of Mullich. "What's he have you thinking?"

She resisted looking at the scans. She focused on the cello music, imagined breathing it. "What if it *is* in us? Some of us."

"You're thinking syndrome?"

"Why not? We have nothing but death and indicators. Maybe we can't find the one thing because there are two things. It happens to us all the time in ER. Maybe it's like Reye's. Working off a common virus. Coryza plus something else. Zoster plus something else."

He almost laughed, no smile but a straightening of the shoulders. "You and Thorpe are still going the same way. He'll like that. I think."

"Assuming the virus is horizontal," she replied. "In us. Then the other factor has to be vertical."

"They've taken all the air filters. All disposal receptacles."

At first she felt a sense of headway, almost a rush. She examined the overhead scans, briefly hers, focusing on Mullich's form, sublimate to profile. That could take forever, to search and test for the vertical factor. It would split resources. They could *never* find it. As in Reye's Syndrome. We just know it's there. We just know the two ends of the equation: pox plus aspirin plus childhood times y equals sudden death. Remove any one additive and we're okay; damn that unknown variable.

She sympathized with Thorpe and hated him at the same time. She was almost able to picture him, to recall which one of those onstage experts he was.

On the overheads Mullich's scans looked better than hers. Sublimate, his form appeared ready, arms and legs evenly spread; in profile, the form was serene, jawline perpendicular to throat. He displayed himself proudly. Both of hers were askew. In profile, her face angled toward torso, a body fearing itself. Sublimate, she had swept her left arm inward, turned the right foot more outward. The form was almost Chaplinesque, or Kabuki.

She returned to Mullich's scans.

"You trust him?" she asked.

Claiborne looked at the scans, studied Mullich's. "All I can say is that I'm glad he's set up down here."

She traced the outline of Mullich's face, squinted, pretended to see something. "Did he ask for these, or did you request them?"

"After I took your blood and your scans, he told me I should do the same for him. Told me he was there with you and Cabral."

Mendenhall clicked her tongue. "Did Thorpe ever find out who called in Meeks? Who found Meeks first and called ER? Used Meeks's cell?"

Claiborne shook his head. "If it wasn't Meeks himself, we figured it was somebody from physical plant who was scared. Scared of infection, scared of quarantine. Makes sense they would call it in quick and then dash, use Meeks's cell."

"But it doesn't make sense that Thorpe can't find that person," replied Mendenhall. "I mean, *I* could find that person. You know what makes more sense?" She pointed directly to the middle of

Mullich's sublimate form. "That. Him. Who else would be poking around the basements? Who would *want* the body to get to ER—to me, then maybe you?"

She knew. She could picture Mullich down there with his laser pointer and range finder, blueprints in his head. She didn't need Claiborne's confirmation.

"Like I said." Claiborne bowed his head and massaged the back of his neck. "Glad I got him down here."

"He's everywhere." Mendenhall kept her gaze on the scan. "Everywhere and nowhere."

34

She remembered to eat. The cafeteria surprised her. All tables were occupied. Groups had set up camp at every one, coats and bags saving seats, table surfaces strewn with empty cups, stacked dishes and trays. Clutter from the booths spilled into the pathways. Three workers from physical plant had been sent to help with the busing and sweeping. The restroom doors were propped open. The bleach smell was singular, sharp, a full erasure. The physical plant people wore tool belts, and the leather hung low on their hips as they pushed brooms and gathered litter into bags.

Mendenhall felt a pang, a crawling behind her eyes. Meeks and Dozier would have been down here. They might have been friends with these others. The bleached air stung tears to her eyes. She used the sleeve at the inside of her elbow to press them away.

Food and water supplies that had been trucked in were stacked in plastic-wrapped pallets. The vending machines were empty. The crowd was noisy, bursts of laughter here and there. Mendenhall broke the seal on a nearby pallet and helped herself to a box of granola bars. She started to do the same with a stack of water bottles, but a security officer touched her wrist with a baton. His uniform had the same piping as that worn by her dislocated-shoulder patient in the ER. This guy was even bigger.

She considered the baton on her wrist, her fingers on the bottle.

She maintained the pose, studied his face. His expression was blank, his gaze aimed at her throat. She removed her fingers from the bottle. The baton tip lingered on her wrist. She returned the box of granola bars. The bleach air and the officer's pale features fit too well and killed her appetite.

"I was gonna pay," she told him. "I always do it this way. I'm from ER. We have to go here and back. It's weird, isn't it, that they put us on the same floor? Food and blood."

She could have left it there. But there was a downturn in his lips. It wouldn't have affected her except that it appeared delivered, a rote response, a passing down of judgment.

"I've seen the dead," she told him. "All six, inside and out. I got them first. I have touched them all. I have breathed their breath." She spread her hand in front of his face.

He didn't flinch. His voice was throaty, boyish. "I know who you are. We all do."

"So what are your orders for me?" she asked. "Like shoot to kill?"

He folded his arms across his chest and centered himself between the pallets, stared at the cafeteria chaos.

"What was it like being sent in?" she asked. She aligned herself next to him, watched, thought of going to parades as a kid. "A thrill, I bet. Telling yourselves you're being sent in to save people, sacrificing. But really it's the power and the secrets. The game."

She studied his jaw. It was shiny, freshly shaved. The bleach scent could have been his cologne.

"Have you ever seen virions? Did they show you pictures? They look like spaceships. Different types of spaceships. They have geometric capsules—some spherical, some octagonal. They have landing gear, tripods, suction cups, drills. But those are only the ones we can find. They hide. In different ways, in different places, in various disguises. They aren't alive, but neither are they inanimate."

She waved a hand in front of his face. His eyes remained still.

"They didn't, did they? They didn't show you pictures of a virus." She positioned herself in front of him, faced him. "But they showed you a picture of me."

She backed away. "Think about that. When you think."

BACK IN HER cubicle, she sipped from a little carton of warm milk she had swiped from a tray. It tasted of chlorine, the chemical still in her nose. She visited the forum. More sympathy from ERs in Mexico City, Denver, and Istanbul. They referred to her cases as the Mercy Six. There were rumors of similar cases emerging. In Tokyo. In Hong Kong. Rumors were to be expected. But Mendenhall had seen the helicopter, and so she worried.

Her mentor had taught her to examine and divide her emotions, especially the surface ones. It was important to learn this in the ER, a way to avoid conflating the stream of patients, injuries, conditions. The worry connected to the helicopter felt new to her, not part of the diagnosis for the Mercy Six. So what she feared was not overreaction but policy. Maybe this was selfish, a fear of losing even more control. Maybe it was objective, rooted in her earliest intuition: not infection, not viral—but we make it so by thinking and acting that way.

A message from the outside invaded her screen. It was a query from a reporter with the *Times*, a T. Ben-Curtis. The presumptive tone led her to believe it was a man. He assumed she would want to respond, couched his message in her need, hid his sex. He just wanted to know how it had started in the ER, how it looked. He wanted to put faces to the names involved. Following protocol, she forwarded the query to Dmir.

The last thing Ben-Curtis asked was, How many more? That

was the one answer he wanted, the patient at the doorknob. Who's next? Who's dying in there?

She forced herself to finish the warm, tainted milk. She wrote out a response she knew she would not send. *It's not a virus. The infection is us. I am the worst part of it because I know and I act and I speak and I don't speak out of fear and comfort. We're all dying in here. We go to sleep and wake up dead.*

Instead of catharsis she felt dread, the same feeling she had whenever she removed a bandage to find that a wound had worsened. She thought of Kae Ng 23 first but recognized her own self-diversion. She almost forgot to delete her message to Ben-Curtis before hurrying off to Pathology. To find Silva. To wake her.

35

She searched the lesser rooms of Pathology. They were empty, peaceful, just as Silva had explained. Mendenhall found her in a small lab at the end of a hall. Within, light fell from a green exit sign. As Mendenhall's eyes adjusted, Silva's form came clear. The tech lay on her back, her lab coat as blanket, her head on a thin pillow. Her hair swept over her face, and her hands rested on the pillow, too, softly fisted.

Part of her wanted to linger and watch, watch for breathing, for a flutter of lashes, a finger twitch. But the part of her that always won swept her toward Silva. I am breaking into pieces, she thought in the movement, a line of vertebrae slinking into itself. Her two fingers went to Silva's carotid, dipped into the warm fold.

Silva's head twitched, turned in the direction of the touch. Mendenhall started, drew her hand back. She sighed twice, the first deep with relief, the second sharp with self-reproach. Silva did not wake. Her lashes quivered. Her lips mouthed dream words.

Mendenhall smoothed the tech's hair clear, placed hand to forehead. Body temp was just below 98.6. Silva had gone into deep sleep. She might have slept for hours. Mendenhall's touch had triggered her toward consciousness, maybe into dream. Silva's fists clenched and released, still pillowed about her head.

Mendenhall pinched the ends of Silva's hair, twirled a thin lock into a delicate yarn. She lifted this and watched the green light slide along the sleekness.

"If I knew what I believed, I would tell you. But it's only in parts right now." She eased the lock of hair higher, weightless between thumb and forefinger. "Maybe that's just what belief is. Parts never reaching a whole, always that gap."

Silva murmured in her sleep. Mendenhall watched the flutter of lashes, followed the black curve, the lift at the end reflecting the lift of the brow. When she fixed her gaze, she found that Silva's eyes had opened. She was awake.

Mendenhall released the lock of hair. Silva blinked, focused, appeared only slightly perplexed. She lifted her head, raised herself to one elbow, her lab coat falling away.

"Dr. Mendenhall." Silva checked her watch. "I overslept."

She started to hurry. Mendenhall touched her shoulder. "You're fine. Everything's fine."

Silva blinked some more, let her stare go blank. "No." She made an *mm* sound. "No. It's not."

Mendenhall pressed her palm to Silva's forehead, then drew a pulse. The tech's eyes appeared clear, remarkably clear. "You feel something? Something off?"

Silva stared straight ahead. "The only time I think clearly is just before waking. Dreams, you know? What they seem to do?"

Mendenhall nodded.

"I'm not off." Silva finally looked at Mendenhall. "You're the one. You."

"I've been scanned. You have my blood. I'm good."

"Still. Something." Silva gathered herself into sitting position, opened a space on the edge of the bed for Mendenhall. "You. You're not the same."

The same? Mendenhall almost felt she was the one trying to wake.

"Not the same as what?"

"The person you were before all this started. Before you called containment."

"You didn't know me then."

"I did. Dr. Claiborne spoke of you often, your work, your charts. He sent me up there often, usually to gather data, sometimes just to observe, to maintain connection."

Mendenhall didn't know why this bothered her. She fought her temper, sat on the edge. "Look. I'm ER. We change for each arrival. We move on. We turn it over to the specialists and move on. Trauma. Think about it. Everything can cause trauma. We can think ourselves into it, *dream* ourselves into it. I surmise and tend wounds."

"While I slept, what did you do?"

"I sutured a wound, reset a shoulder, stole some milk from caf. I told off Mullich and made nice with your boss."

"You shouldn't have done those." Silva swung herself off the other side of the bed, gathered her hair into a ponytail. "Those last two. Those. I could see it in your face."

"You didn't even look at my face."

"I saw it before I woke up."

They faced each other across the bed. Silva fastened her hair, slipped on her lab coat, and pushed sleep from just below her eyes. "I saw you faking." She bowed her head and gave Mendenhall an apologetic glance. "It's not a virus. I do everything I'm supposed to do. Everything I'm told. But it's not a virus. You're the one who's right."

Mendenhall shook her head. "Saying it's not a virus is saying nothing. Saying it *is* a virus is nothing. In ten years we won't even use the term anymore. Not in medicine."

Silva appeared confused.

"We have to operate under a theory. Or we can just go along blind like most, not see the theory."

"Or you can form your own." Silva's arms hung straight.

Mendenhall shook her head again. "It doesn't work that way. Science can't work that way. You have to work off the existing premise, the dominant one, the one that's saving lives. Virus theory. Thorpe's. Claiborne's. DC's. Yours." She opened her hands toward Silva. "Mine."

"I don't see that. I don't see that at all. I see that I must do what Dr. Claiborne says because he knows more than I, has seen much more than I. I'm just an instrument, nothing more—and that's how it should be. But I don't have to believe. In fact, I work better believing you. You and your gel blocks and your ability to see inside without scans."

Mendenhall leaned forward and placed her hands on the bed. "Then maybe understand this. We used to believe in miasma. That disease wafted over our bodies, was born in swamps and bogs. Before that, it was the four humors. We can smirk, but those kind of worked. Humoral theory, miasmal theory. They're not wrong. They're just incomplete. We push their definitions and we find our way."

Silva moved her arms. "Unless the working theory obscures. Regresses. Damages. Tells us to bleed the anemic."

Mendenhall pressed her thumb to her forehead, fending off a headache.

"What do you want from me?"

Silva raised her chin. "I want you to take me with you when you go."

Mendenhall smiled. "Even if I wanted to go, there's no way.

Mullich's built this place for containment. Even the windows don't break. Outside, there are white trucks and helicopters. Inside, there are goons who won't even let me snitch a bottle of water."

"Then you've considered it."

Mendenhall shook her head. But wondered.

Silva moved to the foot of the bed, fiddled with the empty clipboard dangling from the frame. "I saw Dr. Claiborne taking notes—paper notes—after he looked at Cabral's amygdala. He saw something. He even sketched something."

Mendenhall rested her gaze on the green glow of the exit sign. Silva motioned with her arm for Mendenhall to lie down. She pressed her eyes with the heels of her palms, pictured the gray-and-black strokes of Claiborne's sketches, the almond shape of amygdalae, their graceful connection to the hippocampus, a connection too ephemeral-looking to accept its charge.

Then she was lying down. Silva removed Mendenhall's shoes and fitted a pillow beneath her Achilles. She grasped both feet and drove her thumbs along the arches, firm enough to ply the longus tendons. The strength of Silva's hands surprised her, but the warmth did not. Mendenhall relaxed her neck and closed her eyes partway, let the green light of the exit sign blur around Silva's silhouette.

Silva hooked her fingers between the toes, spread them, a delicate force. As she pulled her fingers free, she pinched the web between each one.

"Take better care of your feet, Doctor." She blew a cooling breath then, using both hands for one foot, twisted the left metatarsals together, close to pain, holding there for three long seconds, which she counted in a whisper. Then she did the same to the right.

"They're farthest from our minds, the plantar nerves, all the way out here." Silva ran a fingernail along the oblique arch of each foot. "Firing from here, traveling the length of the body."

She hooked her thumbs over the navicular and dug her fingertips between each metatarsal, counting three for each palpation. All the while Silva pressed the base of her rib cage to Mendenhall's toes, stretching them back.

"From down here," she said, "I could stop your heart."

Mendenhall let her eyes finish closing. She thought of her dog, Cortez, the last time she had taken him to the observatory, let him rest in her lap, placed her palm between his ears, called him "Killer. Hey, Killer."

"Take me with you when you go."

36

Mendenhall crouched in the boiler relic where Meeks had fallen. The heat bubble created by the metal bowl felt soft, something about the copper, the stilled drip of the weld lines. With a laser pen stolen from Mullich's desk, she fired the red beam. The air inside the relic was humid enough to illuminate the line, pink in the mist, almost not there. She positioned herself as Meeks before collapse, given his final pose. She held the pen to her left shoulder, just above the upper lobe of the lung. She imagined the shattered fluorescent above the copper lid, aimed there. Retraced the line.

The line of Mullich's god particle. Not the elegant God Particle, the math of subatomic forces, but the blatant straight line of an architect. On Seven, a fluorescent tube explodes above Enry Dozier as he reaches down from his ladder perch. He collapses over the top step, dies, his shoulders and arms posturing from the pulse that disconnects his brain stem. Within the same second, the same pulse, on fourth floor recovery, Lana Fleming falls across the body of her roommate, dies, her fingers holding a cup of tea, her last breath a dead breath, a residual puff from the spasm in her bronchus. On third floor ICU, Richard Verdasco stares at the ceiling and dies, pretty eyes open, nerve endings just beginning to fizz and break the thinnest of capillaries in the softest organs. In a storage closet on second floor surgery, Marley Peterson holds her last cigarette and dies, the neuropaths throughout her entire body firing.

On the first floor ER—her ER—Albert Cabral crouches near a bed curtain, practicing shadow puppets on the gauzy surface. What does he feel? Is it an emotion? A sudden sadness? A loss of heart? Of meaning? The butterfly silhouette on the curtain reduced to nothing more than the shadow of his hands?

In the subbasement boiler room, she is Lual Meeks. The fluorescent above the boiler relic explodes, and she is struck through her shoulder and left lung. Her last instinct is to slide into the warm copper palm beneath her.

To Mullich's microscopic God Particle, surfaces are liquid or gas, the first state of matter irrelevant due to velocity. Cinder block and bone are hollow matrices. Metal, glass, skin, and vessel walls part and collapse, ripple and recompose. Water. She knows there is a fourth state of matter. And a fifth. But she is ER, trauma, molecular, as rough in matter as the architect's line.

Mendenhall released the button on the laser pen. She backed out of the copper relic, sought distance, looked at the dark panel covering the dead fluorescent and the hard surface of the boiler tank.

A virus is not the thing we see in the electron microscope, hiding in protein folds. That is a virion, a first and necessary cause, a particle that is neither alive nor dead. It is a-life. Other causes and conditions must occur to create the virus. A virus is an event, a collection of actions and reactions between the virions and the involved cells. You do not *have* a virus. You experience it. You can't see it; you see its effects. You adjust. You try. You live. You die.

She aimed the laser at the dark half of the fluorescent panel. The red beam sparkled into thousands of pieces as it refracted through the shards of the shattered tube. They lay scattered across the inside of the translucent panel, reminding her of a kaleidoscope.

"I'm no crazier than Thorpe," she said, firing the stolen laser pen. She was alone and speaking to the ghost of Lual Meeks.

37.

I t had been twelve hours: 0736. Seven thirty-six A.M. on her six-
dollar running watch. According to protocol, a meeting had to be
ordered. Mendenhall was summoned as the physician who had
called containment. She had thought Thorpe would assume this
position. She was also summoned as Floor One leader, a position
she had thought she had deferred to Dmir, or somebody like him,
somebody dressed like him.

The meeting was held in one of the old lecture theaters, a
cupped room with stage and podium, used when Mercy had still
been a teaching hospital. Years ago, before her time, it had become
an informal storage space, its floors and aisles convenient for big
equipment and stuffed files, its nooks ready for illicit cigarette
breaks.

Someone had prepared the room. The podium stood off center
next to a table set up for a panel. An old surgical light cast a serious
yellow glow over the stage. The aisles remained dim, a single thin
light high above, seemingly unattached in the darkness up there.
Old equipment had been pushed toward the ends and rear, looming,
craning, containing. Mullich.

She spotted him in the back row, in a lab coat along with the rest
of the audience, laptop glowing blue. In the rest of the scatter—
no one sitting side by side, no one in the first two rows—she

recognized only Claiborne and a guy from Surgery. On the panel, she recognized only Dmir. The panel chair closest to the podium was empty.

Mendenhall was terrible at meetings, never ready when she was supposed to speak, always speaking when it was best to hunker down and shut up. She climbed past old equipment—a steel X-ray with sharp joints and snagging wires—and took the seat next to Mullich. If not for the blue of his laptop, she would have been invisible.

She returned his laser pen, cuffing it back to him, a passed note.

He raised an eyebrow at the pen, slid it into the pocket of his lab coat. "I think you're supposed to be down there." He spoke softly as he nodded toward the stage.

On the panel with Dmir were two other men she did not recognize. One had broad shoulders and did not fit into his lab coat. Some kind of security head. Mendenhall would leave before it was his turn. She eyed her exit path, over and around Mullich, back into the darkness. There would be clanking.

"I figured that chair was for Thorpe," she whispered. "Where is he?" She scanned the paltry audience, all of them mere silhouettes in front of their laptops and handhelds.

Dmir rose from his panel chair and took the podium. Mendenhall suppressed a groan. She took a granola bar from her coat pocket. The paper wrapping crackled. Heads turned. She put the bar back in her pocket and slid lower in her chair, imagined herself hidden beneath Mullich's tall shadow.

Dmir began. "Six demises in twelve hours."

She whispered to Mullich. "Six deaths in one second."

The architect straightened. Onstage, Dmir paused and peered into the audience. Mendenhall slid lower.

Dmir cleared his throat and continued, "We have reports of other possibles. From the Boston area and Reykjavik."

"The hell?" She looked at Mullich.

Dmir paused and peered. Silhouettes moved.

Mullich turned his screen to her. There was a page set up for this meeting. The first line was about Boston and Reykjavik. She looked at all of the other screens, all on the same page. Her name was all over it.

Dmir proceeded. "Dr. Thorpe is speaking with the Centers for Disease Control."

With DC? *With* them? *Outside?* She resisted another whisper. Mullich was looking at her, the blue light carving the side of his face into angles. Mendenhall's hands felt empty, the space in front of her gravitational.

She stole the laser pen from Mullich's pocket. She fired its beam into her cupped palm. Showed him. Six deaths in one second. She aimed the pen toward Dmir. She could put a red dot on his big forehead.

She pulled Mullich's laptop toward her. "I need to use this." She only breathed the words, mouthed them carefully. "Yours. Not mine. *Capice?*"

Mullich squinted at her. Dmir's speech became nothing more than a drone, a recap of their cases, a vent sputtering somewhere. As Dmir went on, she began her research. Mullich did something to his screen, some function she did not understand. The screen changed color, to a kind of dull orange.

Mullich saw everything.

Mendenhall found one site, then another. Mullich reached over to help. Forty thousand tons of cosmic dust falls to Earth every day. Every day. This was the average. She found the most scientific sites, ones full of equations. She eased her eyes on the calculus, felt Mullich doing the same. They saw a photo of three cosmologists from the Kivla Institute crouching over a collection pool, a type of radar dish filled with water, mirroring the sky. They saw microscopic photos of the particles, some globular, some crystalline.

Somewhere in the middle of Dmir's speech, his notes on Albert Cabral, she found a local cosmologist who was somehow connected to the Kivla Institute. A consultant. Not a cosmologist, technically. An astrochemist. A chemist. Someone who had covered childhood sketch pads with the periodic table while listening to the purple dinosaur sing. Someone crude and molecular.

"Him," she whispered to Mullich. "I need to go *see*. Him." She pointed to the name atop the website: Dr. Jude Covey. Below the name was another photo of cosmologists crouched around a collecting pool, two men and a woman. The caption didn't name the scientists, just said *we*. The sky and its reflection in the circle of water appeared Scandinavian, broken clouds with rims of light.

When it became clear that Dmir was not going to discuss the outside possibles, was not going to take them to Iceland, Mendenhall knew she would not be able to stay quiet. If he wasn't going to present bodies, occlusions, scans, she had to leave. She clambered over Mullich, her breasts skimming his forehead. Mullich took hold of her hips and helped ease her over. She struggled through the equipment in the darkness, her coat snagging on an old EKG monitor, the kind with suction cups. Dmir paused, visored his hand over his eyes. Everyone turned to her.

She found Claiborne's silhouette, scanned the seats, sort of bowed.

"Everything," she said. She firmed her voice. "Everything on One is ready for you. Whatever you need. I have a call. Sorry. ER, you know?"

She finished her exit, let them see her hop, slide, and stumble through the remaining obstacles.

38

The Higgs boson used to be called the God Particle, a force predicted by the math of subatomic physics. The math led to an absence, a particle that had to exist due to the behavior of the subatomic sphere, that behavior defined by a weakening. Mendenhall began reading the math, had to stop herself. She would have liked nothing more than to sip tea and see how far she could follow it, the expression of the Higgs boson.

Thorpe's God Particle was an unseen and unknown virion, submicro, existing outside most definitions of life, not composed of cells but able to reproduce, able to act, those actions defined by hiding, disguise, and opportunistic moving, sliding. Not inanimate but not life. A-life. Thorpe's God Particle was also predicted by absence but not one evidenced in math. It was predicted by history.

Medicine was stacked on history. A correct diagnosis—this man has influenza caused by an RNA virus—can be traced back through medical history, never veering from the text, to a laughable diagnosis: This man is sick from walking the cold, wet heath.

Mullich's God Particle was a hypothetical mass defined by its velocity and its effects on surrounding cells and particles. It would be microscopic. It would be extrasolar, produced by a stellar explosion somewhere in the galaxy. These particles exist, are prevalent. They have been defined by math. They have been collected. They have been photographed. They hide in apathy. No one cares about them except the few scientists who collect and study them. They are pieces of glass or metal. Studying them earns no reward or recognition. Studying dark matter, antimatter, the Higgs boson, earns reward, money, even makes it to television. Studying Thorpe's virions earns the same.

Take me with you when you go.

39.

I t was full morning. They stood on the roof, the telescope relic focusing the sun into a hard white circle on the surface between them. The daylight gave her near-vertigo, the way it always did after night shift, her circadian rhythm awry. Below, blocking the roads from Mercy General, white trucks had morphed into white vans. In daylight she could see that the vans had clusters above them, receivers and transmitters and surveillance. Mullich followed her gaze. He pointed to ones she had not seen right away, the ones in camouflage with armored sides. He pointed to the roof of a far building, about a mile away, where that night helicopter roosted.

"The cases in Boston," she told him. "They're false."

He nodded.

"The one in Reykjavik." Her voice faltered. She had to take an extra breath. "There may be something."

The look he gave her—for him it was a gentle one, the closest to gentle she had seen. An angle of revelation in his expression, a nick of a smile. "Does that break your resolve?"

"It heightens it." She almost took hold of his hand, wanted to feel the coolness of it, the length of fingers. "It gives me necessary complexity. You know?"

"But," replied Mullich, "it indicates possible outbreak. It gives

Thorpe and Disease Control much more power and license. Now their concerns are global. Their audience global. If you still want to do this, you will be heading into something that just got a lot stronger and a lot more vigilante."

"You think it's shoot to kill?" She made her hand into the shape of a pistol.

"I wouldn't joke," he said. He folded his hand over hers and pushed it down. "You really need to see that Kivla person? *See* him? I could maybe get him messages."

"I do. I have to see Jude Covey's reactions and I have to have a full exchange. What I'm thinking is new to me. I need to have an exchange with an expert. My expertise with his. Just like you with me."

He appeared to like this, drew his finger along his jaw. "Okay, then."

He pointed to an area just beyond south parking, where the scrub of the foothills met the asphalt of the lot. "See that little protrusion of stone? That stump just poking out of the brush?"

She thought he was demonstrating averted vision again. She felt way beyond that. But she complied, and she looked, and she saw it. Something she had passed a thousand times and never thought about, never bothered to identify as anything more than an oddly large and upended stone.

"I see it."

"It's a remnant," he told her. "Most likely a sundial. All around it are other stones and pebble lines, almost hidden beneath decades of scrub and brush and soil. But it's in the original landscape blueprints. A therapy garden. The kind still prominent back then, in the 1930s."

"For the loonies." She rubbed her eyes, glanced at the sun for needed sting. "Like me."

"And for physical therapy. And for the doctors. Like your running trails out there."

She could kind of see it, a vague impression in the scrub and hardpan surrounding the stone remnant. Shallow, truncated pathways among the sumac, a line here and there too straight for nature.

She nodded.

"It was named for the mother of the doctor who started this place." Mullich tapped the telescope relic. "The same man who put this here."

"He wasn't happy. Was looking for a way out."

"Probably you're right," replied Mullich.

He straightened his arm, pointed to the sundial ruin, checked her eyes, made sure she followed. He swung his aim slightly and said, "There, two paces left of that stone, is your exit."

The word struck her, confused and clarified. It verified what he was doing—for her. But she could not see how any exit—any literal exit—could be way out there beyond south parking. She feared he was speaking metaphorically, something that would have hurt her, coming from him. But then she knew he couldn't be. He was Mullich.

He offered her a view of his tablet. On it was an old-looking blueprint of Mercy General, a vertical cut showing only the two bottom floors and three basements. Another basement suddenly new to her. He circled his finger around the very bottom rectangle.

"This really isn't a floor, technically. It's airspace between terra firma and the building. Buildings do not rest on the ground, as most people believe. They are tied to the ground. For us—architects—they are structures wont to float, to rise and shift. The pier posts are drilled deep into the earth. They don't just stabilize and offer foundation. They fasten. Get it?"

She nodded, still wondering about *exit*.

"What I'm telling you is that it won't be clean down there. It will be grim and unoccupied. An empty space, a vacuum. It will drain you." He glided his finger along that bottom rectangle, settled on a smudge just outside the wall. "This," he said. "This vague shading is a bomb shelter. Built later. You can guess when. Whoever built it marked the blueprint with this shading. And that's all."

"You know it's there?"

He nodded. "Sure. Right when I saw this shading. It's what I would have done if asked to build a bomb shelter."

"But you verified?"

"Of course. I ventured into the airspace and found the metal door. I used penetrating oil to break the galvanization on the handle. It's a submarine door. I went into the shelter. It's small. Good for maybe ten people. Maybe they had plans to construct more along the other walls."

"So you went in," she said. "It was okay."

"But I'm used to such spaces. Given what I do. Reconstruction. You're not."

She started to speak. He pressed his finger to her lips. The touch felt cool and pleasant.

"There's more. Listen. The shelter has a sealed vent. The vent is also designed as an escape in the event the building collapses. Obviously it opens from the inside. I didn't crawl in, but I know that would have to be the case. I did go and find where the exit would be. I guessed the garden first thing and was right. But that door is now sealed from the outside as well. It's grated over, and there is a bar and lock. And it would have to be dug out some. I left it pretty much intact."

"Why?"

He shrugged. "I suppose I want to keep it hidden. My escape.

I always do that with my projects. Things like that. Gains in knowledge. Secret passages are the dreams of architects."

Mendenhall closed her eyes. "So you would have to go over there and unseal it."

"That's not possible. I haven't figured it out yet."

She opened her eyes, looked at the city, which was gray and white and beginning to shimmer along its far edges. "I know how to do it. I know of someone. Someone who would want to get in. Someone who might know how to be . . . clandestine. Someone who would swap. Him in, me out."

"Who?"

"You'll like this. It's just right for you. Your desire for transparency or redemption—or whatever it is. Democracy?" She wanted to kiss his throat. Just that, just there. "He's a journalist. For the *Times*. He wants to see, to be in here, to report."

"You won't be able to communicate with him without others knowing."

"I'll figure out a code. Doctors are great at speaking in code. To patients, to loved ones, to other doctors. We're great at saying only exactly what needs to be said, to be suggested. And leaving it at that. Trusting that."

He wouldn't look at her. "I know you're right. I know you won't carry a virus out there. Because there is no virus. I know it better than you do."

"I'm ER. An eternal carrier. I will sterilize myself and be careful out there. Just in case."

They stood together, quiet for a moment, watching the horizon, a glance or two toward the ruins. They enjoyed the sunlight, the outside air, the intermittent breeze.

"I'll help you as far as I can. You can't take your phone, and even if you can get to your car, you won't be able to drive it out."

"Look, Mullich," she said, "I'm a good doctor. I'm ER. I might be heading out there just to prove myself a fool. But I really believe I can help alleviate misery. Inform triage. I know you think I most want to get out there and run free for a while. But that's not what I want most. I want to diagnose. I want to treat."

40

I n Reykjavik, a young man strolling with a group of friends fell dead on the sidewalk. The forum noted that he had been in perfect health, had been a soccer star for his work team. His friends thought he was joking when he fell; he always liked to scare them with little pranks like that, they said. They said he hadn't taken any drugs. They had all been drinking, but not a lot. They were in between clubs, strolling and laughing as they walked from one to the other. The night was unseasonably warm, and they had all loosened their scarves. He had fallen just after three A.M., Reykjavik time. The ER there had registered him at 0312, unresponsive.

Three twelve. About two hours after Mendenhall's cases—the Mercy Six. His case had only come up on the forum after the others in his group had been checked for drugs and alcohol. All of his friends described his fall in the same way: from life to death, from laughing and buoyant to collapse, no gasp or seizure or disorientation or stumble. From alive to dead. Brain scans showed very faint, very mild incipient hemorrhaging in the frontal lobes, nothing near fatal. Pathology still thought it was drugs, was waiting on toxicology.

But Mendenhall's cases, there in the forum, had Reykjavik looking at Mercy General. They had Pathology on alert, and they had the friends come back to the hospital for observation in containment. Mendenhall could have sent three guesses to Pathology there, three suggested scans. She was afraid one would be right. She sent nothing.

She fought off images of a group of young friends on a night sidewalk, laughing and turning to one another beneath a Nordic sky, steam and false dawn on the horizon. She saw one fall, the tallest and most gangly of the group, the handsome clown. Struck through. Where? Left lung? Kidney? Perhaps across the torso? Was another in the group, a girl with a secret crush strolling close, struck through in the same diagonal at the same microsecond? Through the thigh or calf or foot? Like Cabral, her sudden quiet attributed to circumstance rather than physiology?

Don't let her sleep, Mendenhall wanted to write. Don't let any of them fall asleep. But she knew it was already too late for that by the time she heard.

IN HER CUBICLE she bypassed the forum and contacted the Reykjavik ER directly. She received an autoreply, bland, suggesting minor technical difficulties. She recalled the flight of the helicopter from last night, Mullich's laser cutting through the exhaust. And she knew the Reykjavik hospital, a third of the way across the world, was in containment, had two deaths. Hours apart. But not hours apart if they knew what she knew, had seen what she had seen, had someone like Mullich and someone like Claiborne and someone like Silva. If they had all that, they would know that both deaths had happened at once, out on that sidewalk, under that sky. Delivered from that sky.

41.

S he began. She replied to Ben-Curtis. She knew others would read it before he did: *As a doctor I cannot divulge case information. I can only carefully offer you a sense of what it's like in here, what it was like when all this began to unfold. But I can only bring you so far. Metaphorically, only as far as, say, the little patch of ruin just beyond south parking. That odd stone you once asked about.*

Metaphor had its place after all. She pushed send. Later she planned to just send him a time, somehow frame it in something that looked fractured, incomplete, and accidentally forwarded. All else she trusted to her skill as a doctor, her understanding of persons. Maybe that would leave her trapped at the dark end of a sealed tunnel.

SHE WENT DOWN to Claiborne's lab and asked to speak to Silva alone. Silva and Claiborne were together at Claiborne's stand-up desk. They were patterning the capillary impacts of each case, composing comparative charts. All six body scans were on the overhead screens, sublimate.

Mendenhall was ready with some lies. But Claiborne didn't ask why, didn't ask anything.

"Her eyes could use a break," he said. He looked at Mendenhall with concern, lingered. Then he returned to the overhead scans.

Mendenhall felt relief. She was ready with the lies. But they were weighted with intense betrayal, personal and professional betrayal of this doctor who believed in her in spite of himself and his expertise. The closest thing she had to a friend in this hospital. A guy who could chide her with that loop of Cannonball Man, pass her with disregard on the running trail.

She led Silva to the small lab where earlier she had found her napping. They left the light off and stood under the green dimness of the exit sign.

"I want you to come with me," said Mendenhall.

Silva's lips parted; her brow dipped. She lifted her hand, began to reach.

"I want you to come with me," Mendenhall said, "by staying here. I'm going out. I'll be back. I need you to stay here and cover my leaving. . . ."

The lab tech kept her head bowed and nodded, expecting Mendenhall's words, knowing them before they were spoken. Mendenhall felt an unexpected pang. Despite this, she delivered her prescription: "I will leave all my stuff in my locker. You go in there and take my cell phone, carry it with you. You must listen to any message so that it appears I'm still in Mercy. You must make occasional calls to the ER desk. You must take my key card and use it in the elevators and doors. You must try to open the roof door with it. Answer my e-mails. Send some e-mails. Move things around on my desk. Drink juice left for me. When Nurse Pao Pao is on break—if she ever goes on break—you must change the dressing on my patient Kae Ng."

Silva put her hand to her mouth. "I can't—"

"Yes," said Mendenhall. "Yes, you can do that. You have to be me. That's what you have to do. And you will find ways that I don't even know. Things about myself I don't know."

"But that nurse." Silva turned away, the green light bending in her hair. "Pao Pao."

"Yes. Pao Pao. She'll eventually figure it out. She might confront you. She might let you continue. She might help you, join you. I trust her. I trust her more than I trust myself."

Silva shook her head. She breathed through rounded lips.

"When?" she asked.

"Today. I need to set something up first. I need to talk to Mullich one more time. When I'm ready, I'll hang my lab coat on the right edge of my cubicle. When you see it there, you'll know it's time to start."

MENDENHALL RETURNED TO her cubicle. She received a reply from Ben-Curtis: *I understand.*

Surrender or confirmation? She had to trust the latter.

She sent him what she had ready, in her head, her fingertips. It would be the last message for him. Thorpe's readers could make of it whatever they wanted. *When we were lovers, two was always best.*

42.

Mullich was waiting for her on the roof. He was not standing by the telescope, stood instead where she had stood that first night, away from him, just before all this happened. She took her place beside him. He stared at the horizon.

"Broad daylight is best. Two is perfect, though soon. You sure?"

She shrugged.

"Night wouldn't work. They'd be on higher alert, would catch movement. He'll need bolt cutters and a spade."

"I can't tell him that," she replied. "I have to trust he'll be ready for almost anything. I have to trust him to be good at what he does. He wants to infiltrate, he'll bring tools to infiltrate."

Mullich changed the direction of his gaze, lowered it toward the running trails. "When you emerge, don't head downhill. And don't try for your car. Don't go away. Use the running trails. Look as if you're going for a jog. I've seen runners and strollers out there during this containment, people coming from neighborhoods in the canyon. They get watched. They are approached if they venture too close and are warned away. Don't think you won't be seen. Hope that you won't be seen right away. Get to the trail and then to the canyon and then to the neighborhoods. I hope you're in good shape."

"I feel ready to run a marathon."

"You ever run a marathon?"

"Not my thing," she said. "I like a fast, hard five. You know?"

43.

She returned to Claiborne's lab. This time she entered and asked Silva to leave. Claiborne appeared a little exasperated, the way he looked whenever she passed him on the trail. Silva complied, said nothing, hurried by Mendenhall without eye contact. Claiborne faced Mendenhall, eased back against the edge of his stand-up desk, crossed his ankles, and folded his arms. He shrugged.

"You have sketches," she said.

"I have lots of sketches. It's one thing I do. When I'm home, with my wife, after dinner."

Mendenhall had an apartment instead of a home, no spouse, didn't really eat dinner. The closest thing to a sketch pad was a set of golf clubs her mentor had bought for her. The irons were still shiny.

"Please don't do that to me." She hugged her shoulders, let her hands run down her arms.

"Do what to you?"

"Hurt me."

He looked at her for a moment, then bowed his head and nodded. He turned to his desk, opened one of the secretary drawers, and removed a sketch pad. He raised it. "Sketches of Cabral's scans."

Eyes closed, she sighed, then looked. "Of the basolateral complex."

"The amygdala." He flipped through the pad. "Don't be coy."

"Why make sketches?" she asked. "Why make sketches of scans?"

He stood assessing his own work before showing her. "It's a way of interpreting. Of getting myself free to interpret. You don't need to do that. With you—up there—it's all about being light on your feet, ready, making quick reads. And I don't always get comparisons. I don't get to see scans of Cabral from when he was alive. From before he may have suffered . . . whatever it is you think he suffered."

He thrust the open sketchbook at her. "So here."

He was a good artist. She could see that. It made her sad to see that someone could be a really good doctor and also be something else. In charcoal, beneath studies of the amygdala, he had written 'Albert Cabral.'

There was nothing for her to see in the charcoal except his interest, his consideration. And maybe he was done with that.

"Anything?" She raised the pad, tried a smile.

"Just the inclination. To draw, to go there with my eyes and hands."

"Hands?" She turned her palms upward. "You use both hands?"

He held up his left hand and pointed to the outside edge of his thumb, where black skin curved into pink. "I shade and feather with this."

"When?" she asked. "When do you do this?"

He shrugged. "When Silva leaves to take a little break. Little in-between moments. It only takes a few minutes." He raised the sketch pad again. "These. Sometimes she catches me, at the end, brushing my thumb over the charcoal."

She felt an unexpected, unclear twist. Had to take a quick breath, underneath.

"You want to tell me something?" he asked.

"No."

"You *need* to tell me something?"

I need to tell you everything. Everything I'm about to do.

"No," she said. "No."

"In medicine," he said, "a double no means yes."

"I'm not your patient."

She looked at him—his lean form at ease against the desk edge. She wanted him to come with her. She needed his expertise, his sketches. His pace. With his lips he shaped the opening syllable of her first name but made no sound.

When she returned to the hospital, she hoped he would remember this moment, remember it right.

44.

On her desk Pao Pao had left a small glass bottle of grape juice—Mendenhall's favorite. How had she found it in all this? Too, there was a porcelain teacup filled with granola, a homemade mix with the scent of burned honey and cashews. Not from the cafeteria or any vending machine.

Pao Pao was in the bay, moving along Thorpe's fever patients. Mendenhall could see that the nurse was recording their body temps, entering them in a ledger she must have started on her own. If Thorpe had ordered that, Pao Pao would have asked Mendenhall. She must have been running trajectories, tracing the wax and wane of each fever, matching it to her floor log. Proving these patients false—or hoping to prove them false, healthy but empathetic. Pao Pao hunched into her procedure, sidestepped swiftly from bed to bed, shedding the thermometer sleeves behind her. It was not hard for Mendenhall to imagine her tending to soldiers lying on a battlefield amid fire and chaos, their eyes wide to her. Her firm and quiet line.

One man dressed in the purple scrubs of ID and two security guards with that special piping on the uniforms approached Pao Pao. They cut her off.

Mendenhall swooped into the bay. In ER mode, she was there in seconds. The ID guy rested a hand on Pao Pao's elbow. The two guards had formed a bracket, and their arms hung restive.

"You," Mendenhall said to the scrubs, "take your hand away from her. She's the floor nurse. My floor nurse. You do not lay a finger on any personnel on my floor."

The guards now bracketed Mendenhall. One put a hand to the hilt of his baton.

"Oh, try us," she said to him. Bantamweight, she crowded him. "You have *no* idea."

She turned to the scrubs. "What are you gonna tell him? She was recording fever temps; we had to stop her?"

He drew his shoulders back, found his height. His glasses were outdated, his hair thinning and losing its color. Behind that was a slight attractiveness, a nice trim in his jaw and cheekbones.

"My advice," she said to him, "do your job, your one job. Keep us from getting out."

MENDENHALL LED PAO Pao to an open space on the bay floor, closer to her line of patients. She squared to the nurse, offered a shrug.

"Sorry, Doctor," said Pao Pao. "It made sense."

"Don't apologize. It does make sense. It's smart medicine. Running comparative charts between their symptoms and floor activity makes total sense for the good of this entire floor."

Pao Pao offered her tablet. "I'll send these, then, to you."

"But then stop. For a while, stop. Let's stay out of their way."

Pao Pao looked back to their patients, her way of clearing. Mendenhall could see that she was confused, maybe a little bit hurt. Mendenhall felt the need to protect her, to keep her from her own good sense, from her capable person. A person Mendenhall was about to abandon and betray. How does a body at once protect and betray another? How torn could she be and still navigate her way out?

She should've just gone, just done it.

45.

Mendenhall hung her lab coat on the right edge of her cubicle. There it was. She hurried to the locker room. Its emptiness disappointed her. She had hoped for some company, a colleague or two to chat with, to test her volition and demeanor. The hollow sound of her locker door and the still air only bared her thoughts. She scrubbed to her elbows, as though for surgery. She put on a fresh tracksuit and running shoes. It felt good to change her socks.

She sent one thing to her aunt: Say my name and scritch behind his ears.

An immediate reply sounded, but she let it go, a first thing for Silva.

She left her cell and key card in the locker. After removing the cash and zipping the bills into a pocket, she left her wallet. She remembered to leave the latch unlocked.

SHE MET MULLICH in the cafeteria. He bought her food and juice and made her eat. She passed on the sandwich but enjoyed a melon salad with mint.

"How did you get this?" She motioned toward the honeydew and mint tucked in her cheek.

"The cook's actually a real chef. If you bring him things, he'll prepare them for you. Gives him something fun to do."

"You know this place better than any of us." She tapped the table with her finger.

He took the opportunity to take hold of her hand. This startled her, but she enjoyed the gentle length of his fingers. He looked at her eyes. He released a tight roll of money, the size of a cigarette, into her palm. He continued to lace his fingers in hers, continued to look.

"Listen," he said, "you're being watched. We're being watched. What you're trying to uncover out there they don't want known."

He cautioned her with his eyes, kept her from looking away, from scanning. The cafeteria was still noisy and messy, smelling of bleach. With taste and touch, Mullich had separated her from that, found her respite in the crowd.

"Then how can I possibly do it?" she asked.

"I brought you here—to the cafeteria—because this is where you start."

She gave him a puzzled look.

He told her what to do. He reminded her of the emptiness she would sense down there, down there in the very bottom, in that dead air between earth and building.

46.

Mendenhall left the table. Mullich remained, feigning interest in his salad. She walked toward the swinging doors of the kitchen, veered left at the fire extinguisher, found herself in the dead end of the little hallway that Mullich had described for her. She checked for followers, saw none. The outline of the dumbwaiter was thin as a pencil line where Mullich had cut the paint seal covering the relic. Hands and weight pressed to the panel, Mendenhall pushed in and up. Nothing gave, but there was a cracking noise. She wondered if it came from within her.

A woman—a nurse, of course—appeared at the open end of the hall, looked dumbly at her. Mendenhall pretended to be stretching for a run. She glared sideways at the woman, scared her off.

With another shove, the panel lifted, pulling Mendenhall forward, a drop in her stomach. She hadn't really believed Mullich until this moment, this little fall of surprise. A musty coolness drifted from the dark cube. Whoever had sealed the relic had left a mason jar, an impromptu time capsule holding a dried rose, a Betty Boop figurine, a Vegas shot glass from the Golden Nugget, and a handful of marbles. When was the last time anyone had shot marbles?

She scooted the jar to a back corner and tried to imagine herself folded inside there. A caf worker slammed through the kitchen doors but could not see her, or made no effort to see her. Mendenhall took a breath, as if readying for a dive, and hurried herself into the cube. She was able to lift her head slightly, to wrap her arms around her knees. The panel fell, and the dark was overwhelming. The flash of phosphenes glided across her vision. She couldn't tell if her eyes were opened or closed.

A man's voice—not Mullich's—sounded from the open end of the hall, the wall muffling the voice. She heard him say the color of her hair. She heard declaration and failure. She held still and breathed through her nose as softly as she could.

And she waited. Time distended with the darkness. She took her pulse. Mullich. Who was he? When she thought about it, who was he, really? What was he? Who would want to know this building the way he knew it, at the level he knew it? All of its bones and ghosts and reasons for existing, reasons for dying. What was she to him? Someone who should be a relic, could be another relic, a piece of time now sealed in this wall. It was easy to imagine her mummy found, sitting just like this, folded away from the place that had become her life, still inside but away, lost, undiagnosed, untreated, unreleased.

She whispered his name, felt it disappear in the utter darkness. Lack of vision was beginning to disorient her, making it feel as though the cube were yawing.

A thunk echoed from somewhere above her, up at least another floor. A cable squeaked. She thought to bounce herself in the cube, to push herself up, let fall her weight. This sent her into a drop that had too much momentum at first before gliding into descent. It was happening. For the first time in a very long while, she felt a whole part of something happening, something she was doing—as a person, as a body.

THE DUMBWAITER CRUNCHED and scraped to a halt, ended up cockeyed, with Mendenhall keeled hard against one wall. The time capsule spilled, the marbles crawling around her. She couldn't slide the panel. Mullich had warned her that she wouldn't be able to. As he had advised, she spun, braced her back against the wall opposite the panel, and kicked both feet outward. Think through the punch, he had told her. Your feet not at the wall but through the wall. The panel flapped open, and she found herself in a little dead-end hall that mirrored the one she had come from.

It was quite dim down here, the subbasement just above the dead space. No light shone in the hall. The faint glow at the open end appeared spent and singular and without color. She crept out headfirst, hands braced to a grimy floor.

A shadow moved across the feathery end of light. Boots scraped the dusty linoleum. She knew it wasn't Mullich. He never made noise. He had told her he would not be there. Definitely boots. Probably one of those guards from the outside. Hospital people, even security, always learned to just wear running shoes.

Mendenhall pressed herself to the wall, into a wedge of pure darkness. Her sound was echoed by his sound, a hiss over the grime. She released a sigh, a near-surrender. A similar response from him startled her, unnerved her. He was frightened—perhaps more than she. She slid quietly along the wall. Let herself appear from the edge. What was the point of hiding? He knew someone—something—was there.

Her form appeared to shock him. He was young, big, almost a twin of the guard from the caf, though softer and somehow reddish. He gave himself no time to really see her, register her. He turned and hurried into the darkness behind the one light, a bare bulb hanging on a wire. The bulb swung in the wind of his exit. She looked down at herself. The reflector stripes of her tracksuit drew bone lines on her black form, angled and ready. God. He must have thought her the plague. He must have thought he had stumbled upon the source in the depths of this building.

She wished Mullich could have seen it.

MENDENHALL RETURNED TO the dumbwaiter and peeled away the broken panel. This was the last stop for the little cubicle. Beneath it, according to Mullich, was a narrow shaft for repairs and ventilation. Mendenhall shouldered herself into the box and pushed with her legs. Again like a punch, he had told her, starting low and following through to the other side. When the dumbwaiter lifted, she was quick to slide her fingers into the opening and pull upward. She used the mason jar to keep the whole thing wedged open.

Tepid air rose from the shaft and sifted around her ankles. She readied herself, emptied her lungs, stretched herself thin, went in feet first, lowered herself with toes pointing, exploring. Above was gray. Below was black. He had told her she would have to just let go, to trust him, his sense of the building. The landing would be okay, he had said.

She opened her hands. The drop was longer than she had anticipated, became a sucking thing. She felt swallowed.

47.

She crashed through the ventilation grill at the very bottom of the shaft, at the base of everything. Her knees buckled and thrust her forward, headfirst, her forearms up just in time. The sheet metal gave, the corroded screws snapping into the darkness, pinging against concrete. She lay fully emerged, shot out, the side of her face against the cool floor, arms boxed around her head.

Mullich had told her it would be safe to use a light down here, that there would be nobody. He had also told her she might want to keep it all dark, to just crouch her way to the opposite wall and then feel for the submarine door.

With raised hands, she tested the ceiling. Metal girders, cold and blistered, grazed her fingertips. As she crept across the darkness, she lost confidence in her direction. Cloth brushed her cheek and neck. She stifled a cry and swung her arm. Something wrapped around it, pulled and cinched her elbow.

"No," she cried.

She snapped on her penlight, a light she had fired down a thousand throats. She saw the man who had dragged himself to her on his elbows, his dead legs behind him, his eyes pleading, Don't let me die alone, don't leave me down here. She saw the patient who had been filed into a half body, planed over the asphalt of a night highway, brought to her. To do what? See the clean side of the brain that still remained, still pulsing and thinking, seeing? Seeing her? His half-mouth grimace failing to lip words to her. Die, she had told him. It's okay to die. She had held his wrist, regretting her gloves, her formal tone.

Mendenhall untangled herself from the insulation that had coiled around her arm. She flapped its dust from her sleeve and doused the light as soon as she had gained her bearings. She crouched lower, fingering the concrete of the floor. Rolls formed on the surface, everything becoming too smooth, a familiar smoothness, the smoothness of skin. Enry Dozier, his beard, the sad backtilt of his head, exposing his throat for her, dead for her. She could not make it past all six. She would not.

She dropped to her knees, palmed the floor.

"Not this."

She reached into one zippered pocket and found a trick passed down from her mentor. A fresh-cut lime often does the trick, he had taught her, snaps you back to the moment, the moment you must be in for your patient to survive, to have a chance. There is so much precedent and history in medicine, so many cases, it's too easy to fall into the past, to see helpless eyes, hear desperate words. On extreme days, when she knew she was going in drained, torn open, she would carry a slice of ginger.

The lime cooled her lips, the scent sharp in her throat, her lungs. Thoughts cleared. She moved through the darkness, stayed low and straight. When she did not reach the wall, found herself again in dark vertigo, she tucked the lime slice between her teeth and cheek, crushed and sucked. She moved forward. Would there be a floor? Or an abyss? Who crawled behind her? All of them? Or just the last six?

FINALLY HER HANDS found the wall. You'll be fine once you palm the cinder block, he'd told her. I'm not like you, she had replied. I don't find solace in archaeology.

The wall gave way. An impression dropped her forward, and there it was, the submarine door. It stood much shorter than she had anticipated, just above waist-high, more hatch than door. Still blind in the dark, she turned the wheel. The smooth spin calmed her. Mullich had unfrozen it, his words true.

The bomb shelter itself will be okay, he'd said. You might even like it. Again, she had said, not like you. Still, he had replied, turn on your light. You'll need it.

The penlight showed the shelter in fragments. The room had recently been wiped down, maybe vacuumed. He had prepared the place. Shelves lined the walls, most filled with ancient rations. The refuge was square, with a Japanese feel that surprised her at first, then made spatial sense: one low table in the middle, rolled mats stacked on a low shelf, block-shaped candles, a teapot next to a mess kit, botanical prints on each wall, one shoji screen for privacy. Mullich could live here. She considered the image, him kneeling on a mat, reading blueprints by candlelight.

Her watch read one forty-three. She found the vent, pried off the screen with the penknife, and began her ascent—a long, dark crawl that took her beneath the south parking lot toward the scrubby hillside, the sundial relic. The slope was more lateral than upward, but she sensed the rise in her effort, sweat. Remember to leave the shelter door open, he had advised. To provide you draft in the tunnel.

There was no draft. Ben-Curtis was not there. Was late. Was not coming. In full darkness, she reached the final upcurl and felt for the concave steel of the hatch. She pulled hard on the wheel and was able to squeak it free, crank it to its unlocked position. This did nothing. She had to wait for Ben-Curtis.

She fitted herself into the cusp beneath the hatch, checked her watch, rested in the darkness. Give him time, Mullich had said. He might have to wait for his chance, his opening. Or, she had replied, he might be stupid.

A rumbling passed overhead, a van somewhere on the parking lot. This discouraged her, erased all her waiting time, made it all start anew. The dark tube began to feel warm toward the top, damp and tepid toward the bottom, pulling her in two. Then something crunched overhead, traveling a line about the length of her body. Silence followed. Her pulse kept time.

"Anna."

It was a whisper. An only child, she used to imagine for herself a brother, sometimes younger, sometimes older. She gave him looks, a sense of humor, an interest in poetry, a voice to match. That was the voice she heard. She couldn't remember the last time someone had called her by her first name.

"Anna," she heard again. The voice didn't seem to come from anywhere. It was just there in the darkness around her. "Are you in there?"

three

48.

S he tapped the hatch, one-two, one-two. Metal snapped and sprang; sunlight and wind fell over her, the scent of brush, warm. Ben-Curtis appeared in silhouette across the circle, then dropped beside her, pressed to her within the tube. She had two impressions: hovering above her, his body appeared small against the light, sheared, slivered, able to soar; cleaved to her in the narrow vent, chin over her shoulder, he was forced to hug her. His body felt wiry, jittery. She couldn't help but take his pulse, which was slow despite the effort and pace of things, indicating athleticism and confidence. But there was something insubstantial about him, or unwrought, his body too inside itself. She couldn't really hug back.

To speak, he tried to draw his face away, but this made things even more intimate, nose to cheek. He relaxed over her shoulder. He wore a ball cap and smelled of whiskey and cocaine.

"In two minutes," he whispered, "it should be clear."

"You're high."

"You're not my doctor."

"But I'm relying on you."

"Have I ever let you down?" He drew back, looked at her face, their breath mixing. He returned to the over-the-shoulder position. "What can I say? I function like this."

"You have enough on you?"

"I think I'm in love."

"I don't care about your health. I care about you blending in."

"It's what I do."

"Okay," she said. "So?"

He removed his cap and put it on her, pulled it low over her eyes. "When I say, go." He wrapped his arm around her neck to look at his watch.

She tapped the bill of the ball cap. "Is this supposed to make me look like *you*?"

"We're dealing with blips and impressions. Too much and you're noticed. That hat and its colors, the wrong team for this city, has been registered."

She started to say more.

"A few more seconds," he whispered into the side of her neck. He crouched and fashioned a stirrup with his hands, lacing his fingers together. The side of his face was pressed to her stomach, his breath beneath her waistband.

"Good luck, Anna."

She fitted her shoe into his hand stirrup, and he flung her into the warm light. She did one shoulder roll into a crouch and peered into the vent. He was looking up, but she could tell he could only see her outline. His eyes were blue and glassy, coked-up with empty sympathy. She flipped shut the lid.

It was easy for her to run.

ONE OF HER most common and gruesome cases, right up there with motorcycles and the DTs, was fishhook removal. Impaled in simple flesh, nothing deeper than epidural, the approach was to continue the puncture, to curl the hook along its natural curve until the barb came clear, then snip off the barb and point and reverse the curl, minimizing damage. But when more was involved—tendons, eye sockets, ear cartilage, scrotal sacs, lips, cheeks—the approach became counterintuitive. She would go in to get out. "Like a funhouse maze," her mentor had said. "In, then back; in, then back."

Some fishhooks were as big as silverware. But the tiny ones that came in clusters were the most stressful extractions, required intricacy, patience, willingness to hurt. She sometimes just wanted to yank these out.

She felt the same way as she began her run, her far aim to the canyon bottom, her near aim Mercy General. Five strides up the slope, through scrub, she was on the running trail. Two white vans were visible, one at each end of the building. Against all desire, she circled nearer the hospital, pacing a hard five, eyes on the track, with outward glances from beneath her lowered bill. Her ponytail struck an even rhythm on her nape.

Something atop the nearest van slowly spun, a kind of metal cup or ladle. In case they had sound, she began a song under her breath, a drinking tune, the refrain "I'm a man/you don't meet/ every day."

The van appeared to rock, though it may have been sunlight tricks on the white surface. She curved toward it. It was clearly pitching with inside movement. She smiled and waved her arms, still keeping her bill low as possible.

"Hey," she called, "can you tell me? Do you know?" She pointed toward the path ahead as she jogged in place, just a fighter's dance. "Does this loop around, or should I turn back?"

The driver's-side window, black, slid down, revealing a guy in a plain black cap. He raised his chin for a better look. Somebody from the back of the van got his attention for a moment, said something Mendenhall could not discern. The soldier glanced into the back, then returned to her.

"You're gonna have to turn around and head back." He waved toward the hospital. "It's restricted up there."

She put her hand to her mouth and ducked. "It's *that* hospital?"

He rubbed his nose. "It's safe out here. But no closer."

She offered a salute with sweep to it. The broad gestures seemed to work. She thought of the purple dinosaur of her youth. The driver's attention again went toward the back of the van, then he looked at her anew. The van pitched, weight shifting to the rear. The driver's door clicked. His shoulders braced for an outward shove, his jaw clenching, eyes lulling.

She looked to the hospital roof. No Mullich. He couldn't risk that. To show any inkling of interest in her would be stupid. Still, she couldn't accept that it was over this soon. She hadn't even warmed up in her run. She was about to ask for at least that. Before they took her.

But something changed within the van. The overhead sound ladle redirected its aim. The driver relaxed his shoulders and turned swiftly toward the wheel. The van's weight shifted again, and Mendenhall stumbled back as the van sped away, the driver still craning his neck toward the other side, over the shoulder, arms rolling the wheel.

She felt abandoned, took a breath, turned, and ran along the trail to begin her descent. To look back, to show any interest, would have been fatal to this diagnosis. But this was not coincidence. Coincidence has no place in the ER. When her mentor had told her this they had been examining an X-ray, a .22-caliber bullet inside a lung tumor.

Maybe Mullich had provided distraction. Others were trying

what she was trying, had been almost from the start. But that would be coincidence, someone breaking through just now. Mendenhall increased her pace, gauging the downward slope. The sting of sunlight on her nape pushed her into the canyon while tire scuffs and dull shouts slowed her, lured her, almost spun her, just to look and see.

49.

Near the base of the canyon the asphalt trail became dust. Mendenhall picked up a follower, heard the pop of running shoes behind her shift from hard to soft. Maybe it was just another runner using her for pace, getting set for a kick. They were on a lower ridge overlooking a housing tract. She risked one over-the-shoulder glance, a racer's peek. Her trailer was smooth, swift, elusive, tracking her blind spot, sliding behind as though part of her shadow.

They dropped into the alluvial fan marking the trailhead. The switchbacks allowed her more glimpses, but she gathered nothing further. She didn't turn and stop because she wanted this run to last as long as it possibly could, again feeling caught, finished. Would they use a net?

She took no rest and loped across the cul-de-sac. The tract was old enough to have grown trees, but its roads were wide and bowed and smooth, the roofs all black, the corners crisp, sidewalks fitted and even. The follower vanished. Immersed in this neighborhood, Mendenhall ran alone. But felt no relief.

In the ER, though predawn always brought the worst cases, each time of day held its own particular dread. Midafternoon was the most tragic, young deaths and self-inflictions from after-school malaise, the sorrowful domestic wounds, when those who don't live alone feel most alone.

She rarely saw this light, only ran it on the hospital trails. The quiet houses and empty streets seemed to move while she ran in place, all coming to her. God, she thought. How have I become so crazy?

The homes, they could be tombs. She imagined a counterpart for herself in Reykjavik running toward a midnight sun. But that didn't work. She was still the last person on Earth.

50.

The bus proved a bad idea. Mendenhall realized this after the third stop. She could see downtown, the gray haze of the ocean beyond. The distant foothills opposite appeared to hover in the smog. Somewhere in that vague gray-and-white triangle the university nestled. After more than ten years, she knew the city only in relation to County and Mercy. The university sprawled behind County. The bus rumbled and stopped in increments, seemed to gain no distance, nothing more than walking speed. She had never ridden the bus. Her patients rode the bus.

Only five passengers rode with her. The driver's elbows were locked, his head angled, jaw chewing nothing. Mendenhall figured his next dose of meth would have to be in less than one hour. She noted his sunglasses case clipped above the side window—his stash. The passenger across from her was passed out, his head against the window, lips squished open and drooling. His ear was yellow, and a tremor quivered the lobe. He would be dead within the year. She might see him die.

The thickset woman with the housecleaner's basket was pregnant, maybe knew this, probably didn't. Mendenhall thought to go sit next to her and tell her, ask her how it felt. The woman's black hair was luxurious, curling with life. Her set jaw and swallow reflex fought tears. Maybe she was sitting there realizing her condition for the first time.

Nearby, an ambulance siren blared and drew closer. The bus lurched to the right and halted. From someplace farther, another ambulance siren began. This one sounded from all directions. Its blue and red reflections caught against a high glass building. The first ambulance passed the bus. Its speed indicated urgency, not a drunk with the DTs, not an invalid with low BP, not anything precautionary. The engine had that high grind of overdrive, chassis in full tilt. She wanted to go with it, to quit what she was trying to do and relieve herself with work.

Another siren called, far ahead, along the bus route, maybe coming from County. One of the three reached its destination, the siren making that final whoop. She always heard it as a question.

Mendenhall hurried to the front of the bus.

"Not a stop," said the driver. "Go back." He started spinning the wheel, ready to swing the bus into traffic.

She nodded to his stash, eyed it, eyed him.

He cranked open the door. She exited with the sound of the brake release, the driver's stare hard between her shoulders. She jogged to the center of the sidewalk, avoided looking back when she heard the driver yell, "Hey!"

Only seconds later did she think his call could be meant for someone else, someone dismounting after her, someone following her. She turned and scanned the sidewalk for anyone who could've been one of the other passengers, one in back she hadn't seen or recorded. The people seemed oddly static, not pedestrians, a mix of loitering and exchange. It all felt pooled, as in a marketplace. Swaths of the city proper were like this, she knew, where most of the population waited. For nothing possible, really, except death. Not for someone, not a lottery ticket, not opportunity, not life. Sunny parts shown in movies and TV, stuck in the minds of travelers and cynics, were insignificant slivers within the morass.

She got the morass. That was what came to her. That was what she found without trying, jumping on a bus with a certain number and location on it. She hated most movies, most TV, most books. She hated what she'd become—a person who loved an awful job, a hideous job. A person who worked as a voyeur, who was paid to peer and invade, see the undignified ways people die. Mendenhall never cured them or even really treated them. The doctors—and nurses—beyond her did that, the noble stuff.

Even now, she thought, look what I'm doing.

THE AMBULANCES WENT silent. The mingling crowd along the sidewalks gave no sense of event, no direction toward any of the emergencies. Mendenhall felt aimless, useless; she longed for the ER. People sang so many bad songs about this city, so many misconceptions and preconceptions. But she knew one good song about it. One that measured the hardness of dreams, dead grass, and concrete spaces, cut the ideals, and then gave the refrain "Don't you wish you could be here, too? Don't you wish you could be here, too?"

She regained focus and decided to use Mullich's money for cabs. The boulevard was jammed. She grew heated just looking at the traffic, saw no cabs. Did this city even have cabs? No one around her had ever hailed a taxi. That she could see.

MENDENHALL COUNTED HER money on the elevator to the fifth floor of Physical Sciences. She didn't have nearly enough to make it back to Mercy General. One professor and two lab techs rode up with her. The techs wore lab coats. The prof wore a tracksuit, not unlike Mendenhall's. He looked at Mendenhall, his eyes lingering on her ball cap.

"I'm going to see Dr. Covey," she explained.

"Are you one of Covey's collectors?"

"Yes." She lied for strength and conviction. She needed both in order to continue.

"Which post?"

Mendenhall blushed, then understood what he was asking. From Covey's website, she recalled the different collecting stations from around the world. "Molokai," she replied.

"You look so pale. I would have guessed the Oslo one."

The elevator stopped at the fifth floor.

"I'm indoors all day." Mendenhall held the door so that she could finish her lie. "I only go out at night."

She could tell from the anxious bend in his brow, his tender fist gripping, that he was about to ask her out for a coffee. Had he been better-looking, not dressed in a tracksuit, a bit more clever, maybe she would have held the door longer, upped the proposal to a drink, seduced the professor to the very brink of this lie.

51.

Covey was not in his office, though the door was open. A tech stood just inside, her lab coat nicely tailored, flattering her thin waist and graceful hips. The young woman seemed aware of this, the way she stood, as though about to dance. She was counting gel samples lined along a bookshelf, using the eraser end of a pencil. She flashed Mendenhall a look and, unimpressed, returned to her task.

Mendenhall leaned into the doorway, checked the office. She was hoping for some volunteer information. The tech ignored her. Mendenhall thought she might be humming, though it could've just been her look.

Covey had a sign-up pad pinned to the door's bulletin board. The cork surface appeared quaint, filled with postcards from various collecting posts. A bumper sticker in the lower left corner: "Matter Sizes."

Mendenhall signed in, startled to find that the pen and pad were digital, her signature and time no doubt forwarded to Covey—wherever he was. She wandered back toward the elevator, that student she once was, frustrated because professors never kept their office hours, always had something else more important to do, to ponder.

A student in a hoodie slipped out of the elevator, headed away from Mendenhall. She couldn't tell if the figure, flinty inside loose clothes, was a man or woman, the hood pulled down by hands jammed into the kangaroo pocket. Earbud wires, one green, one red, looped and flopped atop each shoulder.

"Excuse me," Mendenhall called. She was going to ask about Covey, how maybe to find him. The figure continued walking straight away, not hearing or not caring. In the ER she would have released the hounds. Here she was just that student again, insecure, lost, second-guessing every decision in her life, certainly whatever set of them had brought her to this hall.

She realized one thing, then the other, one in the focal point, the other peripheral. The person ahead of her moved in a familiar manner, a reminding tilt in the walk and carriage. And the woman in the tailored lab coat was Covey. She moved, as usual, to the peripheral.

Jude Covey.

Mendenhall returned to the doorway. The woman with the pencil ignored her, tap-counted three more gels. Mendenhall leaned against the jamb.

"You're Jude Covey. Why didn't you tell me?"

Covey paused and considered her. "You figure it out. Or you don't."

"I knew someone who always said that."

"Knew or still know? It's a big thing to stop knowing somebody."

"Know. Still know. My mentor."

"Did he—or she—show you how to dress?" Covey looked her over again. "Your soulmate is two floors up, by the way."

"We met."

"Schrader. How long before he hit on you?"

"I escaped the elevator just in time."

Covey squinted, drew the eraser along Mendenhall's striped sleeve. "You two might hit it off."

Mendenhall removed the ball cap, shook her hair. "I'm Dr. Mendenhall. I'm from the ER at Mercy General." She let this register.

"You figure it out. Or you don't."

COVEY'S OTHER LAB was in a basement. Part storage room, it held dozens of mechanical microscopes, aligned neatly enough to make them appear alive, stabled. A cement lab table fitted with unconnected plumbing and capped Bunsen burners was covered with five bowls, as big as birdbaths. On closer inspection Mendenhall saw that they were glass-lined—empty collecting pools for Covey's research. Each pool was labeled with its point of origin: Oslo, Reykjavik, Melbourne, Las Vegas, Jakarta. Three had at least one pit mark; two had several. The pit marks ran in a straight line, or close to it.

The desk area Covey had fashioned in the center of the room had nothing quaint about it. The table was titanium with built-in power supplies. The PC had two large side-by-side screens, with one laptop on either side. A green exercise ball made for a movable seat.

Covey eased herself onto it, bounced a little, straightened her back. The pleated tails of her lab coat draped over the back of the ball. Mendenhall thought of the black cocktail dress hanging in her locker back at Mercy, the one she kept for overlooked fund-raisers and retirement parties.

"Have you scanned those pit marks?"

Covey answered by filling the two main screens with side and overview resonance images, or whatever was the astrochemist equivalent. They were not pit marks. Instead they were drop formations, tiny fountains in freeze-frame, liquid heaved up, a single ripple.

"Why are they like that?"

"The glass is very soft—the softest we can make. Almost water."

"Do all the particles do this?"

"Only one in two hundred seventy-five million. The others remain suspended in the water."

"Where are those particles?" Mendenhall nodded to the images. "The ones that do that."

Covey shrugged. The ball bounced. "Somewhere in the mantle."

"The Earth's mantle?"

"Yes. That huge green mass of perodite."

"They make it that far in?"

"They're heading somewhere else. We're just an acceleration, a vector that helps form a crush line."

Mendenhall felt her own earlobes, forgetting. "What is a crush line?"

Covey answered this by putting up a stop-action version of a line of objects hitting Jupiter as it spun. "This is the 1994 Shoemaker-Levy impact. The comet was crushed by the sun and Jupiter's gravity; then the resultant smaller masses were pulled into a line. Twenty-one visible objects. Probably millions of microparticles. All in a line, under a sewing machine."

Mendenhall bit her lip, almost cringed.

"I gave up that fight long ago," Covey said. "Regular people find metaphors smart. Smart people find them amusing, sexy, even. It's a skill with a big payoff."

Mendenhall started to argue, but Covey turned away from her and drew her finger across the screen, across Jupiter. "See, what's interesting is how the crush line creates its own latitude as the sphere spins. It doesn't bend to the equator. It forms a trajectory that extends beyond the planet. To here."

"That's going on? Here?" She pointed to the floor, felt silly

"In a way. There are seven groups in our study." Covey nodded to her collecting bowls. "We're trying to put it together."

"When did this bombardment start?" Mendenhall fell into ER mode. "And how long will it last?"

Covey shrugged. "That's what we're trying to find out, Dr. Mendenhall. It's difficult to gauge origin and duration. I'm a small part of a study that began forty years ago. Now that they're here . . . this city is a crowded place."

"Why aren't you telling people? Us?" Mendenhall clutched herself.

Covey nodded to the images on her screen. "We are. All the time. But . . . they estimate that Jupiter caught the Shoemaker-Levy comet thirty years before crush and impact. For thirty years it was simply that which will be. Unchangeable." She shrugged. "It's the same here."

Mendenhall blinked, looked at the ceiling.

Covey jabbed Mendenhall's shoulder.

"Look, as soon as I and others published our first findings—in just tiny interdisciplinary papers—we were contacted by the NSA. They wanted whatever we had and cautioned—warned—us about releasing it. Assured us they would do it the right way. A safe way."

"You trusted that?"

"I love my work. We love our work. They would have stopped me. That was made clear. I assume you're getting a taste of that now." She nodded to Mendenhall's disguise, the fallen cap.

"To say the least."

"You," said Covey.

Mendenhall gave her a confused look.

"You must know what it's like," explained Covey. "My colleagues around the world take my work seriously, use my field data. All I need to do is offer what I find. No conjecture. Way too early for predictions."

"But what about people?" Mendenhall dipped in frustration, opened her hands. "Didn't you—any of you—think of that? Study that?"

"The particles pass through everything. The ones we're talking about. They're too small and too fast to really do anything."

"You really believe that?"

"It's a virus," replied Covey. "I should put on a mask and turn you in."

"I don't think it's coincidence," replied Mendenhall, "that you're here. That I'm here. Someone like you should have contacted someone like me years ago."

"You would have thought me nuts. You would have dismissed me. You still would if you hadn't seen it firsthand." Covey shrugged. "Besides, there's nothing we can do about it. So it's a virus. I'm turning you in."

Mendenhall eyed Covey's reflection in the screen. Twenty-one pieces of Shoemaker-Levy shot into Jupiter, a straight line of lights, pulsing into the spinning sphere. The event drew a diagonal across Covey's reflection, swept her hair across her forehead, lifted one corner of her mouth, stroked her neck.

MENDENHALL PUT HIGH-RESONANCE amygdalae on Covey's main screens. The laptops continued to show Jovian impacts, crush lines stitching straight seams across bands of orange and cream and red. She explained the limbic system, even though Covey claimed to know it.

With her finger Mendenhall circled the almond shapes inside the coronal view of the brain. "No. They do even more. They use sensorial memory to help the nervous system react to intrusion, pain."

"And pleasure," added Covey. "So?"

"So." Mendenhall again lifted her hands. "So your particles."

"I'm sure people and buildings and trees and animals are hit with them from time to time. More as the planet crowds. But mostly nothing would happen. Just a little ripple." Covey pointed to the bowls.

"What would happen if one passed through a fluorescent tube?" Mendenhall nodded to the low lights of the basement lab.

"The mercury vapor would anticipate a sudden influx of energy. The tube would explode. It's probably happened a time or two."

"We're fluorescents," said Mendenhall. "Not limpid pools."

"I have a colleague," said Covey, looking at the ceiling light. "Actually, I'll call him a friend rather than a colleague. He calls them my particles, too. Jude particles. He claims we should approach them as a-life. But that's only when he's drunk. Which is much of the time."

"We see what we are." Mendenhall felt as she did when the big doors slid open, the ambulance releasing, ramp clattering down. She needed to move, to see, to snitch a pulse.

"They're bullets, Jude."

"Not really, Doctor. They have no mass. Just velocity. A near-infinite velocity."

"Let's not split hairs. Let's not split anything. Show me the line.

The line from here to Mercy. Small scale. Can you do that? Using the location of a hospital in Reykjavik?"

"How small?"

"Street level."

Covey laughed, her smile lingering, almost too pretty, would melt to the touch. "That's not small. I can use Reykjavik and Mercy to pinpoint a line across your thumbnail."

"Will I be able to read it?"

"It'll be a string of coordinates. A bunch of numbers."

"I like numbers. And I have someone who will be able to read them."

"You have someone?"

Mendenhall was tempted to follow that direction, to make girl talk. Just something to convince herself she was normal enough, not mad. Instead she returned to business. "How many crush lines can there be?"

"Not many. Two or three. They would slide into one. The one you suggest would be new to my research. If it's really there, then maybe it just started."

"Just started?"

"Or it's ending. A crescendo of sorts. Time is the hardest thing to figure. Shoemaker-Levy went on for thirty years, and we only noticed it for a few last days. The crescendo. No one looks for this stuff. Just a few trombone players like myself. A thousand hotshots around the world can locate a particle of dark matter for you, pinpoint it in some salt cave deep underground. Smash atoms and isolate their particles. Or they can show you the nearest black hole or measure the microwave background of the universe. But no one looks for regular matter, dust. Even when it's hitting us in the face. Just me and some others. We're just not sexy enough."

"But you're here. Right here in this particular spot. Here now because you know where the crush line is. Today it runs through this city."

Covey offered one deliberate nod, a patient's reluctant answer.

"So," said Mendenhall, "we're either in the beginning, middle, or end?"

"Probably near to the end."

"You mean it will worsen?"

"Thicken," said Covey. "Though quicken is more accurate."

52

Thereʼs someone in my lab."

Mendenhall checked the doorway, the line of microscopes, the collecting bowls. Then she turned to Covey, who pointed to the ceiling.

"The lab up there. Not in here." She motioned to one of the side laptops. The screen showed a man in Coveyʼs fifth floor office. He was scanning the room, looking at the gels.

"But you locked up."

"People get through locked doors." Covey leaned closer to the screen. "Thatʼs why I have this." She pressed her hands above the laptop.

Mendenhall was skeptical, started to speak but was interrupted.

"Youʼre thinking Iʼm nuts. But Iʼm not crazy. See? Someone broke in." With her cell she got ready to notify security.

Mendenhall leaned in, studied the man. A drunk, paralyzed, dragged himself to her on his elbows. A hitchhiker, filed into a half person, spoke to her. Albert Cabral sat on the floor and asked her how she had found him. Lual Meeks curled himself into the brass cup of the boiler, kept his eyes open as his nerves whiplashed to death. The man in Coveyʼs study was from government security, one of those new guys sent in after containment. He wasnʼt in uniform, but he had the same haircut and expression as the others, the ones she had encountered. He wore a t-shirt and sports jacket, like a lot of men in this city. She hated that look.

"He's looking for me."

"Why follow you?" asked Covey. "Why not just *take* you?"

They watched the man look at Covey's gels as he answered his cell. He received a text, replied.

"They want to see what I'm thinking."

"Why don't they just take you *and* ask what you're thinking?"

"Because they know I wouldn't tell them. And they don't want anyone to know, to call attention. Right? Like you said, it's a virus."

The man left Covey's office. Her laptop showed the empty room for a moment, then went blank.

"They probably know what you're thinking now," said Covey.

COVEY OFFERED TWO choices for a change of clothes. Mendenhall took the formal one, a moss-colored cocktail number. When Mendenhall started to slip into the dress, Covey shook her head. "That sports bra thing won't work underneath."

Mendenhall shrugged hard, glared.

"Go without," Covey told her.

Covey watched her remove the bra and fling it across the lab.

"There's no treatment for fate, Dr. Mendenhall. Fate is fatal. Unstoppable, undeterred . . . Did you just need to escape?"

Mendenhall worked into the dress. The fit was close enough to right. "No. I need to show them I'm right. Even if I don't get to act on it. And I needed to bring something in, a patient to make my point. I needed to go see the source; now I have to go back where I can do some good."

Covey offered a thin silver necklace with a chip of peridot. "This goes." She stood behind Mendenhall and clasped the necklace and finished the zipper. She spoke into her ear. "I would want that. In my own work. To see the source and the return. But I just catch helpless glimpses. That's all I ever get to live on."

53.

Covey handed over a map she had made of the crush lines through the city and was about to go fetch some cash for Mendenhall when something crashed against the door. It was the sound of a body driven into the steel door of Covey's lab. Arms slapped against the basement linoleum. Mendenhall had heard it many times on the bay floor, nurses or EMTs tackling and subduing seizure cases, mean drunks, psychotics, or just those who wanted to fight, furious over wounds, death, life. Covey reached for the handle. Mendenhall stopped her, pulled her elbow, shook her head. Mendenhall eased herself against the floor, concerned about the dress, the necklace. She peered through the sliver beneath the door, caught shadows moving swiftly across her view, a mix of dark steps and drags. Flesh-on-flesh noises buzzed her nerves.

Mendenhall rose, pressed Covey to the side, put finger to lips. She kissed her cheek and left.

Again she felt certain to be stepping into deliverance. This time dressed for it, arms open to it.

The basement hall was empty. Two dimes of blood stained the gray linoleum. Doors with hip-handles lined both walls. She could've been in a hospital—the morgue, quiet and abandoned. The lights went off. A hollow sound, either a groan or something dragged, rose through the floor, along the walls. How many basements did this place have? Only the green exit sign above the stairwell door remained aglow. She was okay with it. All of it. They were reading her wrong. So wrong. They were giving her a series of quick things, surfaces, dilations. They were giving her the bay floor.

She took the stairway. Through the little mesh window of the first floor door, she spied one man wearing the t-shirt/sports jacket look. He was standing dead center in front of the doorway to the building. She continued climbing. Between the third and fourth floor landings someone was descending, the steps heavy and athletic, booted.

She did not raise her head and kept ascending at a normal pace, giving herself over to her disguise, letting it work. She pretended to be adjusting her necklace clasp, unhooked it as she neared the government man.

"Pardon?" she asked, looking down, fingering the clasp at her nape. "Could you, please?"

His shadow loomed over her. Callused fingers brushed her skin, the knob of her vertebrae. His fingers were swift, adept.

"Thanks," she said, felt for the clasp after he finished, tugged the peridot into even position.

He let his fingers graze her neck and shoulder as he trailed away, and she continued her ascent. She could sense him looking at her calves, checking her ass. If he gave chase, she felt ready to race, to get to the roof. Let them catch her there.

SHE CLIMBED ONE more floor, then exited to the elevators, just to complicate her route. She pressed the up button, triggered to run back to the stairway if the elevator arrived occupied. The doors parted. It took her a moment to register the emptiness. She never received emptiness in the bay. Every gurney brought her someone, some immediate decision, some aimed expression, some blood or wrong bend of bone, inappropriate gaze or words or tone, sometimes bone through flesh, bloodless and absurd.

It would have been easier to step inside the elevator if it contained a wound—or corpse. She forced herself to go in and press the button to the seventh floor. In the hall a pair of students, one janitor dragging a trash cart, and a professor passed her. She received second looks from every one of them. The professor called her Jude.

Mendenhall figured her options. She could pull the fire alarm and maybe get out in the confusion. That confusion was hard to predict. Or she could give up in the face of fate, turn herself in to the guy on the first floor or his partner searching the halls and stairs, let herself be caught. But she wanted to trace Covey's line—the crush line—back to Mercy General. Did she feel the crescendo only because it had become a possibility? Wasn't that how crescendos worked? Was this thinking in metaphor? Feeling in metaphor?

And there was the blood on the floor, the struggle outside Covey's door. It was no longer just a matter of giving up, of pride. The fight was blood, apparently, to someone—to the ones who commanded the men in t-shirts and jackets.

SCHRADER'S DOOR WAS partially opened. Protocol. A student sat in his office. She was pretty, appeared to be crying. Mendenhall pushed the door all the way open. Schrader looked up, kept his eyes on her. If he had checked the student, Mendenhall would have apologized. Instead she ignored the student, her tears. She leaned her shoulder against the doorjamb and folded her arms.

"I'm visiting from Molokai. I don't want to eat alone. Can you join me?"

Schrader eyed the dress. "It's you."

"Yes, it's me." She held her pose. "I need cab fare. My card's in limbo. We can dine somewhere nice. You know a place? By the ocean?"

"I have . . ."

"You tell me the place, and I'll go there and wait." She unfolded and refolded her arms, kept the rest of herself still, angled. "For you."

She held forth her palm. The student stared into the crease.

Mendenhall waited for the cash but eyed the student. "Can you tell me a back way out of here? I really need not to be seen. Can you show me, walk with me?"

54

The student walked her to the sidewalk after they exited through a loading ramp. Various types of smokers lined the slanted concrete edges: janitors, professors, grad students, administrative assistants. The smoke collected in the still pitch of the ramp. They all seemed proud of that, that production.

One of her searchers stood on the sidewalk, his feet set wide apart, arms crisscrossed, hands on shoulders. Mendenhall was surprised that the student stayed with her, was happy for it.

She showed her the gem chip on her necklace as they neared the man. "See this? Know what it is?"

"Peridot," she replied without looking at the stone. "My birthstone. August. It's associated with fame, dignity, and protection. When it's that quality," she waved her hand over Mendenhall's necklace, "it most likely comes from an island off the coast of Egypt. Really rare stuff comes from meteorites."

"Oh." Mendenhall almost forgot about the man on the sidewalk, peered at the gem and let the student guide her by the elbow.

A cab, as promised by Schrader, slid to the curb. The man on the sidewalk called to them, "Excuse me, ladies. . . ."

Mendenhall did not listen to his excuse for approaching. She hurried into the cab and told the driver where to go. Only after they had pulled away did she realize the student was riding with her.

"That's the wrong direction."

"What?" Mendenhall had to blink to make sure the young woman was really in the cab with her.

"That place is in the opposite direction. Of the beach. Of where you're meeting Professor Schrader."

"I'm not meeting Schrader. I needed his cash."

The student's stare quivered. She chewed her lower lip, red against white teeth, brimmed with youth. "Good," she said finally.

"Where do you want to get off?"

"I thought I was going to the beach."

"I'm sorry." Mendenhall looked away, then back. "We'll drop you off at the next corner."

"No. I'll go wherever." The student fashioned her short hair into a spiky ponytail. "I just needed to go somewhere."

Mendenhall offered confused concern, an ER trick. The student blew at her bangs before explaining.

"Schrader's kind of a wank. I wish I'd thought of your move. All the way to the beach. Who wouldn't want to go to the beach with you? You always dress like that?"

"Almost never."

"Who are you running from?"

"More than one."

"One what?"

"Side. Apparently." Mendenhall eyed the student's black skirt, white t-shirt, and blue Mary Janes. She used to dress like that in college. "What size are you?"

THE IDEA WAS to make it seem as though she didn't plan to return to Mercy. Her thin disguise might misdirect them, keep them following the cab. More likely it would only lead them to underestimate her.

The Mary Janes were fine in the cab but felt tight as she stepped onto the sidewalk. She liked the way they looked, felt insecure in the t-shirt, tried not to think too much about the skirt. She ran a little, just to shake into the clothes more, into herself. The idea was also to stay outside longer, to be away from the bay an hour more, to see what was out here. To be alone.

On the map Covey had marked a bar with a star, a place for Mendenhall. It was getting close to rush hour. Traffic was the same—thick and slow as always—but the sidewalk was intensifying, the pedestrian flow becoming more one-way, pointed, moneyed, with ties and heels and good haircuts. Happy hours were starting. For Mendenhall and the rest of the ER, happy hour was neither happy nor an hour. It was three hours of discontent producing a full spectrum of wounds, stretching into several more hours of outright misery. You name it, said her mentor once said, and happy hour's done it.

She took a stool at the bar corner. This was the center of the universe, a cup of space in a cluster. She felt sent, stung, a mark. The only other remaining seat was on the other side of the bar corner. A man in a loosened tie moved into it, sliding away from his three buddies. Mendenhall could tell that he had underguessed her age. There was a drop in his look followed by reconsideration.

"I'm waiting for someone," she told him, motioned toward the stool.

"I think you're lying."

"I am lying. I don't want you sitting by me."

"Nasty."

"You wanted the truth."

The bartender brought her wine. It was the color of the blood Claiborne had drawn from her. She imagined it warm and lifted it by the stem, got set to take it away to some quiet corner. A woman emerged from the crowd, jarred her way between Mendenhall and the guy.

"Sorry I'm late."

Mendenhall rescued her glass from the interruption. Jude Covey slid in front of the guy, shouldered her way onto the stool, set her tablet on the bar. He hovered close, eyed both of them. Covey gave him an over-the-shoulder glare, and he returned to his former place. She pointed to Mendenhall's wine and made eyes with the bartender, tucked then licked her lips.

"I hoped you'd be here," Covey said.

"Isn't that why you marked it on the map?"

Covey eagerly received her wine from the bartender. "Yes. I aimed you here."

"I'm not going home."

"You are." Covey looked her over. "Nice. Will I get my dress back?"

"I think so." Mendenhall unclasped her necklace and gave it back to Covey.

She waved it away. "Keep it for a while. It looks good with that. Dresses it."

Mendenhall shook her head. "I can't wear this in ER. Nothing that hangs. Certainly not from the throat."

Covey grimaced and took the necklace.

"The crescendo," said Mendenhall. "What might that be? Like?"

"Sorry I used that term." Covey brushed her tablet to life and positioned it between them on the corner top. "I refined some things. Some things on your line. Using what I did for mine. It's crude because you just gave me two general locations. With some travel and a GPS I could be exact. But I did find some GPS readings for your boiler room and that street corner in Reykjavik."

"You can do that? Who has those?"

"Geocachers. Live gamers. Hashers. You look like you could be a hasher."

"Because of this?" Mendenhall raised her wine.

"And your legs."

Covey took a sip, then a longer draw. She spoke facing the bar mirror. "The entire globe is now measured into one-meter squares. If you know how to look, you can do it from your lap."

"So that's your standard of deviation?" Mendenhall held forth the chart Covey had given her. "One meter? Or one meter on each side of the line?"

"Each side."

"So a hallway."

"Kind of." Covey fingered circles over her tablet. "An undulating hallway. I made some quick refinements for you."

On screen was a 3-D gridded globe. The globe was sliced in half diagonally with a circular plane. "In a perfect universe, that would be our crush line." Covey motioned her fingertip around the disc that sliced the Earth.

"*Our* crush line?"

"Yours. Mine." She prodded the tablet, adjusting the brightness to the bar light. The room was beginning to crowd; patrons sought standing space, shouldered between sitters. "Different latitudes of the Earth rotate at different speeds." She tapped the screen and the slicing disc warped slightly.

"I never knew that."

"You could tell me things, I'm sure."

Mendenhall wanted to tell her about Albert Cabral, how he had been struck while fashioning shadow puppets on the ER wall, had spent his limbo trying to help, had died. She sipped and pursed her wine.

"There's the Earth's magnetic field." Covey made another

tap, and the disc became wavy, a rippled slice around the globe. "Solar wind. Current solar prominences, major and minor. Current alignment of Jovian planets. Of inner planets." Each statement came with another tap, the rippled slice growing wavier.

"Inclination." Tap. "Eccentricity." Covey offered a coy peek. "Those aren't metaphors."

"I know." Mendenhall pointed to the equations for orbital inclination and eccentricity. She considered the equation beneath the inner-planets calculation. She thought she saw a shortcut, motioned to it without touching. "Why can't you just—"

"The planets don't circle the sun on the same flat plane. Only in pictures and first grade classrooms. They revolve on their respective orbital planes, tilting around one another, all elliptical. No circles. Nothing's perfect in all this. Still." Covey looked at Mendenhall. "Not bad for a hasher."

"Why are you here?" asked Mendenhall.

"For the good pinot."

"I mean out. Out here." Mendenhall pointed to the floor, angled her wrist for emphasis. "Here?"

Covey looked over her shoulder into the crowd, beyond the crowd. The doors swung open.

"What are you thinking?" Mendenhall followed her gaze, traced her thoughts. "What do you know?"

One of her followers was silhouetted against the late-afternoon light. He was taller than the rest of the crowd, tilting his way through happy hour, his white t-shirt a wedge between dark lapels. Mendenhall checked his flank, saw another who must've entered a few seconds earlier.

She stood. Covey gave her a pleading look, shook her head.

Mendenhall cut toward the left side of the wide doorway, decided, and drew her line. Who could razor a crowd better than she? Maybe Pao Pao. She saw that it was going to be close, the figure quicker than she had anticipated. She pushed through a pawing couple, severing them. The follower appeared to stretch himself taller, sensing Mendenhall meant business. Then something struck him low, buckled him. He was swallowed by the crowd, dipped, a splash. Mendenhall slid along the tangent, swung out.

Bar-fight calls mixed with music spilled out the doorway with her, creating a strange and better song, jumpy lyrics and melody punctuated by dark cheers, yelps, groans.

The sidewalk was almost as crowded as the bar. The late-afternoon light gave everyone a golden-haired look, varied only in brightness, lined by tall shadows, glints off high windows. She reached for a slice of lime, felt more than once for it before realizing, jostled by the crowd, that it was with her tracksuit, two changes removed.

55

Five pedestrians dropped, knees buckled, torso forward, then over to the right, following their dominant side. They were all right-handed. This was what she registered as they fell. They dropped in a line approaching her, parting the thick crowd, only the last two next to each other. Most of the crowd looked around, sure it was yet another flash mob.

Mendenhall at first ignored the dead and hurried to a woman who stumbled away from the middle of the fall line. People shouted. Phones came out. Some covered their mouths with handkerchiefs, hands, or elbows. Some had masks ready. Up and down the sidewalk the mouth covering turned epidemic. Some tried to run from the fallen; some stood paralyzed with fear or disbelief. This created a pool of confusion, rougher and thicker than the ER bay.

Mendenhall was able to clutch the shirttail of the stumbling woman. Her yank broke one of the woman's heels, and she reeled closer. Here Mendenhall felt the pull of the stricken, and she tried to sidestep to the nearest body. Sirens—all types, near and far— were going off.

The woman tried to slap Mendenhall away.

"Stay with me."

"We need to get away," the woman hissed, then cried.

This split response convinced Mendenhall even further. "You

need to come with me." Mendenhall tugged her toward the body, a man in a business suit with white hair. His sunglasses had stayed put. He lay in a Z pattern, with mantis arms.

She sensed helplessness all around and within, the spin-away, a crush line pulsing over the city. The crowd was gathering to help the woman get free of Mendenhall.

"I'm fine," the woman was sobbing, mascara running, making her look younger, prettier, forlorn in a French film. Surprising Mendenhall with her angle, she pulled free. She bumped into someone, and Mendenhall gained ground and then a hold but felt herself giving up on the man in sunglasses. If Pao Pao were here it would've been easy, routine, doctor going one way, nurse keeling the other.

A swell moving through the crowd, an ambulance's arrival, and an extra shove from those wanting to run knocked the woman free of Mendenhall's grasp. She gave up on the chase, just called once more, "You need to come with me."

Covey appeared first, cupping the woman's shoulders, soothing her with soft words Mendenhall could not hear. The ambulance nosed its way through the crowd. More people clustered by the vehicle as though it offered a shield or cure. The EMTs disembarked wearing masks and gloves and goggles.

Covey gazed at Mendenhall, held the woman softly, waited. As soon as the woman realized that Covey was linked with Mendenhall, she shrieked and squirmed away. A hooded figure, skinny and quick, earbuds loose, seized the woman.

It was Kae. Kae Ng 23. Mendenhall was sure she was imagining him, another former patient slipping in front of her mind's eye. But he was there. He took hold of the woman's wrist. With his free hand he drew a plastic strip from his hoodie pocket. Kevlar cuffs. Cops used them to bring bound patients to the ER. Kae had a bundle of them in there, frayed out and shining in the low sun and ambulance lights. He expertly wrapped and locked the plastic cuff around his wrist and the woman's. Mendenhall pictured escaped convicts, movies again.

She kept moving, in mode. She flashed Covey one look, then headed for the ambulance. Covey understood. She called to the EMT nearest the ambulance doors, the one guarding the open spread and ramp. The EMTs with the gurney were confused, not knowing which body to attend.

"Please," said Covey. She used a soft voice that drew the EMT to her. She bent over and held her forearm. He reached for her.

Mendenhall went into the ambulance, saw the syringe she needed, took it and a swab packet, and hopped out. She hurried to Kae and his captive. Kae watched, enthralled by Mendenhall's grip and twist, the way she paralyzed the thrashing limb. She swabbed the woman's forearm, the one fastened to Kae's, and injected the Trapanal. The woman gently collapsed against Kae, caressed his face with her free hand. "Good boy," she said.

"Don't let her go under." Mendenhall escorted them away from the EMTs. "She shouldn't, but I only guessed the dose. So don't let her."

She palpated his shoulder, saw him wince. She noticed that three of his knuckles were split, lines of dried blood. Covey joined them before Mendenhall could say anything to Kae, ask him anything. What could she ask? Who are you? Why? How in hell?

Mendenhall pointed to Covey. "Can you get a cab in all this?"

"I have a car," replied Covey. "Like normal people."

COVEY TOOK THE driver's seat, Mendenhall shotgun, with Kae and his charge in the back. Seemingly unaware of the Kevlar, the woman held Kae's hand as she stared out the window, eyes glassy, the colors of the emergency lights. Three ambulances had prodded their way into the crowd. Sirens echoed from a couple more beyond the high rises. All glass was orange, almost yellow on the highest buildings, darkening toward red in the vertical drop. Half the pedestrians moved toward the flashing lights; half hurried away, an absurd order forming.

"It's like a giant viewing," said Covey.

"It *is* a giant viewing. People always wonder why they go look." Mendenhall shoved her arm. "Start the car." She shoved again, more to stimulate herself than to prompt Covey. She had slept three hours coming up on a full day. She was ragged, quivering, ready to run, ready to nap.

"It's not kidnapping," she said to no one in particular. "I'm taking her to the ER." She pointed to the K-cuff. "You have something to cut that?"

He raised his arm, the woman's lifting along with it. "You need special snips. A knife won't do."

"You have a knife?"

Kae shook his head, barely, gazed at Mendenhall. She stared back.

"You have a scalpel."

He did not respond.

"Throw it out the window." She nodded toward the bundle of cuffs protruding from his hoodie pocket. "Those, too."

She glared at Covey. "And *start the car*."

Mendenhall reached for the woman's wrist and took her pulse. She listed the three freeways Covey needed to return to Mercy General.

Mendenhall understood Covey's trance. Three of the five bodies were on gurneys now. They were covered. The two others had been rolled and straightened into supine positions. The EMTs appeared lost above them, ears to cell phones. Mendenhall scanned the crowd for possible struck survivors, but it was an impossible task. Too many seemed dazed, arms stiff and undirected, steps going sideways, then back, then forward, expressions of understanding—a state of mind that had to be symptomatic, perhaps delusional. The only ones who looked sane, who looked knowledgeable, were the two bodies on the ground looking grimly toward the sky.

"Between here and the ocean," said Covey, "more have fallen."

56

Exhaustion loomed. Mendenhall had slept three hours over the last thirty. Her life felt wasted, she wanted to nap in the car, she was confident she could get back into Mercy, and she knew none of these feelings made sense. She told Covey she didn't have to drive so fast. She checked the woman—her patient. The Trapanal was working. She was watching the sunset over the thinnest part of the city, where they could almost see the ocean. She was holding hands with Kae.

Kae stared at Mendenhall, let the motion of the car lull his body. The lock of hair had returned, covering one eye, the tip grazing his cheekbone. He calculated something, something about her, how many of her features were worthwhile, how many moles he could find, how anything about her came together, eyes to skin, hair to lips.

Mendenhall nodded to the cuff holding Kae to the patient.

"Where did you get those?"

"Not on your floor." He appeared at ease, shoulders folded to the corner of the seat and window, his cuffed arm turned up and relaxed as his hand received the patient's grasp. Mendenhall imagined him gliding through the cafeteria, the kitchen, looking for anything to gain advantage. He would have moved behind the big security guys, no more than shadow and sliver. He had even thought to snitch a visitor sticker. The handwritten name read, "Karlo Singh."

"And drugs?" she asked.

He fished around in his hoodie pockets, showed her a handful of very slim syringes, all capped and loaded. She fingered them, then lifted them from his palm. "Tell me you didn't inject those . . . guys."

He gave a sideways look.

She held up a blue one. "This would've been better if you'd injected yourself. Stronger, more energy, better decision-making, better fight."

"I saw that," he replied. "After the second guy."

"Where is he?"

"Down a storm drain on one of those quiet streets you ran. I liked that neighborhood."

"He's cuffed? Under the lid of a storm drain? With high-dose adrenaline?"

Kae remained still.

Covey adjusted the rearview, angled it more toward him, glanced at Mendenhall. Mendenhall double-checked the freeway and direction. She trusted no one in this car, longed for the open betrayal of the bay.

She held up an orange syringe. "This?"

"That was the last one. He went horizontal. Fast. Back on that bar floor." Kae made a sliding motion with his free hand.

Mendenhall recalled the height of the guy, estimated his weight from the breadth of his shoulders. "A full dose?"

"Half," said Kae. "I put the rest in his wingman."

"Why?"

"Because no way I could take them like that. The crowd would push us together. I need lots of space to take them, move around, like. I'm a boxer, not a fighter."

"No. I mean why are you following me?"

"Because I plan to stay alive. If I go where you go, I have a chance."

"But you see that's not true." Covey spoke quickly, releasing. She glanced in the rearview. "Those people back there? Five?"

"It's more than that," he said. "Bigger than that. I saw more men heading to another part of the city."

Mendenhall closed her eyes, yearned for the ER.

Covey angled another peek into the mirror.

"I hate laying around. She," he nodded toward Mendenhall, "hates waiting around. Waiting around to die. Where she goes, I go. At least we're doing something. Stay close to death, and you live."

"Yeah? And how does that work?" Mendenhall stared at the syringes in her hand.

"It's something I do with my older brother. The one who doesn't do anything wrong follows the one who does, knocks stuff around."

"Stuff."

"People and stuff." Kae smiled at the hand holding his, strapped to his. "My escape trail messes up yours."

"How many did you leave out there? In your—our—trail?"

With tiny eye shifts, he counted. But didn't answer.

Mendenhall recounted. One during escape. One in Covey's lab basement—"the second guy." Two in the bar.

"Four," she said.

He counted with his eyes again, barely breathing. Then: "Six. Yeah. No. Seven."

"They had cells."

"I took those."

"They need ambulances."

"Maybe the one."

She held up an orange syringe. "What other colors? What other colors did you stick in them?"

"Some purple ones."

"They need ambulances."

ovey leaned into the drive, kneaded the wheel. Mercy General was visible from the freeway, windows aglow against approaching dusk. "It looks like a night factory," she said. "How do we get in?"

"We?" Mendenhall checked Kae, Patient X, Covey.

"I still have things to show you." Covey shifted as Mendenhall remained silent. "I didn't tell them where you were going. I didn't. . . . Maybe they followed."

"You showed, they showed." Mendenhall looked back to Kae. "How would *you* add that up?"

"One plus one equals blue." He was looking at the hospital.

"How high are you?"

Kae flattened his free hand, measured it to his chin, up to his nose.

"The stuff I gave you?"

He nodded, then tilted his head side to side.

Covey was watching in the rearview. "What does that mean?"

"Plus two, give or take," said Mendenhall. She sighed, trying to breathe away exhaustion and frustration. She was in a car with two high patients and one free radical. She was taking them into a world that would be twice as mad as when she left it.

"My line," she said to Covey. "My crush line. Is your crush line."

"It's not that simple."

"Don't give me that. I'm a physician. I say that all the time."

"Okay. Yes."

"What happens now? What is happening?"

"Nothing that hasn't happened before. This city—the world—has changed toward it, grown. You know?"

Mendenhall made a fist.

Covey shrugged over the wheel, changed lanes to approach the exit. "I'm not being evasive. I'm not sparing you my expertise. The molecules are too small to have impact. They wouldn't really function in the larger world. They wouldn't be involved. Or we certainly didn't think so. There were times I imagined them passing through me. As I bent over the collecting dishes."

"What about those collecting dishes? The ones in your basement? Those splash-looking things you showed."

"They look like splashes, but they're not. Just like constellations look like they're grouped together, but they're not. Galaxies are not pinwheels; they're more like whirlpools, drains. The universe is not dark and limitless. It's full of light and finite and intricately shaped. We design the surfaces of those dishes to indicate the slightest disturbance, the tiniest spark."

"Fine, but what about the people? Bodies?"

"I didn't know about that until you came." Covey paused. " I work in the crush line all the time, believing they pass through me, wanting that. These must be different. There's a strange amount of sameness in the universe. The periodic table, you know. Everything that's been gathered fits within the table."

"I thought you said velocity was the only factor," Mendenhall said.

"A particle and its velocity can't be divided. The velocity is the particle. And vice versa." Covey eased onto the exit. "It really isn't simple. This time. The line is intricate, in flux, more weave than mere stitch. Calling them particles isn't accurate. For you, maybe, think synapse."

Mendenhall felt drained, hopeless. It would always show virus. Calling it, predicting it would just make her look the good doctor. Her guessing the occlusions for Claiborne. The same population densities that proved her case also proved Thorpe's. She was right; Thorpe was wrong. But people were still dead; more people were still going to die.

"So." Covey eased the car along the base of the hill, choosing an entry, "back or front?"

Mendenhall pressed her lips together, put the corner of her fist there. She envied Covey's—what?—coldness, compression, precision. Her perception, the scatter and gather of it, the way she looked certain while on the run, on the loose. The peridot in the *V* of her blouse rested in the top dimple between her breasts, neat against pale skin, pure.

"South parking," replied Mendenhall. "Kill the lights and slide the car into the back corner. By the scrub."

"What do you have? A rabbit hole?"

"Something like that," said Kae, before Mendenhall could. "But don't drive on the roads. Use the running trail. We come up that canyon."

WHEN THEY REACHED the trailhead at the canyon bottom, Mendenhall became disoriented. The near hill obscured Mercy. She saw two sunsets—one to the west, where the canyon opened into housing tracts; one to the east, where it folded into hills. The one in the east had more glow and color. It spread along the horizon, lifted into thicker clouds. She almost told the others to go on without her, to go wherever they wanted to go. Covey got out of the car first. She stood and arched her back as she watched the eastern sky behind the near hills. Her skirt lifted and made her look very young. She let her bare waist and stomach show, cool. Kae climbed out next, tugging the woman along with him.

"Snow," said the woman. She held her palm up.

Mendenhall watched from the passenger side, thought about shooting up some Trapanal and waiting for DC to come get her, claim her. If she got herself back in, they might not claim her. They would at least have to think about it. If they got her outside, she was theirs.

She saw the snow. It caught in the woman's brown hair, dusted her palm, clung, stuck, smeared into powder where she rubbed it. The horizon reddened; the overhead sky grew dark except where clouds caught edges of light. Distant sirens made whale sounds over the city. They could have been in Reykjavik.

"Ashes, ashes, we all fall down," someone sang as they climbed the trail.

58

Returning was a matter of physical effort, pulling. Mendenhall led. In the vent she used her penlight sparingly, blindness giving them all a single goal. In the bomb shelter she found a note from Ben-Curtis: *This place is nuts.*

"Does he mean *this*?" asked Covey when given the paper. She motioned to the shelter. "Or the whole hospital?"

"You chose to come." Mendenhall took back the note. Had he left? Was this warning or resignation?

She noticed something about Kae. He was still holding hands with the woman. The K-cuff was gone.

He winked, raised hands with Patient X. "You need me. To get her up there."

At the base of the dumbwaiter shaft, he cleared the broken vent and crumpled cubicle, then fashioned himself as a human climbing base, planting his hands against the shaft wall, flexing his knees and spreading his legs.

"Climb," he told them. He appeared fragile, a boy.

"Don't step on his left shoulder," said Mendenhall.

The three women left him alone down there after hoisting themselves into the subbasement.

"Go home," Mendenhall whispered into the shaft. No sound returned. She waited, and nothing rose, not one breath or shuffle.

She wished she had thought of something to say that wasn't a placebo, something with no prescription to it.

They set up Mendenhall's patient in the room Silva had used for napping. Covey made a good nurse. She found an old stand and helped run the IV. Mendenhall fetched a broken EMT cart from subbasement storage, from near the cold cases that held expired saline and glucose kits. The cart still had air function. She recognized the thing from the ER, a heavy roller Pao Pao had named the Beast. Mullich must have decommissioned it. Covey held the patient's hand, folded fingers together, spoke in a plain voice: "What's your name?"

"Julia."

When Covey started to press for more, Mendenhall put a hand to her shoulder. Then she started her chart. Julia Doe, thirty-five.

"What are you—we—doing?" Covey held Julia's hand, curl to curl, thumb stroking her knuckles.

Mendenhall continued making chart entries. It felt good to be working. "Treating her for shock. Oxygen and glucose. We won't really know how she's doing until the Trapanal wears off some. It wasn't the best thing to hit her with."

"That and the cuffs." Covey stroked Julia's wrist.

"Let's forget about those." Mendenhall waited for Covey to look at her. "Okay?"

Covey considered the green exit sign, its glow exaggerating her pale complexion. The only other lights were those of the Beast, tiny yellows, reds, and blues. "What's a virus?" she asked.

"Not this."

"Why not this? That colleague I have who defines these particles—my particles—as a-life. He argues that they have destiny, that they're acting out synapses, that they have molecular structures adapted to carry out both. That they infect solar systems."

"That's just metaphor. Weak, easy metaphor. Following even reasonably accurate metaphors is a fallacy."

With her fingertips, Covey brushed Julia Doe's hairline, fitted a wisp behind her ear. Julia gazed back at her, eyes glistening above the oxygen mask.

"We give her air, fluids, glucose. We allow her organs to function as best they can. If the shock has already cut off oxygen to the vital organs, then we're giving her the best chance possible. Sleep will shift blood flow in the hippocampus. The limbic system will operate on a structure of reality, shifting from a structure of defense and delay."

"How do you know she has it?"

Mendenhall gave Covey a hard stare.

Covey corrected herself. "How do you know she's been . . . struck?"

"In a little, we get someone here who can verify. With me."

She decided to face Claiborne alone. Covey stayed with the patient. Covey's sympathy for Julia Doe remained suspicious. She had to be fascinated by the path, the trajectory and velocity of the Jude particles and all the effects of being stricken by one. The involvement of cells, of specialized cells. And Mendenhall couldn't know whether Covey was risking her health because she believed what Mendenhall had shown her or because she was simply fascinated. If she had betrayed Mendenhall and brought the guards to her, had she acted in goodwill, belief in the virus, or only that same scientific fascination? Mendenhall couldn't read Covey—not the way she could read incoming patients. She was looking into a mirror, trying to see herself, staring and waiting for objectivity, that objectivity staring back.

But now she was moving from this to Claiborne. She was guessing he knew.

HE DIDN'T KNOW. When she entered his lab, he nodded a greeting. His tie was loose, his lab coat off, his sleeves rolled above his elbows.

"Thanks for the last text. I haven't had the chance to reply." He wiped his eye with his shoulder, his hands remaining above the keyboard. The overhead screens showed six scans: three occlusions and three incipient kidney hemorrhages. The laptop showed an MRI of a hippocampus. "Good to see you've changed clothes. At least."

She looked down at herself, dusted the hem of her skirt. "A little dirty. But different." Her feet appeared not hers, the Mary Janes surprising.

"Thorpe forwarded the new cases to us."

"'Us'?"

"Five not far from County. All outside the same office building. The building's under quarantine. Three from inside the Marriot by the park, packed with conventions. Also quarantined."

"The five?" she asked. "Were from the building?"

He nodded. "All five collapsed within the same hour. Close together."

"No." Mendenhall felt for the necklace that was no longer there. "All together. They all fell together. They weren't necessarily from the same building. They were just walking. In the crowd."

Claiborne was distracted by something on the laptop. He double-tapped a key. "You got the same message. Unless there's a new one." He motioned to the overhead screens. She didn't know what she was supposed to see.

Fatigue had her nauseated. She steadied herself, fingertips to desktop.

"You don't look like you just took a nap. You look like you need one."

She pushed her hair back, felt how dirty it was.

He nodded to a far door. "You're welcome to the shower in the chem lab. It's pretty good, but you have to keep the chain pulled down. It'll wake you, at least."

Claiborne returned to his task, not shutting her out but, rather, comfortable in her presence. She thought about keeping it like this, living under whatever Silva had constructed between them, operating under Thorpe's construction as well, forgetting what she had seen, what Covey seemed to know. But she knew she had eliminated all those possibilities when she had touched Julia Doe, taken her, injected her. In those few minutes she had committed herself to a split world of truth and lie.

"You're not as happy as you appear," she said.

Claiborne went still, fingers hovering above the keyboard. After a moment he turned his head to face her, looked at her shoes.

"I mean," she curled one foot, "you're still trying to convince yourself."

"I'm trying to get back to my wife. As soon as possible. I thought you were down with this."

"You should go to her. Right now."

He scowled, did not look away, let his expression soften a bit, brow still furrowed, chin lowered to a more thoughtful angle. "You're different."

"It's not contagious, Claiborne. For now, anyone could fall. For those two reasons, you should go. You probably could find your own way out, you down here in your domain." She began a step toward him, one foot, one Mary Jane, then held it. "There are probably a lot of others like Cabral out there. Right now."

"What kind of nap did you take?"

She opened her hands, held them near her hips. "I brought one to you."

"One what?"

"Just go." She closed her eyes and pictured him on the trail, that way he passed her, shoulders angry, waist thin and balanced. "I can do the scans. From here, I can do everything."

59.

Claiborne tapped his keyboard twice, vaguely looked at the overheads.

"You've changed. Why?"

"I went out."

Claiborne closed his eyes, clenched his jaw.

"I needed to see a specialist. Then I followed the sirens." One truth, one lie. "At the site. Where the five fell. I saw others who looked struck. Like Cabral."

"You *brought* one?"

"Her name is Julia. I have her down here. Oxygen and fluids. Stabilizing. Awake. Alive. I believe she'll make it."

He blinked, tightened his lips, chewed thoughts.

"Look, Claiborne. *You* need to wake up. Thorpe's sending you crap. You know that. He's giving you the lab work but not the context. He doesn't need to give any of us the context. Because the context was predetermined a long time ago. Everyone's blind to anything outside it, especially him. Anything outside virus. But not you. You saw. You drew it. You know. It's trauma. It's ballistic. Those five fell at once. I saw. They came right to me."

"You're insane."

"The woman I went to traces the path. She sent me to a bar right near where the others were struck. She predicted it. Government people followed me there. They know there's something to my diagnosis."

"She sent you? How?"

"She has mapped it all. That's one thing she does. She sent me to the thickest part."

"Thickest part of what?"

"This." She jerked her arms outward, opened her hands. "This city."

Claiborne's eyes lulled.

"You're searching for a virus," she said. "You see its work and its aftermath. You can't find it. You operate under the premise that it exists, that it reproduces, that it spreads vertically, fast, synchronized, then hides. You consider nothing else." She moved in close and pointed at his brow. "Nothing else. *That's* insane."

She looked at her pointed fist, pulled it back. Claiborne eyed her fingers, her lips. She tried to hide any tremor but felt a bundle of pathologies. He seemed unconvinced.

"I went out and found something," she said, close to a whisper. "Something that threatens Thorpe and the wider stratagem."

"So what's he do with you?"

"They will isolate me, Claiborne. They will silence me."

"I'm not so sure that would be a bad thing. For you or them."

She took a tight breath. She wanted to join him fully to her sense of danger, threat.

"Tell me. Where's Pao Pao?" Her lips were thick and dry. *Quarantine.* She had to think it before she could let herself hear it.

"Quarantine."

If she let herself imagine this, she would break. She thought of pacing him on the trail, pushing a challenge. "And Silva, too, right? Although my guess is she was too quick and less trusting. My guess she's moving around, mostly down here but cut off from you."

"She's left a note or two."

"And Mullich," she said. "Mullich you can't figure."

"Sometimes," replied Claiborne. "Sometimes he's here." He motioned to the room. "Sometimes he disappears. Sometimes—" Claiborne lowered a shoulder. "He got you out. Didn't he?"

"He showed me a way. I got myself out." She pointed back to the lab door. "Julia. I had to bring her in. None of the EMTs were going to take her. Were even going to consider her. She's here. With maybe a chance. That's what I have to give her. So go. You should just go."

"I can't go."

She grabbed a nearby glove box and threw it across the lab. She searched for something heavier. "You Path people. Down here in your holy basement. Why are you the only one down here? The others ran. Whoever was on shift down here with you. Tehmul ran on me when he got the chance. Who ran on you? Gonzales? Stuart? Both? Thorpe left a long time ago. Dmir came in. Disease Control came in."

"And it spread. Out there. And it went where you were."

Mendenhall shook her head, bit her lip. "It struck. In a line predicted by a specialist. A specialist like us. It traveled vertically in a packed hotel, like this place. It presented itself in the thickest crowds. Like outside that bar."

"That shows virus."

"They all fell in the same second."

"Then they were all exposed in the same second, and the virus has a precise incubation."

"Despite different metabolisms, different immune systems, different diets, different life paths?"

"Virus works."

"It will always work. We say, 'Go viral. It went viral.' What the hell does that mean? It's just how we see things. It's lazy and inaccurate. It's handy. Common. And powerful."

"You honestly think Thorpe and DC are disregarding evidence?"

"Even manipulating it. Forced observation. It's willful misinformation designed to gain power and control. *The* stratagem."

"And yours? You breach containment. Go into the public sphere. Bring someone in?"

"If you thought I was wrong, we wouldn't be standing here."

"I'm barely standing here."

"So go," she told him again. "Use whatever passageway you have down here. Go be with your wife. Take her to the park. Raise a glass to me." The light was gray; air vents purred. "Raise a glass to me."

THE ER PROVED a mistake. Claiborne had tried to warn her, offered to go gather the supplies for Julia. "They pretty much stay out of the basement. But they know you slipped containment and will come looking for you," he had told Mendenhall. Her patients had been moved to a far wall. Her cubicle was occupied by Dmir. He was sipping from a mug and tapping her keyboard. His furrowed brow tried to convey concern but showed confusion. A curtained partition now cut the bay in two, cutting off flow and sight lines. Extra beds had been moved in, lights added, pale music. Security stood in pairs.

And Pao Pao was gone.

In a few seconds her vantage point would be compromised. She slid to the next corner. Nurses doing nothing at the station recognized her. One pointed, and a security pair turned. Mendenhall charted her path. Behind her an elevator chimed. She didn't know if it was too late to simply retreat, to return to the basements and survive containment there, work there, cooperate. Claiborne could only guess. He had warned her, but she had needed to see. She had thought she didn't.

It was Pao Pao, the notion of her taken from the floor. Mendenhall tried to resist the possibility that she was the cause, that she had betrayed her floor, that she had betrayed Claiborne, was still betraying him by not telling him everything, especially about Silva.

Getting fresh IVs for Julia was definitely not an option. She moved with the open whisper of the elevator, lost her trackers, evaded the nurses. Had they stepped away from their station, two simple strides, they would have seen her. She made it to the old file room. Some EMTs and nurses were in there, sitting on the floor, leaning their shoulders against the wall. The inside fluorescents were off, and the outside parking lamps cast a solemn glow and long shadows. One nurse was smoking; others were sipping coffee. None of them showed any interest in Mendenhall.

A bedpan in the middle of the floor was filled with ashes. Another beside it contained three cigarette butts that had been straightened and reshaped. The smoking nurse passed her cigarette to the EMT on her right.

Mendenhall positioned herself against the wall.

"The ante is two butts or one whole." The EMT spoke holding his inhale.

"I just want to sit here."

"You," said one of the nurses. "You started this."

"You're mistaken."

The EMT released his smoke. The next in line, a feline nurse, her long legs crossed, her feet bare, pinched what was left, inhaled, cheeks hollowed. "No. It's you," she said in slow exhalation, the smoke powdering her words.

Mendenhall curled beneath the cloud. "I just need to sit for a while."

"You mean hide." The long nurse passed the cigarette, a white speck in the shadows. She followed with a languorous stretch, toes pointed, then spread.

"I'm not hiding."

"You should be. Your nurse should've."

Footsteps sounded outside the door, stopped. Mendenhall hunched more against the wall, dipped in the shadows of the others. The door opened, and there was the tall silhouette of Mullich. He took a half step in and spotted her. She knelt forward, didn't know what to do with herself.

"Hey," she whispered. "Hi."

He retreated, motioned to someone in the hall, and made room for two security pairs. One pair remained in the doorway while the others swept in and reached for Mendenhall. They didn't let her stand. Their grip cut the blood flow in her arms. A sharp line of pain slashed diagonally through her left shoulder, just over the heart. She sought dignity, legs together, chin up, thinking of countless ER arrivals sprawling and crying and clawing their arms and legs, shirts or dresses riding up, vulnerable, surrendered, prey for the nurses and EMTs. She braced her arms and double-fisted her hands together, ready to take a swing if freed. She took aim at Mullich's jaw, the angular shadow.

60

She had always pictured it as beds lined neatly behind glass. Mercy's formal quarantine consisted of three adjacent rooms, four beds each, sliding glass doors. She was not there. She was in what used to be a laundry room. The machines were gone, but the concrete platform that had once held them was still there, pipes standing and capped. For her, there was a bed, table with pitcher, and bench. A flatscreen hung in a ceiling corner. The muted channel showed brush fires, then switched to a man in a DC lab coat talking about the outbreak. A helicopter shot of Mercy General filled the screen. It looked festive in the evening light, fires glowing behind the hills.

She was alone, and she felt empty. The fluorescent lighting made a sickening buzz, a pallor rather than a glow, something less than white. She was more angry with herself than with Mullich, not so much for trusting him but just for moving toward him, greeting him, showing herself as a fool.

Through the small door window she could see the adjacent room, another level of quarantine. Pao Pao was in there, tending to those who were still in their beds. Two patients played chess at a folding table. Pao Pao stopped by their game and adjusted one of the table legs, wedged a tongue depressor underneath for stability. The players smiled thanks as she moved to the next bed.

Mendenhall pressed her face to the glass, palms to the door. Pao Pao was helping a patient flex his ankles and legs. She kept him covered as she fitted the heel of her hand into his arch and then pushed. She asked a question, then repeated the exercise.

Mendenhall backed away. She toyed with the copper standpipes as she watched the flatscreen. A newscaster was talking in front of footage showing covered bodies on gurneys being rolled into a building. Mendenhall didn't recognize the area of the city. The story changed to live shots of the brush fire. TV depressed and alienated her. She couldn't translate it, couldn't focus on it because it never explored or even touched what was fascinating. It slid by her, a dream of frustration.

She needed sleep, hours of it, a half day of it. The hospital was approaching the twenty-four-hour mark of containment. She resisted the bed. She didn't want to lie there and feel sick about what she had done to Claiborne, Pao Pao, Silva, what she had allowed Mullich to do to her.

The entire space reminded her of him. She could imagine a few possibilities: an interrogation room, a spa for surgeons and DC people, a gym—a room for crazies. A wave of fatigue passed through her. She poured herself a glass of water and sat on the bench, back straight, shoulders square, a muscle refresher taught by her mentor. Spend a little energy, gain a little more.

She faced straight ahead as she sipped her water. Someone had drawn an arrow on the wall. In pencil, it pointed to a back corner. When she stood to follow its direction, she noticed that the arrow disappeared. It reappeared when she sat back down and straightened herself on the bench. She tested this effect three times, making the arrow disappear with any angle outside 90 degrees.

Mullich.

She stepped through the row of standpipes and turned to the back corner. The walls were whitewashed, bare. She pressed her left shoulder to one and looked 90 degrees forward. Nothing. She touched her right shoulder to the adjacent wall and faced 90 degrees. A thin pencil outline of a square, much the same as the one that had marked the dumbwaiter. With her thumb she brushed the line. Something as if from a moth wing dusted her fingers. It vanished with slight movement, reappeared.

She wasn't sure she wanted to follow this, wasn't sure she was up for it, wasn't sure her legs and brain could make it. She could sleep away containment, quarantine, wake up to the normal chaos of the ER. In the far corner the TV showed fire, then the guy in the lab coat, then the newscaster.

The pencil outline was square, ruled. But it was drawn, not cut like the previous one. She looked behind her, directly facing the opposite wall. Stepping over pipes, she kept her eyes level on the wall as she paced toward the other back corner. Nearer, she watched for an appearance, a shimmering line or arrow, a red dot of light, her tired eyes aching for it.

Her drop began slowly, knees buckling, head faint. The wall eluded her reach. The corner pitched to one side. The floor hinged with a creak and a clang, throwing her into darkness. She slammed inside hollow metal, slick against her clothes, impact acid on her tongue, a blood taste.

And she was falling.

The metal gave whenever she struck and ricocheted, so there was little pain besides friction burns. She covered her head with her arms. The upward blast pushed at her. She almost passed out from the acceleration. The darkness was complete. She was collapsing, going terminal, nerves flaring. She sought to cover herself, to hold the hem of her skirt with one arm while wrapping the other about her head.

She screamed as though underwater, the sound thickened into bubbles. The air gained substance, slowed her, grabbed her. Clothed her. Linen covered and blinded her with white. She came to a stop, then bounced softly, pushed to the surface, sank back. Her pulse was racing. Everything else felt all the more still: the nest of linens and laundry bin that held her, a clean room, the distilled air of the basement.

She was now more angry at Mullich. She stared into the black square, a laundry chute suspended from a white ceiling in a small room. In the distance, from beyond the door, she could hear faint notes from some of Claiborne's music. She remained still, letting the cloth suspend her, letting her pulse normalize. She counted three full and even breaths.

The black square directly above her was silent.

Then, "Anna."

The *A* echoed foreign, almost an *H* in front, soft, deep, down the chute, falling over her.

Mendenhall raised her head.

"Stay still," said another voice, a young woman. Silva. "That's it. Hold still for a while. Sounds come out of it once in a while. The building expanding and contracting. They sound human. Always in two syllables. Mullich says, anyway."

Mendenhall worked herself into a standing position. Silva had removed her lab coat and changed into a dress, blue with vaguely Thai piping. She wore black ballet flats. Her ponytail was set higher than usual. The disguise worked, giving the impression of Eastern, far from Brazilian.

Still buried up to her shoulders in linens, Mendenhall tried adjusting her own failed disguise, tugged the skirt, twisted the blouse, curled her toes to make sure the Mary Janes hadn't flown off during her plunge. Her clothes embarrassed her. She wanted to remain in the bin.

"I stuffed as much as I could up the chute," Silva told her. "Mullich said not to bother. But he's never done it. It's all blueprint to him."

"I liked him better as an enemy."

Silva offered Mendenhall her cell.

"Get rid of it," said Mendenhall. "They'll just track us with it."

Silva maintained distance. Her feet were together, prim.

"How long have you been in here?" Mendenhall worked her way to the edge of the bin.

"About two hours."

Mendenhall looked to the chute. "From there?"

"Yes."

"From Four?"

Silva shook her head. "They never found me. I dropped from Seven."

"Seven." Mendenhall shivered. A double moan came from the chute, a kind of chant.

"He put stuff in it. For me. It slants a bit. Good design, he says."

"Mullich showed it to you?"

"The journalist," replied Silva. "Mullich showed him; he showed me. When I was trapped on Seven. Promised a soft landing. It wasn't that soft. I tried to make it better for you."

"The journalist. He's still here?"

"He found me because he knew you were outside. Knew somebody was pretending to be you. Here. He's really good. But high."

Mendenhall pried herself over the side of the bin, stuck her landing as best she could, tried to look awake and ready. She could have returned to the linens and in their coolness slept for hours.

Silva took a step back. "I'm thinking of turning myself in."

"We have more to do."

"There's nothing left to do."

"We can help Dr. Claiborne."

"If I go to his lab, it's a threat to him."

Mendenhall pulled on her shoulder, tested the joint. "You're a kind person."

"Why do you say that?"

Another chant fell from the chute, almost her name. It seemed to cut across her, shift her, a stick in water. She craved an apple, a slice of ginger, that pinot she had left back at the bar, her work in the ER, arrivals, and sleep, a hard full slam, darkness, blackout.

"How would you have treated Cabral?" Mendenhall closed her eyes and rolled her shoulder some more. "If you had known? How would you have treated him? Before he slept and died."

"Full rest, oxygen, glucose."

"Would you have left him alone? Bedside?"

"No," Silva answered. "That would be the worst. I would think."

"But I mean would *you* have left? Even if someone else remained?"

"No."

"Then don't turn yourself in. Stay down here." Mendenhall tested their distance, took a half step. "Help me with someone. I brought her in. Julia. Her name is Julia."

Silva neatened her stance. Mendenhall imagined her fall, a diver, feet first, arms folded, given over, slicing the dark.

"I'll show you what I found."

61

The basements weren't as open as Mendenhall had hoped. From beneath the door she and Silva could tell a security pair was patrolling the hall.

"I could go out." Silva tightened her hair band, adjusted her flats. "They get me. You get to Julia."

"There might be more." Mendenhall put a hand to the tech's shoulder. "I have a better idea. You play doctor. I play dead."

MENDENHALL LAY ON a gurney, arms straight. Silva covered her with a sheet, hung a toe tag on her right foot.

"This won't fool anyone."

Mendenhall relaxed in the whiteness. She would have to fend off sleep. "They're very scared of death," she replied. "We don't have to fool them. I scared one away by just stepping out of the shadows. Up there they are brave. But very skittish in the basements. When they see you, know this."

"If this doesn't work, then we both get caught. What happens to your patient?"

"Dr. Claiborne will be with her."

"The sheet moves when you breathe."

"Listen. They—the DC security—seem to think the virus is

down here. That it began down here or is being shoved down here. Put on your mask and gloves. Go straight to that room. Hold your breath if you have to, and I'll hold mine. One minute. That's all it takes."

In the hall, she lost confidence. She was blind, the white now smothering. She quickly lost breath and had to gasp, sucking in the sheet. She sensed Silva breaking stride, losing the straightness of the gurney. The wheels skidded sideways. Dead gurneys were different, meant for delivery, not speed, cold and heavy. Mendenhall's back ached. She needed a pillow.

She heard a pair of footsteps, boots. The gurney swayed to the side. Silva took a quick breath.

The steps changed pace, and a low voice asked questions, the answers silent—a cell. Mendenhall felt cold, helpless beneath the sheet. Foolish.

"Ask them for help," she whispered. "Ask them for escort. To open the door for you."

She slipped her fingers beneath her waistband.

"Please." Silva's voice sounded all wrong as she called to them, almost begging.

The boot steps quickened. Mendenhall's lungs tightened. She locked her knees, tried to count, to remember with her fingertips which colors were where. She could hear the men moving fast, the familiar squeak of heels on linoleum, a sound that triggered the best in her. The pair surrounded the gurney. Silva gasped. Mendenhall let them yank the sheet, let them fill their hands.

She gripped a syringe in each hand, thumb on plunger. She had never injected anyone without knowing what, without knowing how much, without getting to assess them at least in a glance. When the sheet whipped off her, she stabbed both men in the femoral triangle, her one clear decision.

They opened their mouths with the pain, made no sound. They both reached for Silva instead of her, an odd gesture that gave Mendenhall confidence. She maintained needle pressure, eyed the colors. The bigger man was getting Demerol. But the plunger there was kicking back against the grip of thumb. She was in the artery. She gave an extra thrust to counteract the blood flow, to get the dose in and through before the gush. He staggered back, snapping the needle, leaving the empty syringe in her hand. Blood spurted in pulses from the needle. Silva dodged the spray and it speckled the wall.

The smaller guard was getting a dose of adrenaline in his femoral vein. He froze. His arms and legs went rigid, his eyes wide. The fate of his partner terrified him. She hoped he had a strong heart. The bigger guy went down and out. Silva tended to him. She removed the broken needle and applied pressure with two fingers. She pressed with enough force to roll the man flat. His arms flopped.

"Any tear?" asked Mendenhall. They were staring at the rigid guard, waiting for him to fire loose.

Silva shook her head.

Mendenhall removed the needle from her guy. She scrambled off the gurney, stood by him, touching his shoulder. She assessed Silva and her guy.

"Main?"

Silva's hair was falling loose from her ponytail. "No," she replied. "Inferior epigastric."

"Good."

"Good?"

"We can stash them. Really push. Tuck the vessel. Count to forty."

With her fingers pressed to the point of the man's pelvis, Silva looked at Mendenhall. Then her eyes questioned the guard who was still standing. His jaw was clenched, and he was breathing quickly through his teeth.

"Don't worry," said Mendenhall. "I have something for him."

THEY PUT THE men in the elevator and sent them up to the ER. They would both be out for at least four hours.

"You're clear of all this," she told Silva.

The tech said nothing, hung her head, gazed at the base of the elevator doors. On the worst nights in the bay, when every drunk falls, every addict ODs, every bar breaks into a fight, the moon is full, great new stuff hits the streets, no questions asked, everybody knows everything, nobody's saying nothing, Mendenhall would take hold of Pao Pao's forearm. The nurse would pause and lift an eyebrow.

Without a word Mendenhall would release and turn and face the next arrival, the next scream, the next sour breath, the next open wound. She touched the cool bend of Silva's hair.

She led her to Julia's room.

"I need you. You're the one to do this. They got me. They get to have me."

62.

Claiborne was with Covey in the makeshift room. They stood on either side of Julia. Claiborne was running a new IV, something fresh he must have brought from his lab. Mendenhall had never seen him—or any pathologist—do this, tend to a live patient. She wanted to start all over, to be as he was, run as he ran. To be what you had to be, do what had to be done. Even in the ER, her world, where she was most confident, she still always felt she was winging it, fighting herself, off center, leading with the wrong fist.

He had also brought a soft light to add to the green exit sign's glow, a quaint-looking lantern set on the nightstand. With her thumb Covey was applying pressure to Julia's forearm vein.

"I drew some more blood." Claiborne kept his eyes on his work as he spoke. He seemed reluctant to look at Silva. "I took arterial blood first. Hypoxemia was pretty clear, anyway. I tried testing parasympathetic—"

Mendenhall cut him off. "Parasympathetic, enteric, and sympathetic will cross-indicate. Forget those." She moved to the foot of the bed to get a long view of the patient. Julia's eyes did not track her, appeared to see her once, then lose her. Mendenhall held her hand out and up, trying to catch her vision. She snapped her fingers. Covey, Claiborne, and Silva looked; Julia did not. "One pupil might be dilated, the other constricted. All three ANSs are vying at once."

Claiborne and Covey watched Mendenhall. She turned to Silva.

With her hand she made slicing motions above Julia's body. "Measure reflex, bottom up." She uncovered Julia's feet and grazed a fingertip along her instep. "Starting here. My guess is she's struck through the upper thigh, somewhere with large muscle mass/lower vessel ratio. It doesn't really matter, though. I think let her fall asleep now. Maintain oxygen, fluids, and glucose. Have Silva hold her hand. Make sure Silva is holding her hand and looking into her eyes as she goes under. Say her name. Say her name. I think she likes singing. Don't let go of her hand as she dreams. If she makes it, others will, too."

She turned and headed for the door. She never heard him coming, he was so silent and quick. Claiborne took hold of her elbow, crowded her into the door, his length pressed to her. He whispered into her ear.

"*You* need to sleep."

"I need to get off this floor, get them away from here. I'll be fine. I'll sleep in Q after they nab me."

"You know what I mean." His lips were touching her ear. She wanted to breathe in his scent, the clean cut of his shirt. "You need to *let* yourself go under." He touched the side of her shoulder, indicating where Julia lay. "Like that. With us around. I brought plenty of IVs. I got the time."

She lifted her eyes to his.

"You were struck with her," he whispered. "But you were more down on sleep. Way down. You're worse off than she is. You know this. Let yourself know this."

"I know this." She rested her forehead against his chest.

"You ER people are all the same. I hate you."

"Left shoulder." She spoke softly against his collar. "No lung, no vessel." She ran her hand up his biceps, over his shoulder, pressed her thumb to the point of impact. She held it there, let him feel, think, imagine. She sighed against his neck.

"Listen. I'll try." She felt his arm across the small of her back. Nothing could have held her better, contained her nerves. "I'll try and set myself up." She nodded toward Julia. "Like her. But Silva stays here, with Julia, because she stands the best chance for survival, and Silva is the best chance, anyone's best chance. I got to Julia quickly. I was on it. You need to oversee. Covey needs to get back to her work."

Claiborne jostled her. "That leaves—"

"Mullich."

They laughed softly together. Together they whispered, "Hell."

Then, for once, she overtook him, got the jump. She made a feint toward the bed, let Claiborne try for the lead, then went the other way, out the door.

HER EYES WOULDN'T adjust to the light. The hall appeared different, as though she had gone through the wrong door. She didn't anticipate the emptiness, the silence. She moved away from the door and farther up the hall, getting to the elevators. Something had changed. She stopped where she had injected the DC guards, where she believed that to be. The elevators remained quiet.

The blood spray was gone from the wall. She traced her fingers along the arc, where it had been. Was she imagining now, or had she hallucinated then? She tried to feel her own symptoms, the push and pull between sympathetic and parasympathetic, her limbic system haywire. There was definitely something off with her vision, but she couldn't discern between constriction and dilation; the light was just wrong.

She faced the elevators, seeking some kind of answer in her warped reflection. When had she known? When Claiborne had said it, she had known, known as though reminded. Oh, yes, when I felt split, when I reached for two, one fallen, one still alive, what I often have to do, every day, several times. When I was ten. Or was it when I was on the roof with Mullich the first time? But no, Claiborne scanned me, found me pure and whole. So the one that pulsed through Julia pulsed through me. Or the one on the roof with Mullich just grazed my cheek, too shallow for any scan but just enough, enough. The one that killed the Mercy Six.

The elevator opened. She stood still, expecting one in DC garb and two security. The emptiness spread through her nerves. She felt herself opening with the silver doors, hollowing. The elevator remained open, waited.

She entered, stood in the center, faced the hall. She didn't have her card. She had two syringes, one in each fist, caps off. With her knuckle she jabbed the button for Seven. As the doors began to close, Covey entered the hall and began running toward her. Covey's hair swung, her strides long and athletic. Mendenhall halted the doors with her foot. Someone running like that, let them in, let them join. Someone looking like that, just the possibility of her wanting to help, hold the door.

Covey drew up next to her, not even breathing hard.

"Who sent you?" Mendenhall let the doors close.

"The woman. She got a message."

"What message?"

"Send Covey, too."

"Mullich?"

"Yes. Who's Mullich?"

"He's a guy on the roof."

Covey eyed the syringes in Mendenhall's fists. "Are those the purple ones?"

"They're what I have left."

"Give me one."

Mendenhall remained still, looked at Covey's swimming reflection doubled on the metal doors.

"You need me. You need me when the doors open." Covey pulled and flipped her hair into a soft knot. She applied lip gloss, looking at the smears of her reflection. "You need me for that guy on the roof. To help him with you."

She gave Mendenhall the gloss, and Mendenhall gave her one purple syringe.

"Under the ribs is probably best. Otherwise the needle could snap. Press with your thumb. Then let them try whatever they want. They'll have less than a minute. Mine will go down right away."

"Will they be all right? Afterward, I mean?"

"If found soon enough. And we leave the empties."

"Did you call in the men Kae stuck?"

"He did."

"How do you know?"

"He's fifteen. He has a brother." And then she knew she was right. "And he's my patient."

WITH THE ELEVATOR'S lift her symptoms intensified. She tried to focus on her reflection, Covey's, keep them distinguished. But Covey's impression appeared to switch with Mendenhall's. Her memory stopped, then jumped, lost temporal order but sharpened in other ways.

The door opened on an early floor. Someone came in. Or the elevator didn't move at first. It was just she and Covey, needles ready. Or the door didn't open. No one came in. Her mind went back down to Pathology, retraced the ascent: They stopped on Four; Ben-Curtis came in, and she knew what he was thinking. She heard what he was thinking. *I'm going out. To watch.*

She told him to go to a room in Pathology first. To see who was there. To talk to them, watch them for a little while. Then go out and find Thorpe.

The elevator didn't move at first. She felt it begin to rise, focused on Covey's reflection in the doors. Her own had folded into itself, vanished, appeared halfway, slunk again into invisibility. No one came in.

THEN EMPTY SYRINGES were on the floor. Mendenhall and Covey were off the elevator and inside the entryway to the roof. The purple empties rolled, made hollow noises. Mendenhall's right thumb was sore, sprained. Covey was trembling. Blood trickled down her forearm. Not her blood. She had no wound. She trembled and did not appear able to move.

Mendenhall's left wrist was sore, also sprained.

"Follow me," she told Covey. She used the hem of her t-shirt to wipe clean the blood. She offered her hand. "Take a deep breath and follow me."

"I don't care if no one finds them," said Covey. She would not move. From the back Mendenhall wrapped her arms about Covey, gently cupping her elbows. They held still together, matched their breathing. Covey's form relaxed against her. She lightened. Mendenhall imagined her rising, slipping upward through her arms.

"Come."

Mendenhall pushed open the roof door. She had forgotten it would be night. She was expecting day. Ashes fell from a black sky. A red laser twirled in the whitefall. They could smell distant fire.

63

Mullich stood beside the relic, his silhouette tall against the orange night sky. Smoke veiled the stars. He was slicing the laser over the backlit hills, the beam made solid by the fine ash filling the air. Mendenhall held her arm across Covey's shoulders, let her lean into their shuffle across the roof.

"Give that to Jude." Mendenhall waited for Mullich to turn.

He seemed to understand as he faced the two women, offered the laser to Covey. She took it, rolled it between her palms as though warming it, then led them to the roof edge. Mendenhall kept her distance from Mullich, sensed him inching closer, avoiding eye contact but still trying to note things about her: her step, posture, hands. She tried to hide her self. Her fists were clenched as she worked out the tension from her last confrontation with security, the one she could not recall. She felt it, though, the quiver in her elbows, the tendons in her hips and ankles still jumpy, her wrist aching. Her blouse smelled of Demerol, Trapanal, adrenaline, and something else, something she couldn't remember from the purple syringes. Covey must have sprayed her during the struggle.

Her vision cleared a bit as she scanned distant points of the city. Covey was testing the laser, arcing the red line through the ashy night. Mullich's dark hair was speckled with ash. The scent of doused coals came heavy on the breeze, and feathers of water shot from the hilltops. The firefighters appeared tiny, without substance against the enormous fire sky.

Covey's aim was adjacent, cutting across the cityscape from mountains to sea. Emergency lights pulsed blue near downtown and the university, where the five had fallen, where Julia had been struck, and where others had been struck in the Marriott. I am not with them, thought Mendenhall. She brushed her cheek.

Mullich saw this.

"We can be more exact for you," he said to Covey. He motioned her over to Mendenhall, then stood between them. Using her shoulder, he centered Covey in the precise spot where Mendenhall had stood the night before. "Here," he said. "At a 67-degree angle."

He took Covey's hand in both of his and helped her aim the laser at the spot between her feet, slanted a 67-degree pitch. He released. She started there and drew the line for them, from horizon to horizon. All the way to Reykjavik.

"How wide?" asked Mullich.

"Three meters either side, if nothing changes."

"What changes?"

"Anything." She aimed at the moon, which loomed behind the ash veil. "Everything."

"Should we even be standing here?" Mullich motioned with his arms, indicating a channel around them.

Mendenhall felt she wasn't there, was just seeing them, dreaming them. She held her hand out so she could look at herself. Of course we should be standing here. It's what we do. Every day we go into ER, into where life happens, life strikes. Every afternoon those people gather on that wide downtown sidewalk, where the bus stops, where the sun ricochets its way between the glass buildings, down to light the faces, hopeful eyes, desperate shoulders.

She spoke while she felt she still could. She nodded to Covey. "Claiborne can get you out. He's your best bet. He'll say he can't, but wait and then he will. If not, then go back the way we came."

She sat down on the roof and leaned against the low wall. The moon appeared to be sliding as the ash blew across its face. She took two deliberate breaths, measured her heart. "It would be nice to set me up out here. But do it right. Pick out a quiet basement room and a nice bed. Claiborne will tell you what to get." She looked at Mullich, tried a smile but felt only a quivering. "I've no doubt you'll be able to get the stuff."

Covey and Mullich crouched near her.

"Stay with me," she said to Mullich as forcefully as she could, whatever was left of her ER voice.

From the waistband of her skirt, she removed the final syringe, saved just for this. She popped the cap with her thumbnail, kept eye to eye with Mullich as she did so. Then, using the moon as backlight, she measured out the dose and snipped the needle dry.

"This much will let me walk but not much more. Basically I go under here. I'll be thirsty when I wake up. Put a slice of lime in my water."

She checked to see if both Covey and Mullich registered this. She wasn't sure her words were sounding. The moon appeared different, closer, clearer, alien. She'd never seen sympathy on their faces, certainly not on Mullich's. They both expressed comprehension, though, and she at least took that.

A low dread brushed along her nerves. If she didn't survive and Covey didn't escape, it would always show virus.

Mullich took her hand, then released it. The heat of his touch lingered in her palm.

Mendenhall tried to start the injection but could not focus well enough to find a vein. Covey took the syringe and pressed it to Mendenhall's forearm, constricted the brachial vessels. She injected the dose to begin everything.

Mullich placed his hand on her arm. The scent of damp coals fell about them with the ash. Covey and Mullich moved to ready positions. She felt herself being lifted and dreamed she was rising.

acknowledgments

Thank you Dr. David Reardon and Dr. Philip Bajo for your expertise and support. The ER imagined here emerged from the many stories told by Dr. Suzanne Town. I am very grateful to my editor, Fred Ramey, for his foresight, openness, and intelligence. I am lucky to be represented by Peter Steinberg, a thoughtful friend and the best agent a writer could have. I have no idea why Elise Blackwell stays with me, but she does, and because of that my life and writing are better.